To MeaBH

From your Goo

Judy

The Macedonian Covenant

Joseph McCoy

authorHOUSE®

AuthorHouse™ UK Ltd.
500 Avebury Boulevard
Central Milton Keynes, MK9 2BE
www.authorhouse.co.uk
Phone: 08001974150

First published by AuthorHouse 11/20/2009

ISBN: 978-1-4490-1331-8 (sc)

This book is printed on acid-free paper.

<u>Acknowledgements.</u>

I would like to take this opportunity to thank a few people who I believe helped me a great deal through the process of writing this book.

Firstly, I would like to thank my wife, Michelle and daughter Katie for their support through the many days and nights that it took to complete this book.

I would also like to thank Brendy and Meabh.

A special mention to my work colleagues for their invaluable advice and wisdom.

Dedicated to my Mother and Father.

The Macedonian Covenant

CHAPTER 1.

In my memory's eye, the June morning my grandfather died is one I am most unlikely to forget. My name is Michelle Fordix and I have just lost my best friend and mentor. As I sat in the old stone chapel in the country outside Orleans near the coast of France, I thought about my childhood with this man, that I loved with my whole being. It was he who sparked my interest in ancient Egypt, which I took to addictively. I was a lonely child, my parents died in a plane crash when I was young and was sent to live with my grandfather in the country. I remember, as a child, the statue of "Our Lady" in the corner that used to scare me, the stain glass window with the beautiful mosaic design and then there was the strange smell of the incense that filled the air deep with the feeling of an after-life that awaited and all the uncertainty that went with it. I was trained as an Egyptologist and as a scientist, so was it logical to believe in any god, one thing was certain I was only here for my grandfather and his memory.

After the burial I returned to the chapel to think in the silence of my own mind when I heard a distinctive sound, the tapping of a cane or a stick on the cold stone floor of the chapel. This sparked a memory from the past, an old man used to visit my grandfather. He was an old friend who served in the resistance with my grandfather during the last war.

As I turned, there he stood looking down at me with a passive smile. He walked with a limp and had a patch over his eye and his coat was worn and slightly tattered. He wore old boots and trousers but with all his short-comings there was still something that made him great in my eyes.

"Hello Joseph, how are you?" I asked.

"Not to bad my dear" he replied. "Sorry to hear about Charles, he was a good man. About two years ago I called with your grandfather he told me an amazing story about a lost treasure in the south of Egypt, discovered by one of your ancestors when he was out there in 1798 with Napoleon's invasion force."

I stopped him there, laughing "that's an old fairy tale he used to tell me when I couldn't get to sleep"

"Yes, he told me you used to be a bad sleeper, now walk with me" he said. As we were leaving the chapel gates he handed me a brown paper package.

"Your grandfather told me to give this to you on the occasion of his death"

I asked him what it was and he said it was just an interesting old

Fairy-tale, he kissed me on the forehead and said "if you are lucky, remember an old man eh?"

And with that he hobbled off into one of the old side streets and was gone from sight. I walked down the road to the old cottage; it has been in the family for three hundred years. I came through the gate, opened the door and walked into the pantry. As I looked around, in my mind I returned to when I was a child. I entered the good room, a room I was never permitted to go into because it was always kept immaculate. I touched the wood of the coffee table, which came from the castle of an aristocrat during the French revolution, the good settee and chairs and other ornaments in the room. I moved to the kitchen, I could still smell the herbs and spices and even the garlic cloves which my grandfather loved cooking with. All the cooking utensils were still in their place, hung up beside the cooker and it was finally then that it dawned on me, I was alone.

I walked up the stairs and turned into a room on the left. It was my grandfather's study. I walked into the room and closed the door behind me. I sat at the table and looked around taking everything in. It was a room filled of wonders with books on vivant denon who accompanied Napoleon to Egypt in 1798, to books on the study of hieroglyphics and studies of non-mono-theistic cultures and also small artefacts from Egypt and the Greek world. This is where I found my calling in the archaeological community. Ever since I was young, I was fascinated in Egypt and her past and also in Greek history, so when my secondary education was over I applied for the University of Oxford in England and was accepted.

After years of intensive study I achieved my degree, and with that my first field assignment in Egypt. It was in the district of Thebes where I helped to excavate Temples and Monuments. I was in Egypt for nine years and loved it.

It was only when I heard of my grandfathers death did I return to France. I placed the package that the old man had given me on the table and I thought of the fairy tale. I opened the brown wrapping that was around the package and gasped. I couldn't believe it, it was the journal of Major Charles Fordix, and was dated 1829. With it was a round shaped amulet which was made of gold. Then it hit me;

"My God," I said aloud. *"It must be true."*

I put the items in the drawer and locked it, thinking 'I am too tired for this,' I will read it in the morning. I walked into my old bedroom and started to undress for bed.

For all her faults, Michelle Fordix was beautiful with long black Mediterranean hair and tanned features with a beautiful slender figure that glided through the sheets like a breath of perfumed air. Many men had fallen for this woman, but crashed on the rock that is called heart break, for the love of her profession outweighs that of any relationship. Not many men had interested her, only the wrong type. The sun had broken through the veil of the linen curtain and touched her face awakening her from her sleep. As she pulled herself upright on the bed she wondered what today will hold.

While getting dressed she thought about the journal and the mysterious amulet that accompanied it. After getting breakfast she went into the study, sat at the desk and opened the drawer and took the amulet out for further inspection. It looked early Greek but it was not her field of expertise, putting it back she pulled out the journal and looked at its cover. It was aged, and the leather was hard to the touch. The contents had been scrolled in beautiful quill handwriting. She turned to the first page and began to read.

This is the journal of Major Charles Fordix, and to god I thank for sparing my life through the wars under the Emperor Napoleon. So that I may live in peace with my family for they are the greatest   treasures of all.

The journal begins in 1798...

We arrived in Alexandria and there we were ordered to march to Cairo to engage the Mameluke army. After the march, we defeated the Mameluke army with only the loss of three hundred men in battle.   It was magnificent! They were utterly wiped out except for factions who fled down through Lower Egypt. Our main force was then split in two, one army was sent in the direction of Jaffa and the other was sent on a 'mopping up' operation after the Mameluke renegades. I was a lieutenant with the infantry and was going through the Nile valley after them. Our unit got lost but we continued on. It was when we were fired on from a cave instead of out flanking them that I decided to use our small canon from close range with grape shot, the mamelukes inside were blown to pieces. Poor sods! When we got inside I looked around. A lot of damage had been done to the cave, as I cleared away the rubble I discovered part of a manmade shaft cut into the back of the cave, cleverly hidden by the false cover, chiselled out to look like the cave wall. As I looked down into the abyss of the shaft, the vapours and steam- like substance slowly drifted into my nostrils. It smelled like nothing I have ever smelt before, almost ancient. A frightening shiver ran down my back. I have heard of tomb's having poisonous gas sealed in the entrance to kill tomb robbers, but as I sat up I knew I was all right. After some time we decided that I and two others would investigate further. The second was an engineer called Jean, a good friend, and Jason my second in command. Jean was a very careful man he did not believe in unnecessary risks, 'I will go first, watch your footing and for traps' I said. As we descended, Jason at the rear, we dropped to the bottom, lighting two torches and all of a sudden, the scale of what we had found was apparent. I studied art in Paris before enlisting in the army, and what I did know was that this was neither Egyptian architecture nor design. I told myself it has to be Greek. There were two massive pillars made out of granite, beautifully carved into two curious figures that I had never seen. A young man and a young woman facing each other with a resemblance of affection for each other sealed in time. We went on down what seemed to be a gallery with beautiful carvings, thinking to myself, 'my god it must have taken ages to build this place' As I walked around, Jean abruptly stopped me, 'My god man, watch where you're going.' As he pulled me out of the way he pointed to a small piece of marble coming out of the side of the stone floor. 'It seems as if they have rigged this place for visitors, observe,' he then pointed to a hole in the wall. What caught my attention was the fact that they were adjacent to each other, reaching for a plank of wood he had taken with him Jean carefully placed it on the marble probe and then pushed down. We heard a mechanical sound almost a second later as a glass projectile sunk into the plank.

With a humorous grin Jean softly said 'careful dear boy, careful.' With that in mind I proceeded slowly down the gallery until we came to a circular anti-chamber, with marble pillars stretching around the chamber. In the centre there seemed to be a dark hole around it and there were steps leading into it.

As we went to see what was in the centre of the chamber, torch in hand, we carefully moved towards it, we saw an antique horror of a scale never before seen. There were hundreds of skeletons heaped into the bottom of the massive hole and on closer inspection I saw hundreds of arrow heads. They must have been the slaves who built this tomb or possibly 'gateway to hell'.

Once built, then, to ensure their silence they were all put to death. What a way to die!

Jean said 'with what I have seen, I can deduct that these people were slain in open ground, look at the way they were thrown into this pit. Think about it, they dug their own grave without knowing it'. As we got to the other end of the chamber we came to another long corridor, we walked along the passage and I observed the old torch holders. It was getting humid and we had walked nearly half a mile when we came to an entrance. Two massive bronze doors stood in our way, so I forced one of the doors open when all of a sudden I felt a clink vibrate through the door, Jean quickly pulled me away from the entrance. Four projectiles slid out of the top of the door, they were about a foot long with a point on the end. They were made out of glass with a green liquid sealed into the tip. As they hit the floor they smashed, burning and scorching the floor, obviously some kind of powerful acid.

'They certainly don't like visitors', smirked Jean. When we got into the room we saw a treasure beyond belief, gold and jewels everywhere in sight. Golden goblets encrusted with jewels, bracelets and what seemed to be personal weapons that had strange markings on them, also, the walls were covered in a strange, almost hieroglyphic writing.

The walls were decorated with carvings depicting a great battle. There seemed to be only one reference to ancient Egypt. By the light of the torch I can still see it now, it was of a high priest accepting a royal decree from a Pharaoh, and leading his people in to the desert. The rest of the chamber resembled what looked like a cross between a royal tomb and a throne room. The centre of the chamber had a sarcophagus that was amazing to gaze on. The corners of the sarcophagus were made from gold and another metal I have never seen before, almost like silver but far purer in form. The sides were made of crystal, polished down to resemble glass, the lid was made of granite with a rectangle cut out of it and sealed with polished crystal but, with a consecrated quality, almost like a magnifying effect.

Inside was a young man perfectly preserved! There were small shafts cut into the ceiling that probably brought the light in the morning into the chamber and finally there was a throne made of the same material as the sarcophagus with decorative carvings all over it. The throne was built into the floor along the first step of the encirclement of steps leading down to the sarcophagus, it reminded me a little of the classic Roman amphitheatre. The corners of the throne were shaped like lions feet and had jewels where the toe-nails should be. It gave me a feeling of something that my country had tried to wipe out; there was something imperial about the whole atmosphere. As those feelings wore off and we settled down I realised we were all very rich men. We made a pact to blow up the entrance and conceal the truth from our superior officers, so that we would not lose a fortune. There are a lot of officers out there who would hand this vast treasure over to further their careers and standing in the Republic of France.

We each took one small item from the tomb, small enough to fit into our pockets. I took a small piece that looked like a coin of some kind and as we were leaving the tomb Jean stood on a trap as we were getting out of the last chamber. I heard a clink and a cold feeling ran down my spine as I turned around I saw Jean being driven through by one of the glass tipped spears. It had broken inside his shoulder and what I saw next terrified me to the bone. The strange liquid started to eat him in a line from his shoulder to his waist; it was like an acid I have never seen before. His body slid apart and landed in two different places so we left him there, his resting place this would have to be, so with a sad heart we got out of the complex and blew the entrance with gun power and got on with the war. As for Jean, we reported him missing, most likely a victim of an attack at night.

Jason was taken prisoner towards the end of the Egypt campaign, and as for me I am a survivor. I got back to the mainland and was promoted to captain and got land for my bravery in the face of such odds.

As for Jason, I had heard that after the war he was taken to England where sadly he died of the fever. Not a night has gone by that I have not prayed for his soul, for it is a soul I miss. The land I received had belonged to a baron's estate. Within it is a small thatched château that used to be what the ruling class called, a gatehouse, and a few fields.

CHAPTER 2.

Michelle closed the journal, set it down and it dawned on her, that the fairytale must be true.

Lifting her coat she walked outside and headed towards the orchard, she thought about the mysterious journal and how it had been her grandfather's dream to find the treasure.

She thought that most people would jump at the thought of an adventure, but her better nature told her that it was going to be very difficult to set up an expedition team and as well as that, it would be very expensive and dangerous and if the manuscript fell into the wrong hands, people would most certainly get hurt or even killed.

With this in mind she thought about who she could trust, really, really trust. As she walked back into the house she grabbed her bag and put the journal into it along with the gold coin, then locked the doors and climbed into her car, a battered Renault five. As she drove past her gate she saw something out of place, a car parked down on the hard shoulder about fifty yards from the château drive way, ignoring this, she drove on.

She pulled into an old gateway and drove on up the lane. It was plagued with potholes and in some parts it was eroding at the sides, thinking that this place has not changed over the years. She drove around a corner with a mound on the right that obscured the view when an old house with rose gardens at the front appeared into sight and in the garden was an old man tending the flowers. She stopped the car, pulled the handbrake on and opened the door.

The old man approached her.

"Hello my dear, I was wondering how long it would take you to come up here. I believe you have some pressing questions for me" he said.

"Yes" she replied.

The pair walked towards the house.

"Why did my grandfather give the journal to you and why did he want me to have it?" she asked.

"Your grandfather was an extremely superstitious man and he believed he was in danger. I was the only person he could trust."

"He said that one day a man came to the front door and offered him a great deal of money for the journal and the artefact. When your grandfather asked how he got the information about his ancestors past, he replied that he was a wealthy businessman who owned a number of construction companies as well as an antique business.

When one of his teams were gutting out an old church in England they found a reference to an entry made in 1805 in one of the old parish records, that the local priest who helped out in the Napoleonic prison camp that a dying French soldier told him of an amazing treasure sealed in a tomb in Egypt and of a great friend who he missed. Before dying he placed a gold coin in his hand and smiled, and then he slipped away."

"Along with the record they found the other coin. Your grandfather refused to part with the journal and the coin which made him angry, your grandfather then asked the man to leave. Charles was a good judge of character and thought his presence was too powerful to be a simple businessman. So he came to see me the next day and gave me the journal and coin for safekeeping and said that if anything was to happen to him then it was to go to you and you would know what to do."

"What to do!" she exclaimed.

"Well you are the archaeologist my dear and you could form an expedition and go off in search of the treasure yourself?!"

"Do you have any idea what it would take to put a team together besides expense? And time?" she said.

"Well, it looks like you will have to find a partner to finance the expedition. But, whom?" he replied. "Sometimes it is better to stand beside the devil than stand in front of him, for the meantime anyway."

"You don't mean!"

Grinning with a devious smile the old man calmly said, "Yes why not?! Our mysterious businessman obviously wanted the journal for a reason. With your contacts you could arrange a meeting with this man; it may be a reasonable assumption that he could have the financial and material backing required for the journey my dear. Everyone needs a professional in the field. And that, my dear will be your leverage, apart from the treasure there is something else going on, I would think."

"How can you be sure?" she asked.

"I'm not, but my heart tells me there is something much bigger going on behind this masquerade. Keep your eyes and ears open, but most importantly don't endanger your life. Now my dear, time for tea, I'll get the pot on the boil."

As I strolled through the rose gardens I wondered at the beautiful colours, as I touched one of the roses I pricked my finger on a thorn, it was then I heard Joseph say; "every form of beauty has the ability to hurt you." He was standing behind me as he spoke, "a good lesson to learn don't you think my dear? Tea is ready, do you take milk or sugar." He took her by the arm and started to walk towards the house.

"So where will I start," I asked him with a mouth full of cake.

"Start at the top my dear; we have to get this business man's name. It shouldn't be too difficult" he replied.

"What do you mean?"

"Men with his power and money have a tendency to stick out a mile. There is however another way, we shall fix it to make sure he will come to us, with today's technology and the Internet..." the old man stared at me the way you would only get with a school teacher attempting to pull the answer out of the student.

"Oh I see, post the artefact on an information page and see what fish bites the hook."

"Precisely my dear." He said. "Now, it is time for you to go, it is getting late."

Looking at her watch, "my goodness look at the time. I have been here all day."

Kissing Joseph on the forehead she said goodbye, "I will be in touch."

"Take care my dear and remember what I said, be careful of who you trust. Look after yourself my dear."

Pulling out of the lane onto the main road, stirring images and emotions filled her mind, the treasure and anticipating the adventure that lay ahead and also fearful of the danger she might put herself in and others. It was late and it was raining, the wipers were on full and the white lines on the road rushed by with a distorted flash. The car was doing sixty when she released that her daydream was interfering with her driving so she slowed down to forty five and then realised that she was pulling into her entry. She drove up to her château, got out of the car and locked the door of the Renault and walked up to the door. She unlocked the front door and walked into the hallway and suddenly went stone cold, she could smell the scent of aftershave. Her heart thumped in her chest as she closed the door. She walked into the good room and picked up the poker and walked around the house to make sure no one was there. When she was sure that nobody was about she put the poker back in its stand, there was no visible trace of a break in. Everything was in its place or so it seemed but as a safety precaution she had, earlier that day, pulled the carpet up on the stairs and placed a thin slab of soft putty covered by two pages of blank paper on the top and the bottom and slid it under the carpet. As she pulled the slab out from the carpet she saw the out line of a male boot, quickly going over in her mind where everything had been she realised that all is where she left it.

All the valuables were still in the house, so what is going on, she thought. As she climbed the stairs she turned into the study, she sat behind the study desk and took the journal out of her bag and started to conjure some sort of a plan. Obviously there was no other way, she would have to go to the wealthy businessman and try to broker a deal. The next day was Friday, it was a cold morning as she rang the old man and asked just how to get in contact with this businessman and to tell him about the break in. He said it sounded like a professional job and to be on her guard.

He gave me a number, the same that he had given my grandfather. As I sat down I picked up the phone and nervously dialled the number, it was a foreign number perhaps German or Austrian, the person answered the phone "Hello Heir Strauss' personal secretary how may I help you?"

"Good evening, my name is Michelle Fordix. I'm ringing in connection with Heir Strauss' interest in my late grandfather's journal..." as she was about to go on the secretary broke in with the words; "oh yes I will put you through to Heir Strauss right now", at that the phone went on to an answer tone and on the other end, a very well educated voice answered.

"Miss Fordix it's an honour to speak with you. I heard about your grandfather, a brilliant man who will be missed by the historical community. How may I help you?"

As I explained he suggested we meet for a business lunch in his headquarters, so the meeting was arranged for Monday morning. His personal jet would fly Michelle from Paris airport to Berlin at that he said; "I'm looking forward to meeting with you. Remember to bring the journal and the artefact with you. Until then goodbye my dear"

As she walked away from the phone, she rushed with anticipation and excitement at the adventure of a lifetime that lay ahead of her.

Stepping out of the car at the airport car park she walked towards the airport and through the terminal where she was met by a woman in a suit; "Miss Fordix I presume? The private jet is waiting for you."

"But I have to check in with airport security and customs and all that" replied Michelle.

"No need, I have it all taken care for you."

She was in her early thirties, sleek and professional looking but deprived of a personality owing to her professional lifestyle. At ten thousand feet the curtain behind me opened and the woman came in and introduced herself as Margaret.

"I am Heir Strauss personal secretary we shall be in Berlin in fifteen minutes. Would you like tea, coffee or any other refreshments?"

"No thank you, I'm cutting down."

"Very well, if you will excuse me," and with that she vanished behind the curtain.

I heard the wheels touch down and the plane came to a halt, from behind the curtain came Margaret who politely asked me to accompany her to the awaiting transport. Climbing down from the jet I saw a black limousine accompanied with the chauffer who was standing holding the door open for me. I climbed in, the interior was leather and it had all the latest Hi-Tech gismos. It had the feeling of absolute power.

Heir Strauss' personal secretary Margaret accompanied me in the limo.

We drove through a small suburb of Berlin and headed for the outskirts of the city, we then pulled into a massive industry estate and through what seemed to shadow renaissance architecture. We then drove up the central avenue which was beautifully landscaped, running up both sides were fully matured oak trees. We drove up to the entrance of a building which was signposted 'Strauss International Headquarters' thinking to myself that this place reeks of power. At the door were armed guards wearing black uniforms and luminous security badges. Something told me they were ex-military and very professional; they had heckler and cock machine guns and side arms. Wondering who or what they were protecting, I walked through the front doors and was stopped by a security guard with a hand held metal detector, then I was taken into an audience chamber where Margaret told me that Heir Strauss would be with me momentarily. Then she left through the massive gilded doors with a Greek pictures carved on them.

All around there were glass cabinets with Greek and admittedly some ancient Egyptian artefacts which were good enough for the best museums in the world. Among the ranks was a very impressive piece, a funerary amulet from the tomb of Tutankhamen wondering how such a piece got into his possession, I heard a voice behind me say; "Impressive and beautiful it is". As I turned around I saw an old man who was very well dressed.

"Miss Fordix I presume? Forgive me, I did not expect someone so young and beautiful, I trust your journey was comfortable?"

"Yes thank you, it was very comfortable."

"Please my dear, take a seat," He said. "As you can probably work out, I am a very wealthy man. I run businesses all over the world and as you can see some countries can be very generous because of the work contracts I offer, for example Egypt, the amulet was a gift from the government in power at that time for setting up factories and electricity stations. Due to your profession you may be forgiven for thinking it was stolen," he laughed.

"If I may be so bold to ask what type of companies do you run?" asked Michelle.

"Everything from car parts to highly advanced computer components for military equipment, hence the state authorised armed security. The reason I have asked you here is obviously your grandfather's journal. When I was in the army during the last war I was a signals officer in the Africa core at the time. One day I got a very interesting dispatch through the enigma code machine. A re-con patrol who had advanced through enemy lines claimed to have discovered some kind of tomb that was covered with rubble, they did not go inside but they covered it over and headed back to base. They forwarded the location but before they could get back they were taken out by allied air cover. Knowing this gave me an idea that the information was not relevant to the war so I did not share it with my superiors as I was not obligated to, so I put it to the back of my mind and got on with my life. I heard the story of your grandfather's journal from a priest who found the records of the amazing story of a pair of Napoleonic officers, with your insight and expertise and my financial backing what a discovery we could make! Do you accept? Take your time of course, think it over."

"I don't have to, I accept" replied Michelle.

"My dear you will have the best of everything, equipment, travel etc, the team however, you will hand pick yourself, and if anybody has work commitments you'll find my wallet is very appealing. Money, you will find is the best means of motivating people, you could say the same about greed. The difference in the two is one is for necessity the other is for over excess and that my dear normally causes trouble, be wary about who you pick for your team. You will have to be able to trust whoever you are working with. There is one other condition to this, my head of security will accompany you to Egypt for your safety, he is a very experienced man and utterly professional. His name is Jack Toner. He was a soldier in the French Foreign Legion, an Irish man in the right place you might say. You will find him fascinating, I have arranged a meeting, I hope you don't mind."

"No not at all, I like to know all the people who work with me," she said.

 At a restaurant in the suburbs of Berlin, Michelle sat quietly waiting for the mysterious Mr Toner.

Slowly walking towards the restaurant Jack Toner wondered what his contact looked like. He walked in through the door of the restaurant and he then began a casual sweep of the room, first there was a group of Japanese business men enjoying the night, next on the left was a family having a meal, eyeing the next table down however lifted his spirits. He walked towards the table and he was confronted with the front end of a pair of stilettos curving up into the heel, brilliant white in colour. Remaining casual, he followed his line of sight which took him from the ankle upwards to a slender pair of legs shaded by stockings that radiated a weak marble effect, as his eyes slid slowly upwards a cream skirt and blazer appeared, she had beautiful long black Hair and tanned appearance, a long neck, small nose and piercing eyes.

"Excuse me?" a female voice interrupted his stare, "Are you Jack Toner?"

"Yes that's me." replied Jack.

As they sat down he said; "I expected somebody a lot older and not as attractive."

"Not disappointed are you?" replied Michelle with a stone cold but confident expression.

"Not in the least, pleasantly surprised would be correct. So Miss Fordix, have you ordered anything yet?"

"No I am not that hungry but perhaps I will have a drink, and please, call me Michelle." as the waiter approached she asked for a glass of white wine.

"Very well Michelle, please forgive me if I forget from time to time. Formality and professionalism were drilled into me when I was in the army so I am apologising in advance," with that he ordered a malt whiskey and began to tell Michelle about the travel arrangements. "I am handling all the travel details, when you arrive there however, I will not be with you but you will have two security experts accompanying you.

"That's strange, why aren't you coming with us," asked Michelle.

"Michelle, I have a lot to think about, tactical and strategic ground work to complete as well as the political landscape to take into consideration. The two major ethnic groups have been fighting for domination of the area for the last ten years so let us just say that I will be an invisible equation." And with that he finished his whiskey and bid Miss Fordix a good evening.

Her eyes followed him as he made his way out of the café, he had a muscular tone and a face that was laced with an air of experience was chiselled almost to the bone, she had noticed a scar on his left wrist which was covered with a leather bracelet. He was wearing a white shirt and a pair of trousers; he carried his blazer over his shoulder and walked with a competent step. As she got up to pay, the waiter said that the gentleman had already paid. Looking around she saw that at a distance stood Jack Toner with a smile, he nodded and then turned around and walked away.

The next morning Michelle was driven back to the Strauss headquarters. With her, she had a briefcase and within that were the names of her intended unit. She was met at the door by Heir Strauss;

"I have a surprise for you. This is Martin, your personal secretary."

A young and innocent looking man walked out from behind Heir Strauss and shyly said, "Call me Marty. Miss Fordix, I will be taking care of all your secretarial needs," with that Heir Strauss dismissed himself and left. "Come, I will show you your office" said Marty. They came to the doors of an elevator and stepped inside, the doors had a colonial look about them although the rest of the building was relatively modern. The elevator came to a halt and the doors opened and Marty ushered Michelle to a door on what seemed to be the basement level. The office had an ultra modern look about it and Marty explained that he had chosen the décor.

Michelle opened the briefcase and handed the list to Marty.

"I will call two of them and you can take care of the rest Marty"

"Yes right-away" and with that he scurried away to the room next door. Lifting the receiver I wondered back in time to when I was at a unique lecture by the eccentric Professor Kevin O' Dougherty. He was an expert in early Greek and Egyptian hieroglyphics as well as numerous scripts. The lecture was at Trinity College Dublin and was many years ago, suddenly, brining me out of my day dream, at the other end of the phone I heard a voice answer;

"Hello"

"Hello Professor, its Michelle Fordix here"

"Oh, how are you darling, keeping well I hope?"

"Well enough Professor, well enough," she said.

As I told him about my tale it was like throwing petrol on a naked light. After the conversation he informed me the he would be out on the first plane. I replaced the receiver and looked at the next name. I smiled, Alex Monroe, the American, he was one of the worlds foremost carbon 14 experts.

In a research lab in Washington Alex Monroe was scrutinising something under the microscope when a research assistant walked over and told him there was a lady on the phone. He lifted the phone;

"Hello, Alex speaking."

"Hi, its Michelle Fordix here and do I have an offer for you?!"

When she hung up the phone she lifted her briefcase onto the table and out of it she produced the old leather diary of Major Charles Fordix, and beside that she placed the gold amulet. Looking again through the diary she found a small section at the back, it read;

... With all we found in the tomb I still think it is more than a tomb. The strange booby traps, the strange circular hall with the skeletons in it, the hole in the middle of the hall, the room with the sarcophagus that almost doubled as a throne room. It's as if the burial chamber was a gateway between the living and the dead.

She closed the diary, a shiver ran down her back, almost as if Charles Fordix himself had pulled her shirt out from her neck and playfully blown down her back.

At that same moment, Jack Toner was in a room with nine other men going over tactics, times, local phrases and expressions and brushing up on Arabic. Also that evening there was weapon's training. Jack was a very experienced man who had served all over the world in the legion as well as having the skill to make some of his own weapons of his design for close quarter combat.

As Michelle was going over notes Jack suddenly appeared;

"Sorry for disturbing you Michelle, when I go into the field I always insist on a small weapons training course for non-combatants, in this case yourself and your archaeological team. In my business it's better to be safe than sorry."

"This is highly irregular," protested Michelle.

"Ms Fordix, in the small chance that we end up in trouble and I or my men are occupied in operations at least you will be able to defend yourselves competently and affectively. Let's say, Wednesday evening?"

"Ok then, Wednesday evening it is then."

Tuesday morning arrived and Michelle was sitting at her table. There was a memo addressed to her. Opening it she scanned the words;

"Everyone has been assembled, as you wished and they are being collected at the airport right now and will be arriving at eleven o'clock, signed Marty."

My gods, thinking to herself, some of these people do not come cheap; Heir Strauss must have a lot of financial and persuasive muscle. Hearing a knock on her door she turned around and said "come in," With that Marty came in and said "did you get the memo?"

"Yes, very impressive," replied Michelle.

"Thank you and by the way I have cleared the lecture theatre for today," said Marty.

"Yes, I will need to explain why they are all here and that is an excellent place to explain it from. Marty, would you grab all my notes and bring them down to the lecture theatre."

Michelle started towards the lift and pushed the button with the number two on it, the doors opened and she walked down a corridor until she came to a set of double doors. Pushing them open the theatre opened out like a round hall with seats all around and at the front and centre was the podium from which she would either convince her audience or worse, have them thinking she was clinically insane. Just at that moment Marty stumbled through the doors with her notes.

"I have taken the liberty of organising everything in alphabetical order, I hope you don't mind it's just that it will make it easer for you to pull files when you need them," he said.

"You're a star" said Michelle happily.

With all the papers in his arms he grinned and said "Yes, I know." Michelle watched him shuffle down to the table at the front of the hall. Walking down towards him I asked about Heir Strauss' own intervention on the subject and at the same time explaining to Marty that I needed to know everything in order to get as much information to help me locate the cave with the false back on it. Marty walked over to the file locker he had wheeled into the hall earlier, opening it he said "Heir Strauss said all the information should be in this". He threw an old German army intelligence file to her, "He told me he could have been shot for withholding this intelligence file but understood there was something bigger afoot." Looking at the file, Michelle ran her hands over the leather front with the Africa core insignia on it. Tilting her head to one side and thinking to herself, what could be so important he had to obtain especially during a war? Opening the first page marked commutation records it read *'May 15th 1942, while carrying out re con in Libya near the border our orders were to find a mountain path and to see what the roads would be like for armour. This was when the time came we could send reinforcements around while our main force was engaging the enemy and cut them off from the back thus affecting a cut off pincer movement. The mountain paths were primarily for hill top fortified bunkers ensuring that our armour had a level of security and also for moving troops to the other side, the thought being, if we were spotted, which was a possibility because the British had air superiority they would perhaps only see one and not the other. Once this was in place we would strike with commando forces and knock out their aircraft in one night allowing us to rip into our enemy with the vigour expected of the Africa corps. I am Captain Hans Müller and am presently writing this report in a place called Al Jawf, near the Egyptian border. This evening I received a report from my young lieutenant. While on patrol in this god forsaken place he came upon a strange place when sheltering from enemy aircraft for fear of being strafed or bombed as the danger passed he realised the back of the tomb was covered in stones and boulders. There he could clearly see the outline of the manmade shaft. Upon closer inspection he saw where someone had blown the back of the cave, obviously in an attempt to conceal the entrance. We cleared the entrance and went further in to investigate, as we let ourselves down the shaft we were met with a beautiful sight, two massive statues of what seemed to be in the Greek style. As I was admiring them I saw a terrible sight that filled me with dread; an old skeleton with what seemed to been cut in two, the top half was uniformed in what seemed to be an old Napoleonic tunic. Carefully I went through his pockets and found old dispatch letters and then I saw something gold. It was an old coin, a very old coin and with this I ordered my men to carry the remains outside where he got a decent burial. I, with my men, then sealed the entrance and returned to my unit.*

Lifting her eyes Heir Strauss was standing in front of her with a gentle smile, he produced a gold coin from his pocket and with confidence he flipped the coin in the air, caught it and slapped it on the back of his left hand then said, "heads or tails my dear?" He was the lieutenant from the report.

"As you've probably worked out, I was the German officer; I took a considerable risk hiding the file during the war. It has been in all sorts of interesting places, even in the graves of fallen comrades, unfittingly I was never able to carry it with me. If it had been discovered I would have been shot as a spy, it was that simple. Finally, I buried it in a forest close to where we surrendered to the American army. After my repatriation to Germany I dug it up and it has been with me ever since. So Miss Fordix, this tale is a familiar tale to the both of us, don't you think?"

"Yes indeed, I see now what drives you, however, I can't believe it's just for the treasure as you are more than wealthy," replied Michelle

"Yes my dear," he said looking at her with a strained face, he turned to Marty and said "show her the artefact."

"What artefact?" asked Michelle.

With that they lead her into the basement where there was a massive safe with an optical scanner. Standing forward, Heir Strauss bent over and allowed the contraption to scan his eye, then the wall of reinforced steel opened up and she walked in the middle of the floor. There was a large granite block, she walked up to it and looked at the inscription. It was in Greek and had a picture at the bottom of it, looking at it a chill went down her back, it was the same picture her ancestor had wrote about. The one he had found in the tomb, it had the Pharaoh sitting on a throne handing a high priest some kind of decree, head bowed and clad in what seemed to be a leopard skin accepting the decree. Looking back at the old man he smiled and said, "it was discovered in an ancient Greek burial site near one of my construction sites, according to the inscription the tomb belonged to a general of Alexander the Great's army.

"We need Kevin here to decipher this correctly and most importantly fast," said Michelle.

"I concur, we all need a nights sleep," he said.

"First I want to get the rest of my team on board," walking back into her office she lifted the phone and dialled a number an English accent answered.

"Hello James is that you?"

"Yes speaking.

"It's me, Michelle Fordix."

"Oh hi Michelle, how are you?"

"Not too bad. How's that scoundrel of a brother of yours?"

"Oh you know, just the same," he laughed.

"Listen, get yourself on a plane for Berlin and collect the rest of the squad on the way. Let's just say that in a few days you'll be involved in the biggest find of all time."

"Ok then see you in the morning then sweetie"

Chapter 3.

Standing on the platform outside Heir Strauss' main building a small minibus pulled up along side and Michelle greeted them. They were a funny lot. First was the American who was wearing a baseball cap- he was about six foot tall and holding a sports bag stuffed with clothes and in the other hand was a laptop case. Behind him was a well dressed man with a hat and an old briefcase, his shoes were shined and he had a walking stick, "Michelle, darling, how are you?" with that she gave the old man a hug, "my dear you'll make the rest of the guys jealous."

After meeting the rest of the team, they were escorted to the lecture theatre, at the moment Michelle was preparing to perform on to probably the biggest stage of her life. Although she was accustomed to giving archaeology lectures, she found this time to be very nerve racking, she was making a move to go out when she felt a hand take hers. It was Jack Toner, "it'll be Ok, don't worry about anything you'll be fine," with that he slipped behind the curtain and took his seat in the lecture theatre with the rest.

"Ladies and gentlemen, thank you for coming here at such short notice. Some of you already know why you are here and others do not, I will now try to explain what is going on. Long ago an ancestor of mine who happened to be a Napoleonic officer stumbled into what first appeared to be a tomb but on further inspection of his dairy it appears to be much more, take for example, he discovered different chambers which appear to be completely out of Egyptian architectural character for instance a large percentage would appear to be of Greek origin of Alexander's time. From what the diary explains, the burial chamber appears to have been built for more than internment, it also appears to be a map room of some sorts, I have all the artefacts on the table for your closer inspection if you would like to come down and have a look."

The team started going through the artefacts while Marty explained the rest of the story. Michelle turned to Kevin and handed him one of the coins, the moment he saw it you could see the eyes lock on to the coin, "oh my god it's Alexandrian coinage, do you have any idea how rare this is? I have only seen a few examples in my life; it's as if it's been struck only yesterday."

"I have something else to show you," turning around she introduced Heir Strauss to the ageing but charismatic old Irish man.

Standing in front of the slab of granite Kevin took a seat and started to translate the inscription.

"*Hail to you who look upon this and know it is the tomb of General Aloun. I who served his majesty with honour and distinction at the battles of Hellsspontine then at Issus and most gallantly at Gaugamela. The ground I soaked with the blood of my King's enemy...*"

Michelle interrupted, "he likes to blow his own trumpet."

"Yes Michelle you have to understand when he was living the King just wasn't a man he was considered as a God and the Macedonian and Greek very much so considered every body else their subordinates, the mind set was very different nothing we would recognise."

"*... After the Persian campaign I was ordered to leave for Egypt with me went our best engineers and an architect and slaves, numbering five*" *hundred. The reason which must remain a mystery, however I will say after it was accomplished I was ordered to slay all except our officer core and sworn to secrecy. Along with us was a high priest from the sanctuary at Ammon, my greatest regret is that we had to leave behind a brilliant young officer called Excios, an unforeseen situation saw to that. I am hopeful when the next people will heal him and return his life back to him all I can say this is bigger than any of us , for the future of man kind could one day need their wisdom and advanced methods"*

With that Kevin removed his glasses and turned in the general direction of Michelle, "in my research I have come across perhaps what you would call references to what this man is talking about. Long ago in Egypt, a land was said to have been discovered like nothing that has ever been seen before, the inhabitants were supposed to have had advanced technology. In the rule of Pharaoh Akhenaton in around 1345bc there was rumoured to be an underground world with great mysterious qualities, they say if you had drank the water you would have lived to old age and the earth was so fertile you could have bumper crops all year round it was so amazing that Akhenaton was supposed to have sent a delegation to this world to ask consideration of co-colonization. According to sources his offer was accepted, fifty of the greatest minds in Egypt and engineers, soldiers, architects and scribes were chosen to join the strangely named 'the people of the light.' A short time later the Pharaoh died and if any of you know your history you will know that after his death he was proclaimed a heretic and his memory was nearly erased from history by his predecessors. Luckily, we have the parchment with this story in Dublin, it was discovered not far from Amana at the turn of the century it seems a loyal priest hid it after the decline of the cult of Aten, and you could say it was hidden before the house was cleaned."

Down at the firing range was the metallic sound of empty 7.6 gun shells hitting the ground echoing through the empty cubicles. Placing the AK47 down on the table in front of him, Jack Toner pushed a button that brought the target paper towards him, the target had a human silhouette shape and the head had three bullet holes neatly grouped together between the eyes. He lowered his safety glasses and hit the forward button waiting for the target to get about twenty foot he then as quick as lightning un-holstered his side arm, the black glock 9mm, bringing it flush to his right eye he had knocked the safety off on the way up to his firing position with a bang followed by two quick cracks in succession, safety on and proceeded to clean his weapon and with that he retrieved the target. There were three neatly placed holes where the heart is, in his mind he was still making preparations and calculating things.

The rest of the team was chatting almost in a frenzy when Heir Strauss walked in and announced everyone will be leaving early tomorrow morning, normally this would have begun protests at such short notice but there was not so much as a word, these people were ready for their upcoming adventure .

Early the next morning on a private air field, as we walked from the bus that had brought us there, I saw a massive air hanger and two C-130F Hercules supply planes taxied out on to the run way, an army of men began to load the planes with 4 wheel drives and what seemed to be two armoured hummers finally they drove what seemed to be a mobile command centre onto the planes, black in colour it had no plates and no make or model, I'd never seen anything like it in my life. We were ushered into a small briefing room where Jack Toner addressed the team that had gathered;

"You have a long flight ahead of you so get as much sleep in the planes as you can, we will be landing at an Egyptian military controlled airport in an undisclosed location. From there you will be blindfolded and escorted from the base to another undisclosed location where the team will be assembled and there the adventure begins. Myself and a small tact force will leave a few hours behind you."

With that came protests at Jacks absence, looking at every ones expressions Jack said, "god forbid if you do get into trouble, it is normally what the enemy cannot see that makes the difference, now please board the plane."

Walking past Jack, Michelle lightly ran her finger over his on the way out and with a calm expression; she smiled and got on to the plane. As the mighty engines roared, the Hercules began to climb into the sky and as she closed her eyes she whispered, "Egypt here we come."

The wheels screeched as the pilot applied the brakes; almost jumping out of her sleep Michelle woke up and yawned. She looked out the window and to her surprise she saw Egyptian military personnel dismounting an armoured patrol carrier

They had Kalashnikov rifles and were armed with side arms and appeared to be very well trained. The door on the side of the Hercules flung open and a well dressed Egyptian officer stepped on to the plane and said in well spoken English;

"Good morning ladies and gentlemen, my name is Major Smith and I am your host for the next hour. As you have probably already been told about the blindfolds, here they are, in your position I would protest but let me assure everybody it is for your own good as well as ours. Egypt is an unstable country at best but our people have the greatest hearts please enjoy your time in our country."

With that we were blind folded and led in a single file, it reminded me of the old cinema reels of the first world war of the wounded hobbling arm on shoulder, from the front line we were led out where my feet touched the concrete run way, suddenly the heat hit me I had forgotten how hot Egypt could be. We were led to a bus and were taken to seats and asked to stay there as the bus started up. It left the runway and we drove for two hours and then we heard a voice say, "please remove your blindfolds now", as I did the sun was almost like a blinding light but it calmed and my eyes went back into focus .

"My dear, no sign of the other chaps?" said Professor O'Dougherty.

"They will not be far behind." reassured Michelle.

As they looked out at the desert, it had veiled a red colour and had its own beauty, suddenly, the rest of the fleet pulled up beside them and everybody mounted the 4x4s and they started off. We drove for a couple of hours then suddenly Kevin spoke, "Michelle I think were on the outskirts of the Arabian Desert, not far from the Nile."

"Yes I agree I have seen this territory before we're not far from Al Minya" replied Michelle.

Driving the 4x4 was a well built man in his late thirties, who vaguely smiled as if to say, 'you're good, really good'. It got dark very quickly and the convoy travelled through a small town with white washed houses and narrow streets. It seemed if one were to get out one would get lost in the alley ways and streets and where if the right people were to get you, your money and possessions would probably get lost too. There was a stray dog sniffing around for scraps, it was thin and vexed looking but had the sense to scarper once the head lights caught the dog. On the outskirts of the town, the driver finally broke his silence, "we are stopping for the night ten clicks up ahead and if I am correct the camp has been built and you will all get good nights sleep."

Everything he said had a touch of the militaristic, you would know he was a mercenary and, at that not long out of the army or perhaps marine core. As we travelled along the road he suddenly knocked of the head lights and put on a pair of night goggles.

"Are you trying to kill us young man," the Professor said in protest.

"Sorry sir, orders when they don't know where you've gone they don't know where the camp is or for that matter where you are going"

Then we went into dunes it was a bumpy ride and the first one we came to the driver just hit the gas and we went straight up and over, then the terrain levelled out and we drove for two minutes and the camp appeared. The convoy were all covered in a camouflaged net as the driver turned off the car he turned to Michelle and said "meeting in the command room in five minutes ma'am."

As we walked into the command room the smell of coffee and biscuits hit us and as we walked over to the table it was the first time I saw the inside of the strange looking vehicle, the table was in the middle of the room, the sides of the room were covered in stainless steel panelling that had monitors at the top of them, at the far end of the room there was a communications centre and it seemed to be manned twenty four hours a day. It was all very strange looking, almost technologically advanced, I asked one of the guards about it only to be politely told that we did not have the correct security clearance. At the head of the table a man sat down and introduced himself as Richard, "as you probably have gathered I am English..."

"Ha, ha, we won't hold it against you dear fellow," joked Kevin.

"Ah, Professor O'Dougherty, you were in the armed forces yourself..."

"Yes young man, many years ago I was a lieutenant in an infantry battalion in the Congo serving with the Irish army, upon which I ask isn't the fact of my military record supposed to be secret?" with that the Professor started to laugh his whole body reeling from the mighty laugh. "So young man how long has it been since you've been through the gates of Hertfordshire?"

"Ah Professor, not that long, you sir are not as slow as you look."

"Indeed, now what is our situation?"

"We are currently camped outside the small town of Al Minya and are still a few days from our target. The cave is believed to be at jilf al kabir or in the surrounding area; there is no evidence from the journal to get us there so Heir Strauss has supplied us with old whermact maps to rely on. Alex said, "My god jilf al kabir is adjacent to the tropic of cancer, deep into the desert, we would need to be well supplied."

"Yes, we have everything sorted out and the world's foremost security experts and a superb supply back up and all the vehicles have sat navs to guide us and other gismos to help us, so ladies and gentlemen if you want to go to bed please go ahead, if you want supper go to the canteen tent and help yourselves."

They went to the tent and were sitting around the table when out came the chef with menus, "if you would like to pick something to eat please go ahead."

"So, what do you think so far Alex?" asked Michelle.

"I'll tell you one thing; I have never been on such a well funded field expedition in my life. There's something about these guys I don't trust, it reeks of government but the question is which one."

Across the way was a table of very hard looking ex soldiers who very much kept themselves to themselves, they were part of a squad doing guard duty and were being relived, watered and fed before going on guard. A man walked in and the man at the head of the table stood up and said "officer on deck."

"Sergeant major, you were always one for tradition, so old friend no need for that here," tutting and nodding the sergeant major agreed.

"Well sir, anything to tell us for tonight's guard duty?"

"No, just like Germany keep your units tight and close knit," with that the men got up and carried out weapons checks and then they left the tent.

Kevin turned to Michelle and said, "I can tell you one thing for sure, there's no way those guys come from an infantry regiment, they're all Special Forces. From what I can make out there's foreign legion, airborne, US marines, also rangers, a few SAS and then there's the illusive Jack Toner, and while were on that subject has any body seen him?"

"No," said everybody.

"I have a hunch he is a man of honour", said Michelle.

"Don't let your feelings cloud your better judgement my dear Michelle," said Kevin.

With that Alex looked over at her, "Michelle, is it ok if I take the coin for a few tests, it would surprise you what something can tell you under the microscope. I might even carry out a carbon test with your permission."

"No problem," she reached into her pocket and produced the coin, she then handed it to Alex saying, "happy hunting Alex."

Around a camp fire, walked the leader of the rebels. His name was Aseare; he was a battle hardened guerrilla leader and had about fifty men. He was preaching his usual sermon about corruption in the Egyptian government and how they would overthrow this weak government and reinstate their own. To forage for food they would sometimes cross into Libya to loot and take what they needed, as he went about the current government he was almost laughable except for the fact that he was so heavily armed. The Egyptian army had tried to apprehend this hapless villain but on hindsight they forgot that this half whit had a better insight of the desert and better survival skills. His skulduggery knew no boundaries, his usual method to finance his mad operation was to kidnap someone of great importance them, to ransom them off and heaven help them if they were not insured. He would normally send body parts to the family and that would normally be enough, as he was turning around a lookout ran into his camp, out of breath, the young man turned to Asere and said; "general there is news from al minya, my cousin said there is a mysterious caravan of modern vehicles camped there tonight and they are coming this direction." Taking the boy he looked him in the eyes and turned abruptly and said "did I not tell you that providence favours us my brothers, let us prepare."

Early the next morning the sun was high in the sky and a strong wind gently brushed across her face, it was a lovely April morning and she was the first one up that day. As she walked around the camp wondering where Jack was and how he was doing she had to admit to herself secretly that she was falling for him but for the minute professionalism had to rule her heart, heading back to the tent she passed a burly guard who greeted her.

When the camp was struck we all got into the four wheel drives and started on our way, we were heading west into the desert and with every mile it became ever more baron. The Nile was now behind us like an old friend saying good bye with a kiss to the back of the neck.

Sitting back on the back seat Alex asked Michelle, "what do you really think is out here?"

"The ancient Egyptians believed that the desert contained the underworld and all the monsters connected to the depth where they belong."

"Hey that isn't a bad way to keep the populous out of the desert."

"Yes at first glance it is but what you have to understand is that they believed it without question, the only people that dared go into the desert were the high officials on Pharaohs business, heading perhaps to another country or the army, from my research they did a portion of their training in the desert, some kind of death march and the only other people I can think of are the fort commanders on the border and of course the Bedouin marauders." She said

"They were some lot, the Egyptians, fascinating culture, what would it not be like to be there." Michelle then sat back and relaxed into her seat and replied "yes if only."

Driving past the ruins of what appeared to be an old temple the caravan stopped for a break so everybody stretched their legs. Michelle walked back to the ruins of the old temple accompanied by a guard, looking around the guard turned to her and said "so which god is it dedicated to?"

"Osiris I believe" looking puzzled at her he said "how do you know?" smiling she turned around "the statue on the ground that was smashed into pieces," she then pointed out that Osiris was the only god that had two identical sceptres across his chest and lying on the ground was the reminisce of the sceptres lying smashed all over the floor. "Very good lady, very good" he said.

"The sad thing about this is that it was most likely destroyed by one or the other of the great faiths."

Heading back to the convoy she remembered her time in Egypt with great joy, it was always the one place she felt at home, the desert was turning a lighter red almost tinting a yellow colour, there were rocks all around and it was starting to resemble to an extent the under world that the ancient Egyptians would have recognised with no problem. As she walked up to the group Alex waked over to her he said "the results are in and baby, wait too you hear this. The coin you gave me is the right age but this is were it gets interesting I ran a metallurgy test I hope you don't mind, there's more than gold to this coin there's a foreign element in its make up that doesn't match anything on planet earth and what's more it seems to be able to stand up to fire, weather and time a lot better than its other counterparts for example here is a coin from Alexandria, its about fifty years older but I think you get the idea."

He placed an old looking coin in her hand, "it was found in a funeral tomb and was sheltered from the elements but you can hardly can make out its description and was wafer thin," in her other hand was the coin from the tomb as if it had been minted yesterday .

Looking at Alex she said, "I don't understand".

"Michelle, that makes both of us."

We were handed our military food rations, though I have to say they were not too bad, they were manufactured by Heir Strauss' company and according to the security personnel they were delicious compared to the rations they had in the army. With that we headed off again deeper into the desert, we passed a Bedouin caravan, his magnificent white galabiyah and his sandals the gown sweeping from side to side and he had a beautiful head scarf behind him was three camels and a few goats... Kevin interrupted the moment of tranquillity with the sensible question "where is he going to find water? Would be a good guess he probably knows the location of an oasis that's been in his family for generations, the difference between life and death in this country gentlemen is water to the Bedouin people its worth its weight in gold and nothing else has the same bargaining power".

As the Bedouin tribes man walked past our four wheel drives we slowed down so as not to scare the camels the man responded with a acknowledging nod and a subdued wave, his eyes were Atlantic blue and but for the head scarf you could almost see the smile. The deeper we got into the desert the calmer and relaxed the security got, we stopped for a smoke break and I got out to stretch my legs. This desert was a very strange place; I walked a bit and turned back, with my bodyguard of course. The 4x4s and command vehicle were in a neat column, as I looked at the rest of the camp I felt as if we were all ghosts walking in a forbidden landscape and something not of this earth was hanging over us. Walking back to the vehicles the driver came and delivered some good news, "camp is about ten clicks west ma'am, we'll be there in approximately fifteen minutes." We headed off in a westerly direction and drove over dunes until we saw the lights of the camp. It was the same again, everything was set up as standard, you would think it had been airlifted in one piece, then I saw their secret two Chinooks sitting side by side, they must have striped the camp and then air lifted everything to the next location were it was assembled and ready. The thought of it was a logistical miracle. As we pulled into camp the smell of the canteen flooded our senses, overwhelmed, I ate with a controlled air of dignity and surprisingly so did the rest of the team. We then sat around the table and the canteen staff came down with a tray of alcohol beverages which, to our surprise had all of our favourite drinks on it. The canteen man said "with the complements of Heir Strauss". As we crowded around the table I asked Kevin about the legend,

"Well my dear, as I told you the Pharaoh Akhenaten had his name erased from the list of Kings, in those days, that alone was a death sentence in the after world, and assured one thing we can depend on the other Pharaohs tried their dammed hardest to eradicate the memory of Akhenaten for which we can be thankful. You see, the existence of Akhenaten was only discovered relatively lately, that means that after his death the capital was moved from Amarna back to Memphis and all the statues and steel he had erected and every mention of his name was wiped out, meaning that all contact with the lost world was forgotten. We can assume that whenever Akhenaten sent some of the greatest minds in Egypt to this mysterious land, the entrance was sealed and after his demise his followers were ether ejected from court or worse executed which was probably more likely. Nothing more was heard from this lost land until the rise of Alexander, legend says when he was in Egypt he visited the oracle at Siwa where the priests parted to him a secret said to be so great it made Alexander shiver, yes shiver, what secret was so great it could do that."

"I don't know Kevin but its starting to make sense after he walloped the Persians; it seems he sent the illusive General Aloun and other brilliant minds into this abyss."

" Yes but the thing I don't understand is this general I have never heard of him in all my studies, its as if he never existed, as if his very being was deleted from the history books, as it seems that's what Alexander did or ordered someone to do."

Looking over at Alex, he looked at the both of us then looked at the coin, "what I can tell you is that we don't know what this race of people are capable of, are they peaceful or war like, what are their aims, what I can tell you is that looking at the make-up of the metal of the coin we are dealing with a very advanced race to have that level of metallurgy. Of course we have counterparts to that now developed just a few years ago, now ladies and gentlemen this coin taken from a tomb that was about in Alexander's time, the thing you see that gets me is the older one is far superior and if they had that level of technology then what in the name of god would they be like now!"

Laughing hysterically he put to them that their means of transportation is probably teleportation, the rest of the room exploded into laughter, the Professor was nearly bent in two and the guards that overheard the conversation were doubled in two and it took a good moment until everybody regained some kind of composure and quickly the air of sincerity came back again and they were once again locked in conversation.

"Right, we know that Alexander built the tomb but why, and its layout, I have never seen and that's including the tombs in Egypt which are to an extent very different to what I have read in my grand fathers journal. This circle chamber in the middle is very complex and where we need to be careful is with all the traps that seem to be very well designed and constructed. The only one my grandfather came across was the glass spear with acid inside it," said Michelle

"Yes," replied Alex "the fact that glass doesn't rot gives you the idea that whoever designed them knew what he was doing and if any of you have read the diary you will know that they are deadly. So let me give to you on a serious note a word..." looking very grave, the look of comedy now gone from his face, "...and the word is caution. Whoever designed this tomb was at the top of his class Michelle said that the only traps she heard of were the gases trapped in the tomb before you open the tomb, standard practice is to leave the tomb for a day so that the bad air and the gasses can escape, they were placed there by the ancient Egyptians on purpose, the offerings moulded over time and the body of course, bacteria built up over thousands of years and the rest you can guess."

Chapter 4.

Meanwhile, thousands of miles away in London, a black limo pulled up outside the front door and a man got out he was a tall thin man with a scar on the right cheek and black short hair, his name was David Blake. He was well dressed in a Seville row suit and considered himself to be a highly professional man, the one thing he hated was his personnel being sloppy, he looked sternly at the doorman as he entered the building he walked up a flight of stairs and into an adjoining hall it mirrored something like a conference hall but this was no conference. As he walked in, the man at the top of the table looked at him impatiently, "well Mr Smith how are things progressing?"

"As I said in the phone call, everything is on track; our man in the Egyptian army is at this minute engaging a daring plan. As you know the so called rebel Aseare has been receiving intelligence reports on the movements of the Egyptian army, this alone has given him the advantage of knowing were they are and knowing they knew nothing of his location he was able to amass a small fortune under the pretence he was a gorilla leader. In return he and his followers will attack and hopefully capture the team, he will also secure the journal and coin if possible, we should have them both by tomorrow."

The old man at the head of the table was pampered looking and had a beard he belonged to a secret organisation called the line of Ammon. Standing up, the old man addressed the awaiting members "what we have strived to achieve is now achievable, as you know Alexander.." pausing for a moment with an air of reverence for the Kings name, "... entrusted our ancestors with this great task that now rests upon our shoulders, to protect the people of the light from the corruption and perversion of this world, before Alexander died in Babylon he recruited his elite guard to one last task the preservation of this wonderful world at any cost. He set up treasure deposits and instructed his guard accordingly, whatever empires came and went them and their forbearer's were to infiltrate and assimilate into any cultures and religions that were in power at the time and they had access to the treasure so they could well equip themselves and bribe any officials towards their own end. They of course kept to their real faiths and worshipped Ammon as Alexander had commanded."

Looking at them all the old man looked at a younger man sitting on the left and reassured him, "worry not my friend."

Nicolas was the descendant of General Aloun, he, as his ancestor before him, worried most about the young man General Aloun had no choice but to leave behind. This was the young officer Excios, left behind to open the gates between the two worlds; the young man nearly paid the ultimate price to open the mechanism. It required courage at the entrance of the gate, there was a stand there about waist length and on top of that was a strange device, there were two holes on both sides and beautifully carved handles on the inside, the idea was to put your hands into the holes and grasp the handles and when you did that you pulled the handles back and away from yourself, at that moment blades came out of the shafts of the handles and cut into the wrists just as you were completing the technique so you would not notice that you were then starting to bleed into the stand. It's then that you notice the blood filtering in with the mirror liquid on the gate which activates it but the only problem was the lack of medical experience and it often turned into a death sentence for those who wished to use it. Never-the-less, this young officer took it upon himself to open the gate against the wishes of his general but, as he lay dying the priests of Ammon placed him into the strange sarcophagus that they had just built and placed the lid on top again and inserted strange crystals into the slots. The sarcophagus started to fill with a translucent fluid, the priest said to the general, "When the world is ready he shall be awoken and healed."

Aseare looked at his men and gave the order, "are you ready do your duty?"

He headed back into camp and went into his tent; only he was allowed into this area. He walked over to a laptop and powered it up, he then activated the web camera, then rolling his head back and forth and side to side almost as if he had done a hard days work thinking to himself that he had been at this for years and after this job he would be wealthy enough to retire to the continent in Europe. He fancied France, just one more job and he would be free of these morons and could take flight in the middle of the night while every body slept. He had a car fuelled up and hidden on the other side of the caves where the car was covered in an old tarpaulin that he got in a raid on a Bedouin caravan a year ago. If anybody suspected anything they would have his throat cut and leave his body to rot, but he had thought of that, after the raid he would throw a huge party and get the alcohol flowing as well as some cannabis for the men to smoke and by the time he left there would be nobody in any fit state to do anything about it. Laughing to himself he looked at the laptop screen and said "we are nearly ready to deploy." The man on the screen said "good, I have got some details you might like to know, the target is camped about twenty miles east of your location, they have around twenty armed guards and the rest are all academics so I trust it shouldn't be much of a problem." Looking back towards the rebel leader a man in uniform sat comfortably on his seat, Aseare could see that the soldier was in some kind of office, probably in a barracks somewhere on the far bank of the Nile, he was smoking a cigar and laughing loudly. Then he said with a serious look, "after this raid my friend, my advice is to get out of dodge as fast as you can, this is the last time I can help you, military intelligence is closing in on me so after tonight I am burning all my information on you and closing down this web link. Our friend has instructed me to tell you that you shall be paid through the normal channels", with that the officer looked at Aseare and said "farewell friend." With that he closed the connection, leaving Aseare looking at a blank screen. Nodding and smiling with a crazed look in his eye he ejected the computer disk. He had copied the whole conversation, just for insurance purposes of course. He would post them to his sister in Cairo just in case he was double crossed, not that he ever intended to use it. After he was gone, the Egyptian army would be tipped off with the location of the camp and the populous would most likely end up getting slaughtered. If this happened it would be to his advantage. Over the years he had slowly turned everybody into fanatics, without a doubt they would all fight to the bitter end and with them all dead nobody would know what he looked like and then he would have no problem bribing a corrupt official to supply him with a new passport and papers.

Back in London the old man got out of his chair and said to the gathered, "let us go in to the sanctuary we have built to the god Ammon and make an offering to the success of the mission." He headed towards the double doors at the back of the room. Just as he walked towards them they opened and in the room in front of them stood two priests of Ammon wearing leopard skins and with shaven heads. The members walked in and the doors were closed behind them.

After the nights comradely, Michelle was tired and was in a mind to go to bed, so she excused herself and headed into the desert for one last look before bed. She loved the desert at night, the stars shining bright and the light air that touched her face in the gentlest way. She walked in to her tent and sat down on her camp bed. She lay down on the top of the blankets, normally it would be freezing but they had thought of everything, the tent was heated. She fell into a deep sleep and dreamt of her grandfather, as a child he would have played with her. What happy times she thought, as she was looking at her grandfather he gently turned around to her and said "everything will be all right; all you have to do is trust your heart."

She woke up suddenly as she was being thrown out of the camp bed by the force of an explosion. The roar of gunfire was all around, crawling on the floor she realised she was in shock and stood up and went outside. They had struck when the guards were being relieved; they took out all the perimeter patrols with ease and moved in with speed. Aseare had trained them well, a grenade was thrown into the guard house and nearly everybody was killed. They lined everybody up against the command centre, the mercenaries were in shock and some were in tears, the injured were carried over beside them and Aseare mockingly shouted, "you useless fucks are supposed to be the best," he laughed out loud, the English soldier we knew as Richard shouted over "what about our injured?" as he was cradling a young man who had a gunshot to his abdomen. Aseare just tilted his head with an evil grin walked over to the injured man, pulled out his pistol and shot him between the eyes; he slumped down dead to the desert floor. Richard shouted, "You bastard, that man could have received medical treatment!" With an arrogant tone Aseare replied, "he got all the treatment he needed." The rest of his men laughed at his sick antics. He then turned to Richard and motioned him to hand over his side arm. Reluctantly he did so and then with a grin Aseare pistol whipped the English man, he fell onto the ground, crimson spittle came from his mouth as he recovered. Aseare stood over him and said "don't ever insult me or it will be lights out for you, do you understand?" Looking at him Richard nodded.

We were forced into the 4x4 by two of the rebels, their Kalashnikovs were shoved into our backs and one said in broken English, "you no escape we no shoot." As I watched through the windscreen I saw a man go through my tent, he came out with my grandfather's journal in one hand and the coin in the other, he pulled out a mobile phone and was jumping with joy, he was laughing and speaking in Arabic. From what I could hear he was saying something about having the package. They then stole our Jeeps and along with their own vehicles headed in a westerly direction. As we headed to our secret location in the desert one of the captured guards looked at me and said "these are the rebels I have heard of, they're supposed to be very dangerous." I asked him "why could you not protect us?" The man looked confused at first but then said "they came out of nowhere as we were changing the guard, grenades were thrown into the guard house, the rest of us were easy pickings for this scum." He looked down in total disgust, almost ashamed of himself for getting himself and the others into this mess and not for reacting fast enough.

The 4x4 banged and tyres spun as the inexperienced young Arab man drove along in a reckless fashion until we came out into a flat open plain. Thank god, I thought, at least where flat ground was concerned we would have nothing to obscure the way and cause an accident. Driving along it was still dark and I could see in the distance a rock formation that was shaped like the horns of a bull. It had one way in and one way out. The soldier looked at me and a small smile broke out on his face, for what purpose, I knew not. This situation was getting worse by the minute. As we drove into the horns of the rock formation, the vehicles carrying prisoners drove right to the back of the cavern. Stopping abruptly the two guards jumped out and shouted, "Cage, into cage!" We were all hoarded into the make-shift prison and subjected to the taunting of our guards. As the night went on, for some reason there was a heavy mist and the leader appeared to heap praise upon everyone in his twisted circus. He turned around and walked over to a pile on the ground, he pulled off the blanket and underneath there was whiskey and vodka and in the other pile there was beer, about a ton of the bloody stuff.

They intended to have one hell of a good night, terrifying thoughts ran through Michelle's mind, of being multiply raped and that alone sent shivers through her spine. An hour passed and most of them were paralytic and stumbling all over the place and vomiting. For those who appeared not to drink, they smoked cannabis and lay around the camp fires, smoking and bursting into occasional fits of laughter.

Aseare walked over with a swagger and introduced himself, "I am Aseare, the commander of this battalion of liberation rebels.   We captured you because you are of great importance to someone and they will pay well."

"Why are we here?" asked Michelle.

"As I have told you already, you are of great importance to someone. Who that is? I know not." He replied.

Driving through the desert at night was hard at best but when there was fog, it dampened things a bit. Two vehicles pulled along side each other; one was a small truck with a tarpaulin on the back. Jack Toner stepped out of the 4x4 and surveyed the site that met his eyes. He was just in sight of the rebel base, their fire glowing in the mist. Twenty five heavily armed men jumped out of the truck and giving the command, "gear up," they began putting on their night-vision goggles and then they all fanned out in the direction of the rock formation. As they closed in they saw two guards on the outskirts of the horns. Toner took them both out with his heckler and cock machine gun that had a silencer. Thud, thud, as the bullets hit the guards; he then fired off another couple of shots into them as they lay kicking on the ground. He put his hand into his jacket and pulled out a strange looking object, it was black in colour and was a new innovation from Heir Strauss' weapons research department. Around the fires, the rest of the rebels saw the attack begin and they mustered their weapons. But before they could move, a strange looking object landed in the middle of the crowd who were still reaching for their arms. The device went off, it started with a high pitch sound and then went off, it was packed with ball bearings, and the device had in fact measured the diameter of the circle and then fed the device enough explosive power to deliver its pay load to the enemy. They were riddled with ball bearings as the camp flooded with Toners men, the sounds of the dying and the injured over-whelmed the misty atmosphere. Aseare saw what was going on and turned to run in the direction of the entrance, Michelle saw this and screamed at Toner to catch him. He just smiled at her and then, as quick as lightning he turned and pulled out his knife. He flipped the blade into his hand then with all of his might he threw the knife, Aseare was running past a tall post that had been used for restraining hostages. If they had been too hard to cope with during the day, the post usually pacified the prisoners, and now it was his turn, a numbing pain went through his body, he turned his head to discover Toner had nailed his arm to the post with the knife. Casually walking over to him Toner said, "Well, well Aseare, you've certainly been busy."

Screaming at him in broken English he said, "I do not know what you mean!"

"You will," knocking him out and retrieving his knife, Toner walked away and Aseare slumped to the ground. He casually looked at two men standing behind him and said, "Take this piece of shit away and clean him up." They picked him up and dragged him slowly to the command vehicle until all you could see of him was his feet comically disappearing behind the door.

As Jack Toner walked over to the cage he shouted, "Stand back," then pulling his pistol out, he shot the padlock off. Michelle came running out and jumped into the arms, he kissed her hard and said, "Did I not tell you that every body would be ok?" Looking over at the guy who had been beside Michelle, Jack asked, "how many casualties Jim?"

"About eight sir, I'd also like to add that that slug Aseare murdered one of our people out right," replied Jim.

"Ok Jim, once we get Intel out of him he's yours for about fifteen minutes before we hand him over to the authorities" said Jack.

"Thank-you sir" he said.

Just at that moment one of his men came running over shouting, "someone's coming sir."

"Ok, get the bodies out of the way and tidy up the camp quick" said Jack.

"Yes sir"

"Adapt your clothing to make it appear we are the rebels"

"Yes sir"

Jack Toner took of his black combat jacket and replaced it with one of the rebel's. He also put on the traditional head dress and started to walk in the direction of the lights. It was almost morning and you could just about see the tip of the sun. It was beautiful. As the lights came closer it became clear what the mystery vehicle was, it was a land rover country, one of the old ones. As it got closer you could make out the driver and his accomplice, as he walked forward a bit the vehicle got closer and closer until he could see who was driving it. It was a European man and in the passenger seat sat a middle aged man in his late forties; he had an eastern look about him. As the land rover came to a standstill the passenger door opened and the middle aged man stepped out.

He said, "ah Aseare, my friend, have you got what I want because I have got what you want."

All this time, Toner kept his distance and played with his head-dress as if he was fixing it.

Toner said, "You must be the illusive captain Al Hasher?"

The man turned around and said, "How do you know my name, you're not supposed to know my name!"

With that Toner threw his head-dress to the ground and said, "you got a close friend of mine killed, a major in the Egyptian army a few years ago."

"Yes my friend, to make progress in this world you have to walk over a few corpses" he replied.

With that Jack pulled out his gun and shot. The captain's head almost exploded. He had used hollow point rounds in his 9mm. The man slumped to the ground and rolled over in his own blood. The driver got out and introduced himself, "My name is Mr Collins, I am Mr Smith's assistant, owing to the situation it looks like you already know who I am."

"Yes, you work for the secret society called the line of Ammon. I have a proposition for you, from Heir Strauss, I think you should listen to it!" said Jack.

Walking over to the command tent, Jack said to the tired looking soldier, "my men will get you in touch with anybody in the world from in there." Taking the ear piece and putting it into place, Me Collins typed an address into the computer and finally there before him was the mysterious Mr Smith, "there has been a development. It appears Aseare has been incapacitated and his mission has failed however, there may be a compromise."

"Yes, tell me more," replied Mr Smith.

"Heir Strauss' head of security, a man called Jack Toner, has asked for the help of the line of Ammon".

After fifteen minutes of the meeting Mr Smith agreed and went to consult the chairman.

"I'm not sure about this, not one bit, but it's for the best it's for the best. Tell Mr Toner we will meet him and Heir Strauss tomorrow in Egypt at the rebel's camp" said the chairman.

With that Mr Smith said, "yes sir" and gently bowed, turned and walked into the office adjoining the main conference room. He looked at the computer screen and said, "You're on, tomorrow at the base, see you there," with that Mr Collins closed the line and went to find Toner, "we're on for tomorrow Mr Toner."

"Good Allister" said Jack.

Jack walked over to Michelle and said, "How are you feeling?"

"Oh, I have been better, being kidnapped is all in a days work for us," she joked.

Toner laughed and said, "Would you have preferred it if we hadn't have rescued you?"

"No Jack, I prefer it just the way it is."

Jack looked deep into her eyes and said "good I am glad to hear it."

"Sir we've rounded up the rest of the rebels, what do you want us to do with them?" said Richard.

"Let them go," replied Jack.

"What! Are you mad Jack?"

"No Richard, bring out Aseare."

One minute later, the remains of the rebel force was gathered outside the command tent, Jack was speaking through an interpreter, two of his men took Aseare out of the vehicle and his men started to cheer him as if he was a hero. Jack started his speech, "gallant people of the desert, understand, that this man before you is not the charismatic leader that you think he is or that he does Egypt any good. For the years that he has lead you, he has deceived and corrupted you for his own selfish goals. He has amassed a small fortune of his own, with the help of a corrupt army official." Two of his own men walked over to the crowd with a laptop and three carrier bags of loot, stolen credit cards, jewellery and a large amount of cash. He pulled out the briefcase that the captain had, it was full of American dollars. Looking at the bewildered populous he said, "Do you know what this money was for? It was for turning you lot over to the Egyptian authorities and you would have been slaughtered in a hopeless gun battle with the Egyptian army. Now, to an extent this is not your fault, it's his, so I am making you a deal. There are two trucks over there and this money and valuables are rightly yours. I reckon there's enough in there for you all to have comfortable lives, also, the fate of Aseare, I leave to you."

With that the armed guards backed off and handed the keys over to the crowd and then threw Aseare into the crowd, they began kicking him to the ground then one of the older men said stop and produced a rope. "O fuck," Aseare thought, "they're going to hang me." But he was dragged over to behind one of the trucks and hog tied around his boots; the rest of the men got into the trucks and started to sing. It was almost comical watching them drive off. They were still singing while Aseare screamed as the truck moved off, his screams eventually died off in the distance.

"Oh well," said Richard, "there shouldn't be much of him left by the time they reach the dunes."

Laughing out loud Jack said, "where I come from, there's an old saying, 'what you sow you will reap,' I do not believe I have ever had the pleasure of meeting such a bastard."

"Yes," replied Richard, "they say that there is no creature crueler than the human being."

"Right," said Jack, "but on a serious note, this chairman and Heir Strauss are meeting here tomorrow and I would like everything to be ok. This was an unforeseen set of incidents and it seems that the line of Ammon have no choice than to meet us for talks."

The day gave way to the night and this was the only time Michelle could feel relaxed in the desert, the rest of the team had been annoyed at what had happened and a few of them had threatened to resign but she had convinced them to stay and reminded them to be aware that they were on the threshold of a great discovery and they would be part of history. To her surprise, Kevin had intervened to reinforce her position by saying that the reason they had been kidnapped was because what they are looking for is very valuable.

As she walked through the camp, the fires were all lit and the men were around them laughing and engaging is some kind of banter, games were also being played. Just then she looked across and saw Jack. He was looking at her, sitting on a wooden box he had a cup of tea in one hand and a diary in the other, he said, "tomorrow is going to be busy you know, the two head honchos are attending," she laughed and said, "have you ever heard of this line of Ammon?"

"Yes, but only in myth and legend, it's said they kept there belief of the Ammon on the instructions of Alexander himself," he replied.

"So you think this is for real?"

"I cannot be sure, on the other hand, I have heard too much now to dismiss everything I've heard."

Michelle said, "Why don't we ask Kevin what he knows about this lot, it would fall into his curriculum."

Jack said, "why not, it would do no harm."

They asked Kevin into the command tent and they all sat around the table, "we need to pick your brains on something," said Michelle.

"No problem, what is it?"

Jack pored him a glass of whiskey and replied, "The line of Ammon?"

Kevin gently laughed and said, "My goodness that is an old fairytale, a myth. You can only find them on the fringes of legend, they are strange and difficult to define, and there are some scholars who believe they exist. Why do you ask about them?" he asked curiously.

"Have you ever heard of their leader?" said Jack

"Yes, the name varies from century to century; he was known as the general, before that he was captain of the shields, as the order progressed into the future. I believe they now call him the chairman," said Kevin.

On hearing that Jack Toner turned in his direction and said, "Well tomorrow you are going to meet him."

"What?!" said Kevin.

"It was the line of Ammon that tried to acquire yourself and the rest of the team, in, as you remember, what was quite an ungentle manner," replied Jack.

"Oh my god, so it's true, I don't think there isn't anyone I wouldn't kill to have five minutes with that man. Imagine still being under Alexander's orders thousands of years later. What an honour."

"Don't tell me you look up to them?"

"Yes I do, how could one not admire them, but it's strange, nowhere have I read that they have ever used violence to achieve their goals."

The next morning a fleet of 4x4s pulled up outside the camp, a handsome man got out of the vehicle, he was slightly well built and had blonde hair and had an air of confidence about him. He walked over to Jack and introduced himself, "hello Mr Toner, my name is Nicolas."

"You have me at a disadvantage sir," replied Jack

"No, no you're very well known in the security and intelligence community," replied Nicolas.

"Ah, I see, you have done a background check on me."

"Yes it helps to know who you're dealing with, and on that note the chairman should be arriving very shortly. He's on route in his helicopter," said Nicolas.

"Nicolas, this is Michelle Fordix, Egyptologist, and this is Kevin O' Dougherty from Trinity he's a Professor there."

"Yes I know, I've followed your work for years I believe you know an ancestor of mine?"

"An ancestor yes, General Aloun, I'm his direct descendant," said Kevin

"My god that's incredible, you and I have a great deal to talk about Professor, I do believe it will be a pleasure."

As they talked, Jack heard the low purr of a high rotary engine. The noise got louder and louder until it engulfed all the peace of the desert. The helicopter finally landed and Heir Strauss walked out of the command vehicle. Michelle turned to Jack, "How did he got here so fast?"

"He got here early this morning, he owns a leer jet, I have been on it once, and I tell you that thing can move."

She looked to the side of the formation and saw a makeshift airfield. The thing about this part of the desert is that it's so flat, flat enough to land a plane, at the sides were two strips of landing lights.

Heir Strauss walked over to the helicopter and awaited the door to open. An old man stepped out and shook his hand, and they greeted each other and exchanged complements. As the rotors powered down then they came to a standstill "I trust you had a good flight," said Heir Strauss.

Laughing the chairman said, "Oh I have had worse, I used to be a pilot for the Greek air force," they both smiled and continued to walk over to the command vehicle. Heir Strauss walked beside him as they talked casually until they reached the vehicle and Heir Strauss said, "after you dear fellow, after you." They were sitting around the table and it was the chairman who spoke first. He mentioned that they thought there was no other way to gain entry to the tomb and had underestimated how complementary and civil Heir Strauss had been, acknowledging this Heir Strauss said "let us be friends in this adventure, you have a world of knowledge to offer and it's not every day you get to meet a legend, especially one that has connections to Alexander himself."

The old man said, "We have some old blue prints of the trap systems of the tomb but some have been lost or misplaced. The only thing I don't know is the location of the tomb, you see before he died Alexander ordered General Aloun to destroy the only map which showed the location. Some have known about the tomb but have never managed to find it," looking puzzled, he continued, "I have always wondered why Alexander ordered the destruction of the map, it has always been a worry for me."

"What do you mean chairman? Heir Strauss said that the tomb was sealed and the workmen slaughtered and the very location was concealed, have you ever thought it was for a reason, like maybe the tomb was never meant to be opened and the people of the light, they were considerably advanced when Alexander ruled, what are they going to be like now? Have they ever crossed your mind what will their civilisation be like now? Are they a war-like people or a harmonious one? Because if we open this portal between this world and theirs we are risking everything. But at the same time it might be the best thing to happen earth in two thousand years."

With that they agreed to carry on with caution, "we also have to be on the lookout, there are several government bodies that want the treasure and would be prepared to kill for the privilege. They of course know nothing about the true origins of the tomb; they just have a lust for treasure and ill-gotten adventure. I would like to show you all something I have been working on, so here is the prototype."

They drove the command vehicle into the desert and it started to transform into a larger block than it had been, then this discus shaped object fired out of the top of the command module, it went about one hundred feet into the air and then the top and the bottom of the discus opened and there seemed to be rotors. It was powered like a helicopter, the outside of it was a groove and in this groove was a lens that went around at great speed. Down in the command module, Heir Strauss stood in the middle, a technician handed him an ear piece and a set of virtual reality specs, this enabled him to see a panoramic view in every direction for three hundred miles.

"Don't worry chairman, here you are perfectly safe," with that he handed the glasses over to him, "it's the latest in discreet surveillance technology. Also it's as good at night vision and thermal imagining this way we can see an enemy coming a long way off. It's a handy piece of kit that gives you advanced intelligence on the spot."

In the breakfast canteen, the Professor, Nicolas and Michelle were talking about the tomb and Nicolas was filling them in on what he knew about it.

"Nicolas, is it true about the order Alexander gave the line of Ammon to stay true to that faith?"

"Yes, we still to this day worship Amun-Ra, you see to Alexander he was the reincarnation of his father Philip and was also the god of war in Egyptian mythology. To affirm the trust that he had imparted to us and to reassure us how important the mission was, he insisted that we convert to the Egyptian religion and they even say that as he died he made General Aloun swear to carry out his wishes. We had only one rule that was not to be broken at any cost, in no way, were we allowed to interfere with the government or culture of any civilisation for the world had to progress naturally, this we have done."

Kevin asked almost in a childish manor, "What was he like?"

"My ancestor?" asked Nicolas.

"No I mean Alexander the man." asked Kevin.

"Well according to my father, General Aloun spoke of him very affectionately. They say that he could on occasion, be mistaken for an ordinary soldier. On one occasion at a siege at one of the sea ports he stripped of his armours and jumped into the line of soldiers pulling one of his siege engines and in other occasions he was chopping trees down for other uses. He was never idle and at most of his battles he was the first soldier into the enemy ranks. It's true he took unbelievable risks with his life, his soldiers worshipped him. On another occasion he was leading his troops through a desert when he heard reports of water shortages, he stopped his whole army and said, 'when you men find water on the other side of this desert then I will be obliged to drink when you do,' with those words he lifted his water canteen into the air and poured out his water. So, Professor you can see it's quite clear that anybody who came into contact with Alexander was deeply touched," with a stern look Nicolas went on, "there was also another side to him, he could be ruthless, utterly ruthless, and in today's accounts he would have committed ethnic cleansing in a great scale. In some instances he had whole cities erased from the landscape and the population massacred, he always spared the people who found sanctuary in the temples in these cities. He was, I suppose, an extraordinary man, you see he was educated by Aristotle the Greek philosopher, it is said that Philip spent a fortune to ensure that it was by Aristotle."

Just at that one of Jacks men ran in and said, "All ready to go sir."

"Right then," Jack stood up and said, "Everybody to your vehicles," and off they went. They travelled for days, almost as if they were crossing over into Libya, the sun was beating down, they say it could kill a man in less than a day if he did not know what he was doing the desert. At this stage the dunes almost appeared to shine as if beckoning us to our deaths. There was a snake, it was a strange looking creature, "look a royal cobra," said Michelle, "a sign of protection for the Pharaohs and his family, because in ancient Egypt there was nothing as important as family and children, it is said Rameses the second had over one hundred children."

Jack coolly said, "a real ladies man by all accounts, and let me see, he also went on a mammoth building project and managed to defeat the Hittites and proclaimed himself victor of oh let me see, everywhere!"

Michelle laughed out loud and Jack said, "You're not the only one who has done a bit of research."

"Can I ask you a question Jack? How did you end up here?" asked Michelle

"Oh it's a long story, a very long story."

Looking at him lovingly she said, "Well I'm certainly not going anywhere!"

"As you have probably have guessed, I am Irish, I come from a small village in Northern Ireland, no work prospects and plenty of personal trouble so I joined the French Foreign Legion," he said.

Looking at him seriously she said, "Was she pretty?"

Brush strokes of red broke across his face as she asked the question, "Yes," he said, "she was very pretty, it was so very long ago, almost another world you would think."

"What happened?"

"Oh, she married somebody else and my romanticism ended that day on a very sour note. I was very young then and now that I have years of experience behind me I can understand what I did wrong with a tinge of regret. I often wonder what she must think of me now."

"As far as I understand, time is the greatest healer and some say the greatest forgiver also," nodding with approval Jack said with a grin, "I don't need to ask you what your story is."

"Why is that?" asked Michelle

"Because I have read your intelligence file," laughing loudly his chest resounding with booming energy, then the chat died down, looking at his watch Jack radioed to the command vehicle, "anything afoot Heir Strauss?"

"Nothing yet Jack," shouted Heir Strauss into the radio, "Our friend the chairman has warned us that he believes that his organisation has been infiltrated by a government agent, who's government, he does not know. Jack listen to me were going to camp up ahead tonight not far from these old runes, some kind of temple I believe."

As we drove over the last dune, it was like a sea of sand, and there it was, the ruins of the old temple he was talking about.

"It's actually the remains of an old border fort with Libya once run by Pharaohs men, then after the decline of Cleopatra the Romans rebuilt it as one of there supply forts during the Graeco Roman period," said Michelle confidently smiling at Jack.

Grabbing him by the hand Michelle said, "Let's go and take a look."

So he drove the 4x4 over to the old fort and they climbed out of the vehicle and started to survey the old ruins. Michelle walked seductively beside him. Hidden under his professional exterior his lust was fighting a war with his cold hard discipline and his lust was winning inch by inch, like a piece of metal being eroded by acid and the only thing that denied victory right now, was time. As they walked into the front gate of the fort they saw signs of habitation, Jack said, "Don't worry, the Egyptian army sometimes use this place as stop gap when they're patrolling the desert." They walked over to the back of the fort and there was what seemed to be a subterranean vault that had been dug into the ground, as they walked into it, they could see that it had ancient graffiti, they both laughed and Jack turned to face Michelle. The battle of lust had been won, the acid had eaten at all of Jacks reserve, he swung her around and kissed her, hard and long, it felt like they had been hit by a bolt of lightning, they stopped and looked into each others eyes, then the overwhelming desire took over and they started taking each others clothes off. His wore a silver ring, shinning and glittering in the light, he slowly moved down over her neck and down to her breasts, and he circled her nipples until they were erect, it produced a rippling affect and it went through her like a shiver. He grabbed her by the waist and then, with his lips he started his decent using his tongue, tasting every inch of her and caressing her with care. Passion overcame her and she started to unzip his trousers and with her boots pushed them round his ankles. With her fingers she caressed his perfect stomach and she began kissing him. He grabbed her, laid her on the ground and began to make love to her. She moaned in pleasure, grinding her pelvis against his and as they both climaxed the sun seemed to beam through a small hole in the back of the vault and it bathed them both in sunlight. Their sweat soaked bodies lying on top of a pile of clothes. Jack turned around to see the vault and the small room had small particles of dust floating around the air, which had a sparkling effect that made the efforts of the young lovers seem worthy. They got dressed slowly and headed back for the vehicle, they jumped in and Jack started to drive.

CHAPTER 5.

"So, what you think of the Greeks version?" asked Michelle.

"Yes it's very interesting. The only thing I am asking myself is why Alexander would go to all this trouble. Think about it, he sends one of his best generals into the desert along with some of the most brilliant people of his time but for what reason?" replied Jack.

"We could ask Nicolas?"

"No" said Jack, "we will consult Professor O' Dougherty and play it calm until we get to know this mysterious Nicolas," looking at Michelle smiling he said, "remember what I said about caution, it always serves the sensible well."

As they drove onwards they saw the lights of the camp, the other cars were parked in the middle of the camp and she could see commotion. They were all around the table in the canteen and Kevin came up Michelle and said, "We're about two days off the discovery and the excitement is starting to set in."

Looking at Michelle, Jack said. "I have got to go and sort out the patrol shifts tonight, see you later," with that he winked at her and walked off in the direction of the command tent, playfully slapping her bottom as he went.

After his dinner Kevin took a sip out of his pint of Guinness, "not bad," he said, "not bad indeed. All this trouble for a few brilliant academics!" laughing he said, "My dear I think we've set the trend for all field explorations," giggling at Kevin she said, "what do you think of Nicolas?"

"Well apart from the fact that he has some very old ancestry and he belongs to a secret organisation, not really much, though I am normally a good judge of character. Something tells me he can be trusted, as for the rest of them? I don't know."

"Kevin, what do you think Alexander has got to do with this?"

"Well, let's look at what we do know, he conquered Egypt and most of the ancient world, he was an extraordinary military genius..."

"I know but what really gets you about him Kevin?" sitting back he said, "there is one thing about him I could never work out, the fact he never chose a successor, all that power and nobody to hand it over to. It's not to say there wasn't heirs because there was, it's the only thing I can't work out. Most people who built empires always had heirs for succession. Why?"

Looking at the Professor she said, "I see what you mean, at the moment Nicolas is the only person who can shed any light on this."

As they retired to the heat of the fire they saw Nicolas heading from the command vehicle. Michelle beckoned him over and said, "There are a few things I don't understand, perhaps you could shed light on them?"

Smiling, Nicolas said, "If I can."

"We don't know what purpose the tomb has? Have you ever come across what they took into it?"

"Well from what I have heard, they sent some of the best engineers, up-and-coming scientists and scribes; they obviously wanted to know about the world outside their own."

Jack walked up to the group who were standing around the fire and said, "Nicolas is there anything you feel they tried to hide from the rest of the ancient caravan? For instance, was there anything that General Aloun was not at liberty to disclose?"

"Well come to think of it, there is one thing that I always wondered about. There was a sealed part of the column and it was always the heaviest guarded, it was the only thing that we did not know about for some reason or another and the only person that knew anything about it, was the general. But you see Alexander swore him to secrecy and what I know abut his mission, great care was taken to ensure that this was achieved. After the tomb was built, the slaves were taken out and executed in cold blood, for one of my kind to do that, it still runs chills down my spine"

Intervening Kevin said, "What you have to understand is that it was a different time, your ancestor probably committed much worse atrocities under the command of Alexander. Please remember this man was one of an elite officer core trained by Philip Of Macedonia. There was no such thing as not following orders."

"I wonder if he had little choice in what to do."

"You forget Nicolas, he was under the direct command of Alexander the Great," with that Nicolas said, "yes but I can tell you one thing Professor, there are old letters to his wife, you can translate them if you like?"

Jumping at the chance he said, "Yes please."

Walking over his tent Nicolas reached towards his briefcase and opened it, he reached inside and produced this old looking papyri, he handed it over to Kevin and said, "Knock yourself out."

"Nicolas did you never have them translated yourself?" asked Kevin

"Believe it or not, they could not be translated because they might be too sensitive and we could not take the chance. So Professor you're about to become the only person in about two thousand years to read it."

Everybody crowded around the Professor and awaited the translation. Looking through the document he scanned everything for about five minutes and then he began.

To you my darling, I send love, and to my children I send my wishes, to my little boy remember your lessons and honour your mother in three moons you will enter the military academy that I once attended. Serve them with honour and obey the master and the gods will see that you live to join the falanks and one day serve our great King Alexander. To my little girl, a fathers love and kisses and assurance that I will return once my duty is complete. My darling, we set of from Babylon and I cannot say where we are going, of all the battles we fought this is to be my most important according to the King. I will be gone for about five years, possibly longer, until then I shall send you letters of affection and think of you my darling wife.

Putting that papyri letter to one side he picked up another one and began to read once more:

I have arrived at my destination and by the gods I have never seen a more desolate place in my whole life and I have been to quite a few. The heat is overpowering and there are other dangers to be considered. Last week I lost a man from a snake bite, a strange creature with two horns on the top of its head; we killed it and gave it to the man of science we have along with us to study. Personally I was glad to see the thing dead, the one strange thing I can say is, this private caravan is doing well. I see a woman and child go out at night to catch the cool air of the desert night, then they are taken back into the closed off area and that's all we see of them, the son of Ammon will live through him forward into the ages .

The Professor took his glasses of and set them on the table he looked at Nicolas and said, "It could mean any one of a series of things, what was the connection between Alexander and this woman and child and... no ..." he sat back on his chair, "no it couldn't be."

Michelle looked at Kevin and said, "Couldn't be what?"

"Well think of this as just a theory, why did Alexander not choose anybody to be his successor?" looking up and pointing his finger at Nicolas like a school master to his pupil, hesitating a little about the possibility of changing the future he then said, "now this is a long shot and I mean a long shot, just imagine that the woman and child were his woman and his child in the sealed of part of the caravan," looking around he said, "cant you see he was protecting his prodigy his biological line, my god, then if everything went to plan he should have descendants to this very day. Imagine somebody walking around with his DNA and genetic make up! No wonder he never chose a successor, he had a son and another family who were eventually all assassinated, no wonder he died happy with a smile on his face. He knew that whatever happened in this world his son would be ok with the people of the light. The tomb is full of gold, it is a diversion, the real treasure is behind the portal, my god he was one clever man."

Nicolas sat down beside him and said, "I now see, I understand what our mission is now?" he looked at Jack and said, "Now I know what the stakes are, we need to be vigilant."

"Agreed," said Jack

"What about the Greek soldier in the tomb?"

Jack thought for a moment and said, "We have the best medical facilities that can be built into the tomb and if the legends are true and this man can be resuscitated we will be ready."

"What you are talking about is cryogenics, so then they were more technologically advanced than we are now?"

"Not by much, perhaps fifty years."

"It makes sense Alexander would never have attacked a civilisation more advanced than his own. He must have started negotiations through the priests of Ammon?"

"The way you have to look at it is, their weapons technology would be way more advanced by this time, Alexander had no other choice than to hold peaceful diplomatic talks."

As the morning arrived the security guards were running around, Jack walked over to us, "somebody is following us."

We walked over to the command vehicle and Jack handed Michelle the v r glasses, she looked around in astonishment as she saw the landscape. She could see everything in about one hundred miles; she turned to the tech and said, "Can I zoom in?"

"Yes here you go," hitting a few buttons on the console her vision zoomed in with clarity, this technology was amazing she saw six vehicles driving in what seemed to be military formation they had about forty men on two trucks and there was two old Russian armoured personal carriers that had a canon and a heavy calibre machine gun parodying out of the turret.

"It looks like a serious threat," said Michelle, "what are you going to do?"

"Well they're about seventy miles from our location and at their speed they will be here in ninety minutes so we need to act quickly. On our way here we set some remotely controlled e m p charges, they're about ten minutes from them now. They were developed by Heir Strauss originally for the US army. They send an electrical magnetic shockwave and can knock out any car or lorry engine in close proximity. With that the technician in the command vehicle started to type on his lap top then suddenly the front of the screen started to flash, he then selected his targets and after electronically painting them directly using the eye in the sky, he hit execute the first thing that happened was that a timer came up on his screen and the charges were on tracks, they were calculating the distance and time of impact, they then automatically placed themselves in the road of the hostile convoy. Then as they were driving over them they went off, the first vehicle that was affected, the engine folded in two and the rest followed suit, watching from the safety of the command centre gave her a false sense of security. As we watched the men get out of the vehicles and walk around, one of the security men in the room asked Jack, "Do you think they know what happened?"

"No, not a hope not unless they have access to the technology we have and that is very unlikely."

With that the room went silent, Michelle turned to Jack and said, "Why have all the security guys gone quiet?"

"Because when we took out their vehicles it also knocked out all their commutation equipment, its almost ironic we use humane technology to immobilise them, only with no commutations they can't send out for help, if they don't have somebody that knows his desert survival they will all die and now that's their affair," with that he slid off Michelle's glasses and put them on the table and walked out of the room. Looking at Richard she said, "What's that all about?"

"It's a long story," looking at the screen he said, "that has a very similar story to what those guys are about to go through," staring at Michelle Richard said, "A story best left to another day."

With a clump the eye was returned to its home on top of the command vehicle, everybody mounted their rides that were to take them to the tomb and the archaeological discovery of the age. The desert was now surrendering to a baron landscape that was full of mountains and hills, it was peppered with boulders and rocks, and the terrain was changing to wilderness that had sweeping bends and mountain roads. We reached the point that we had to get to then the security guards got out to manually clear the way. The chance of a sniper was too great, never mind one with an r p g rocket launcher. His men wove through the small hiding places that could be a hidden threat until the terrain was starting to become less hostile and it started to lighten off a little. The men laid personal alarm systems so that if somebody was still following us we would know about it. The heat was beating down and the sweat was running down everybody's face and it was getting hotter by the day. As the day turned into night, they thankfully had a love of the night and the cool wind it brought with it. Kevin sat back and pondered the similarity in General Alouns letter home to his wife about the cool nights that they all loved saying, "we must be close to the tomb by now, less than a day I'd say, I tell you one thing this place has no shortage of caves and its plastered in the dam things but how can they find them?"

Michelle sat down beside him and said, "I think the location will be in that old German log book."

Standing beside the 4x4 Heir Strauss took out the old wermacht file, the leather folder was creased at the edge and it still stank of leather. The old man held it up to his nose and gave it a deep sniff and said, "soon old friend, soon," with that he took out a sheet and unfolded it into one large sheet. There before them lay a map lined with a grid reference, he then walked over to the command vehicle and motioned to Jack and Michelle and her team. As soon as they got to the command vehicle he said as he coughed, "How do you young people say, yes, do you want to see something cool?"

Looking at each other in wonderment he then gave the order, "activate the eye in the sky." The technicians started the device and he walked over to the notice board and pined the military survey map to the board

He then took his position and placed the v r glasses on his head he said, "Take it up to the height of ten thousand feet and hold it there."

Jack said, "Can it do that?"

Heir Straus looked over at him confidently and said "Yes, easily," he then took a remote control out of his pocket and hit a button. A round shaped object came out of the roof and the windows went a darker tint, the object started to produce light it moved around and around before it kicked in. We then realised it was a projector and it was laying out the landscape before us, behind her she heard someone say 'god that's cool.' Heir Straus said "Now look at the map and see if we can cross reference them with the Ariel projection in front of us."

With that Jack shouted over "Here I've found something."

They all stood behind Jack, as not to stand in front of the projection he pointed to a small area about thirty miles up in the hills, "it's the profile, can anybody else find them?"

"Yes," said somebody from behind, it was at the side of a valley and with that Heir Straus took out his remote control and hit the directional button and it shifted it over towards the map pined up on the wall. It was a perfect match.

"Yes!" shouted Heir Straus, then he said to his technicians, "take a sat nav reading," the man sitting behind the chair said in a deep voice, "sat location acquired sir."

He then walked out of the command vehicle and clapping his hands together he said, "Tomorrow we will be there, tomorrow god willing."

Nicolas smiled, "indeed if the gods smile upon us, we will get there."

The men continued with their sweeps of the local area, prepared for close quarters combat if called upon. The terrain was starting to get worse, the boulders were starting to look like a building site, a very large building site indeed, its rugged terrain almost seeming to have collapsed into the side of the valley to give the impression that it was caused by thousands of years of water erosion, if there was such a thing out here though one got the impression that rain was extremely rare. The heat had a tendency to stick to you like a sweat with the quality of a weak honey, the conditions were starting to get atrocious and it was starting to show on everybody, some had short tempers and a few fights started to break out but Jack handled it with the same vigour as a old sergeant major would have. He made the guys do sit ups and press ups in the wavering heat then he pulled them out of the sun and the two men were still at each others throats so, he devised a plan, he walked over to the command vehicle and walked out with two empty bins the two men looked at him as if he was mad. He looked at them and said this will soon put the hostility out of you two, now gentlemen, if you want to fight you can. The men looked at each other with a renewed hatred almost ready to rip into each other when Jack said, "stop, it will be by my rules," and the others looked around in amazement as they circled the two men about to go for each other. Heir Strauss came over and laughed, "He got this idea from me. When we were in the Africa core we had this kind of thing inflicted upon us, it incorporates two rules which you are about to witness."

Jack ordered the two men into the bins, they were roasting hot but the two men jumped into the bins anyway, "now," shouted Jack, "the rules are; once you are in the bin both opponents will crouch down into the bins, thus your bodies will remain safe from harm, but here's the catch, while in the bins you must be placed four inches from each other."

The two guys egging each other on to take the first swing, one of the men started he smashed into his opponents face, blood dripped from his fist and ran of onto the sand were it almost dried out before the other man returned fire, it was then that Michelle saw Jacks point because they were so close and practically immobilised, that meant that they could not move and parry thus meaning that all their training was useless, without the mobility they needed there would be one of two possible outcomes. The first one being that one of the men would knock out the other or they would slug away at each other until they were exhausted and the only winner would be the pharmaceutical company selling them the bandages and plasters for their injuries.

As Michelle looked at Jack he laughed, almost knowing she had the intelligence to understand what was going down. The two men beat chunks out of each other, one had a broken nose and the other man was bleeding heavily, they were starting to lose their strength very quickly and when they were exhausted they finally knew that what they were doing was folly.

"The moral of this story, gentlemen is quite simple, do not allow the sun to get on the wrong side of your tempers. If you have a problem work it out with each other," he then walked over to the men and helped them out of the bins that were now covered in blood. He stood the two men up against the under crop of the cavern edge, he then looked at each of them and said, "Do you two understand if you were stranded you would need to count on each others help?"

With that he reached into his bag lying on the floor next to him and pulled out two freezing cold beers and put them into their hands, "Now go and cool off."

As he walked away from the crowd Nicolas said, "He is quite something isn't he."

"Yes," said Michelle, smiling as she walked off.

The Professor was still in his 4x4, he was still reading the documents that Nicolas had given to him, he reached over to the cold box in his vehicle and opened a bottle of beer, he looked at Michelle and said, "He had quite an extraordinary life," taking a swig he started to explain, "the general had written down everything, he was a pathological record keeper. There's everything in there from the battle of gaugeable to the port siege of Java and other battles. These papyri are worth a fortune! There's even a report on how to conduct economics with a city state that has surrendered to Alexander without a fight. All the nobility of said city kept their positions and were handsomely rewarded for their good choice, their King if they had one was put under the direct command of Alexander and the country then became a part of the empire but most interesting was this," he produced a set of papyri, "These, believe it or not, are the sword and shield drill of the officer core elite of Alexander's army, according to this they did these drills every day until it became second nature."

Jack walked over to the jeep and overheard the conversation he said, "Sounds like any normal military manual for basic training."

"Yes," said the Professor, "All military can trace its discipline and military tactics from the Greeks as well as the Romans," he laid each sheet out on the bonnet and they looked in disbelief as they clearly saw the diagrams of a Greek hoplite. The first move was shield tight in to the body and the sword kept back from the shield until he needed it then when the enemy was under the shield he used the sword. There were twelve in all, different drills that used the same weapons or, in some cases there were spear drills and a drill showing you how to use your shield as an offensive weapon on an oncoming enemy. When they had had a good look at it they all headed off towards their vehicles. The Professor put all the manuals into a folder and put them into the back of the jeep, they then headed off in the general direction of the tomb site. At a crawling pace they advanced into the valley, it was covered in small stones and you could easily have lost your footing. The men were still sweeping through the valley, weapons at the ready, until they heard somebody shout, "Over here I think I have found something."

They converged on the sheltered place and one of the men held something up, Jack walked over to them and he took the object in his hands and looked at it. It was covered in sand and rust he shouted at the Professor to survey what they had found. He took out a brush set he had had, while on archaeological digs around the world. It was bound in brown leather and tied of with a leather strap, he untied the strap that was around the pouch and rolled it out on the ground and selected a brush about an inch thick. He began to brush off the sand and rust until he could see the rusted piece of metal then he took an eye piece out of his pocket and examined the mysterious object. He took the eye piece out and blew at the piece of metal he then replaced the eye piece and he then looked up and said, "Yes, its French, without a doubt, it's a piece of a musket." With that Jack walked over to Michele and said, "In your great grandfathers journal they ran into Mameluke resistance. When their column was attacked by the small group of Mameluke resistors camped in a cave. Well this story is starting to eerily take a true twist."

Standing were the musket piece had been found, he and Richard began to study the battle field, "If this is where the French was and there were fatalities, according to the journal, hold on a minute I have got an idea..."

He stood in the same place the musket piece was found and he drew his side arm then thinking out loud he started to theorize the situation, "If I was a turn of the century French infantry man and I was under fire what would I have done..."

Jack interrupted him and said, "Yes Richard but you forget only officers held side arms back then."

"Yes Jack that's exactly my point," looking at Richard he suddenly understood what he was getting at, "It was an officer, and he was taken out before he could react..."

"Exactly," replied Richard, "That means that the entrance is within musket range of this position."

With that, he ordered his men to fan out and look for a cave or what looked like what would have been a cave at one time. They looked everywhere, Jack went back to see Heir Strauss, "Can you remember how they sealed the entrance?"

"Ah, now, let me remember, yes they turned a field gun on it," they all fell silent, Jack turned to him and said, "Heir Strauss what calibre of field gun?" Jack turned around and said to himself, "O god let it not be an 88 mill, oh please god let it not..."

Heir Strauss suddenly said, "Yes! I remember now, there were no 88mill in short range recon just 50 calibre weapons and mortars, so they must have sealed it with a mortar shell, so everybody look for debris or what looked like a out crop at one time."

With that Jack sighed a breath of relief if it had have been an 88 mil it would have most likely have destroyed the whole complex. Jack turned to Strauss and said, "This Captain Muller, what kind of man was he?"

"He was a professional soldier and he hated the Nazis. His main worry was the men under his command. I am still alive because of this man; he saved my life many times. I sometimes think of him at night, may god be good to him. He's not buried far from here, perhaps later on you will accompany me to his grave?"

"Yes Heir Strauss, it would be my honour."

CHAPTER 6.

They were looking over a piece of land about three hundred feet from the musket site and they started to see scorch marks on pieces of boulders and around the immediate area. They looked at Michelle who was standing with her diary, reading the map, she said, "From what I see here, this appears to be it. Right everybody, because we know there is no serious archaeology in the entrance of the cave we can go about the removal of the debris in a robust fashion."

With that, Heir Strauss pulled out the mobile phone from his pocket and made a short phone call he said, "There will be a Chinook here with a JCB here in ninety minutes it should lighten our load a little."

Jack looked at Michelle and said, "Good show, it will clear the cave back to the shaft, then we will have to clear the rest by hand."

"Yes, the old fashion way, and it depends how much debris is deposited down there. I have been in tomb excavations that have lasted years with countless numbers of Egyptian workers coming into the tombs with straw baskets and wheelbarrows, a continuous line of workers in and out, then all the debris is sifted through to see if the archaeological team has missed anything."

Jack said, "I understand that we could be here a long time, if there's a lot of debris in the shaft, then again you never know how it will all level out."

As they were speaking they heard an engine, Jack found it instantly familiar. It was the sound of a Chinook. Because of his service in the army he had used them many times and had come to admire this monster of a machine. The Chinook had, under its undercarriage, a steel harness attached to a JCB digger. The dust and sand were flying up in the air and the JCB was lowered onto the ground and the cable snapped free. Richard got into the cab and started the engine, it roared into action and Richard poked his head out of the cab and said "I spent many hours on a building site before I joined the army. It's now coming in handy as you can see!"

With that he headed to the area and started with the smaller rocks, scooping them up, he dumped them at the other end of the site so that he was sure he was not blocking the shaft. The smaller rocks turned into bigger ones as he continued the digger which was new, was starting to have problems with the bigger loads so he offloaded the biggest load. He then turned the digger around and used the back bucket to move the remaining boulders he extended the arm and used it to move the bigger boulders. The digger was starting to rev and over heat but the large boulder was moving. He managed to get it across enough to see that there was a corner visible. It was the shaft, everybody's hearts were in their mouths as they brushed around the entrance still knowing that the whole entrance of the shaft could be blocked and that would mean months of back breaking work to clear it. When they stopped brushing Richard moved in with the back of the digger, there appeared to be two large slabs of rock blocking the shaft so they moved back and allowed Richard to extend his back hoe and pull out the first of the slabs. It fell back with a crash and broke into several pieces, which he moved with the bucket of the digger. He then moved back into position with the back hoe again, this time it would be harder, he moved back towards the second boulder and he started to move the second huge slab, it was touch and go for a while but he got it out enough for the men to latch a rope around it and tie it off to the back of the digger, so he pulled up the stabilising legs and pulled the back hoe into position. He looked at Jack and shouted, "We have only one shot at this!"

Jack nodded and gestured him to put the foot down and he did, he raced forward and the rope strained under the pressure. It made a number of strange noises, then, suddenly the huge slab came out of the shaft, it smashed into pieces on the ground. Everyone gathered around the entrance of the shaft to see if it was clear but the stir and dust was coming out of the shaft which made it hard to see. Michelle moved beside Jack, took his hand and said, "It looks like we won't have to dig." Looking down, Jack saw that as the tunnel cleared of dust, it was in fact clear of any rubble. A shout of joy went out amongst the group that had gathered around and Heir Strauss walked over and congratulated them both, "We've done it, I tell you, we've done it!" Everyone was delighted as champagne was delivered to everybody in the expedition. They all drank up and smashed the glasses in a comical Cossack poise. Afterwards Heir Strauss walked over to Michelle, "Well my dear, we've done it as promised, all yours," with that she turned to her team and said, "I want a tent over this entrance and a generator to pump air into the tomb if necessary we will also need the skills of an engineer to deal with the traps."

The first thing they did was to fix a rope ladder onto the mouth of the shaft, they then descended, they dropped a flare to the bottom of the shaft it was steep, about forty feet in all and the rope ladder just reached the bottom of the floor. Climbing down Michelle looked at the shaft; it was roughly cut out in a hurry, and as she got to the bottom the quality of the shone cutting improved greatly. As she dropped to the bottom Jack came down behind her and they switched on their torches and what they saw was beyond belief.

Before them stood two of the most beautiful carved statues they had ever seen, they were magnificent and stood at the entrance of a round chamber. Michelle turned on her short wave radio and told them up above to send down the Professor. Hobbling down the rope ladder he finally made it to the tomb floor and said, "God I am too old for this." A voice from behind him said, "how about this?" He turned around and could not believe his eyes, he gazed at them for a good hour then he said, "They are a mystery, and a beautiful one at that!" He went to step forward and Jack stopped him, "Remember the traps."

"Ah, yes!" he replied "sorry."

Alex came down and he had a remote operated vehicle that had censors on board, he carefully made his way around the front main chamber right to the first set of doors, they were copper and looked like they weighed a tonne.

Alex said, "We're all clear here, up until we hit those doors, behind them I can't vouch for."

When the remote operated vehicle was pulled back the whole area was then lighted and a command centre was established. Alex pulled out the cables attached to his ROV and attached a remote control unit so they could work wireless and it would be easier to move about. He then built up a table and chairs which he placed monitors on and other technical equipment, while this was going on Kevin and Michelle were walking around the room. Kevin remarked that he had seen architecture like this before in Greece, it was in the Macedonian style of Alexander and there were many paintings on the wall one of Alexander him self walking through a garden with a young boy and him laughing and being affectionate towards this young man on the other pictures it showed him in front of his troops at what seemed to be the battle of Gaugamela. In another he was leading his men in to a fortified city and was being greeted by the leaders of that city state, they were giving Alexander tribune in gold jewels and livestock in one it was quite odd, he was standing talking to his mother Olympas and they seemed to be sharing a mother son moment from the early days before he chose to avoid her, "They say that Alexander loved his mother very much but after his fathers death he kept her at arms length, there are some scholars who still think she had something to do with his fathers death. You see, Alexander was very fond of his father and his mother hated him so you see the problem Alexander was up against." Just as they were talking about Philip of Macedonia, there he was, towering over Alexander with his hand on his shoulder and over looking a battle field. Philip dressed in black leather armour and Alexander in a child's white set, "His father was teaching Alexander the tricks of the trade even before he went to Philips military academy and was educated by Aristotle. It's as if he wants to show someone what's happened in his life. It's like a reminder for a relative," when he said that he looked at Michelle with stern eyes and said, "What in the name of god is this place for?"

Thirty miles from their location two men hobbled over beside a spring and fell head first in to the water. The men drank with all their might, one of the men who was dressed in black said to the other who was dressed the same, "We're the only two to make it, the others are dead of heat or exhaustion it appears it is up to us to complete the mission."

"Listen Joe, they're all dead, nobody is alive, what's the use of going on, we would be better off radioing headquarters and telling them of our failure."

"Are you mad? We would be working like dogs for the rest of our careers. What we need is a vehicle and some food, also something to carry water in."

They looked around the oasis, there were a few palm trees, the place had a beautiful serenity about it, they both took a few minutes looking around the site then they saw what appeared to be a small town, it was about one mile away. Joe and Bob had worked for the Antiquates office of Egypt; there was a general feeling that this mysterious force was out to rob Egypt of its treasures. Joe and Bob were both captains in the army, to be precise, paratroopers drafted in to take care of this simple case of robbery. They had by this stage lost their best men, the only thing they were armed with were their side arms. Joe turned to his subordinate and in a commanding tone said, "We will proceed towards the town and commandeer the appropriate supplies and vehicle and then my friend we will continue our mission."

Given the circumstances the Professor was acting like an excited school boy. He had set up a desk to work from and it was heaped with papers and ancient papyri. He was trying to make sense of the round chamber they had named "the octagon," it was pillared with a court yard and had seating around it made from marble. The Professor walked over from his desk and sat on the marble seat, he stared at the two huge bronze doors that according to Michelle's diary led onto a corridor, the same place that the young Napoleonic engineers life ended. He stared at it for a while then stood up and walked over to it, he casually turned to Jack and said, "Give me a hand Jack."

As he walked over towards the huge doors Jack said, "It may be booby trapped."

"No it isn't, it's just the corridor. Remember the old man's journal; they had both doors open so theoretically they should open easily."

"Yes in theory," said Jack holding him back, "Alex," he shouted, "Check it out. Just in case Professor you understand."

"Of course Jack. No problem."

Alex came over and looked the doors up and down, "Well there's one thing we don't have to be afraid of, there's gaps between the door and stone frame so that means there's no gas inside. That was my main worry, from what I hear they can be very nasty." He slipped a fibre optic cable through, attached to the other end was a camera so he could check for any locking devices, after half an hour he gave the signal all clear. Jack then radioed for two men from above to come down to assist with the doors, he made it clear that when opening the doors that no one was to step into the corridor for fear of setting of a booby trap. They grabbed a handle each and started to pull the massive doors open, they made a cracking sound, everybody had thought that the door had been broken but relief came when they heard the squeal of the hinges working, it was a noise that would have cut a man in two, when they got the doors tight up against the wall they took a well deserved break. Jack and Kevin looked into the corridor, they waited until the dust and old air had cleared, it was like an army of ghosts marched past. Alex was standing behind them and said "Right lets see what we can see," he shone his torch into the shaft cut into the rock there was a data rail cut into the stone and below there were holes cut suspiciously into the rock. Jack started to count the holes, "Twenty, twenty of the bastards," he looked at Michelle and said, "That ancestor of yours was one very lucky man."

"Yes, but not his engineer."

"Let's just see what were up against."

Jack walked up to one of the tables and lifted a heavy book; he turned to Kevin and asked, "Is this book important?"

"Well, not really," he hesitated.

"Can you do without it?"

"Well, I suppose so; it's just a reference source."

With that Jack walked over to Alex and said, "I need you to pick out a dodgy flagstone. Can you pick one out?"

Alex looked down the corridor and selected one, he said, "Tenth one down, third one in."

With that he threw the book that was fairly heavy, it slammed down bang on target.

"The impact itself may not have been heavy enough to make any difference," said Jack

"No the impact would have definitely been enough to trigger the device," Alex said.

With that they heard a sound that sent shivers down their spines, it was a loud clank, it was then they heard something slide down the hole cut into the side of the wall and out came a glass spear it had green liquid in its tip where the spear head traditionally was. It slammed into the book and was left sticking out of the book, looking at Jack, Alex said, "Yes we've got one intact," he started to assemble a reach and grab device, it was telescopic and worked through a sensory glove set.

He mounted it on top of the tripod that had been specially made for it, at the end it was counterbalanced by a heavy weight. Switching on the machine, he put on his gloves and voice activated them. The reach and grab came on line, with one hand he controlled the telescopic out reach and the other hand controlled the grasp. With his right hand he moved out the arm and with the other he opened the grasp he grabbed the spear and lifted it off the ground along with the book and began to pull it back towards them with his other hand. The book was dragging on the ground and Jack said to Alex, "What about the other traps?"

"Don't worry it's not heavy enough to do any harm." He looked at Jack and said, "Get ready to catch our spear!"

Jack stood beside the tripod and as it came closer he held out his hands until it was in reach. Just then Jack said, "Ok let it go." With that he released his grip on the gloves and Jack had the spear in his hands with the book still dangling on the end, he pulled the spear out of the book and handed it back to the Professor, "Sorry about the damage."

"Don't worry old boy, it was only a third edition anyway."

Looking at the spear he admitted to himself, "It's a thing of beauty all right, after all this time it's still gleaming like it came out of the factory yesterday." It was wet to the touch. Jack looked at the corridor and said, "If this was in water all that time, my god there's more of the bloody things. It's a supply system they could have hundreds of them..." Alex interrupted and said, "I have to admit, I have never seen anything like that before."

Chapter 7.

Hearing a voice behind him, Alex turned to see Nicolas, "I have it" and in his hands were again old papyri. He held it in front of them and there was a drawing of the glass spear and what seemed to be a diagram of how they were made. Kevin walked over to Nicolas and stood beside him he started to decipher the Greek on the papyri, "Well it tells how the thing is made, it's heated up in two pieces, and the first is the shaft and the second which has a strange substance injected into the spear point while it's hot. From what I have read it turns acidic over a period of time, the two pieces are then soldered together with glass."

"Ingenious," remarked Nicolas, "and of course very dangerous."

"Yes this general was quite a genius."

"Yes, what my father told me about is that this side of the tomb was protected by technology only from our world, beyond the throne room is theirs." A chill ran down everybody's back at the thoughts and expectations that Nicolas had arose in them.

Shouting at the two men, "Disgrace, this is extortion!" said the old man looking helplessly at the two. Joe said to the old man, "You will be reimbursed by the government for the supplies we have taken." He walked over to the old man standing with an old hat and galabiyah and slippers.

"He looked like he didn't have very much as it was," said Bob.

"Shut up will you, he will be reimbursed, as I told the old man." He produced a card from his pocket and handed it to the man and said ring this number and ask to speak to this man and he will organise your money for you. Looking at Bob he said, "Get in to the pick up," and they set off on their way. Bob said to Joe, "How do we track them?" Turning around he said, "The old way, with your senses." He then set off in the last known location of Heir Strauss and his minions.

They were trying to figure a way out of the corridor when Jack came on the radio, "I think the boss has thought of something when he was studying Michelle's diary. He had the helicopters drop off aluminium sheeting along with steel supports to lift the sheeting off the ground; hence nobody would be on the floor to activate the device in the first place."

So firstly they took laser readings of the dimensions of the corridor and he then had the sheeting cut to size. The supports were raw plugged to the stone floor carefully, it was an operation that took several hours which Jack did himself, even at the protestations of Heir Strauss he went ahead and did it himself, and sighting the fact that nobody had his mobility and speed. With all the supports down he signalled for the first piece of the aluminium platform to be put in place. Nicolas and Kevin carried the back of the platform, both wearing gloves, and Jack was in front. It was a dangerous operation, one slip from Jack and he would die. Finally they got to the place intended for the platform, when they had got it down Jack stepped safely on top of the platform and began to screw the it down to the steel supports. The first of the platforms had been laid and they could see the other set of doors, these doors were different they weren't bronze they looked like they were gold with a classical depictions emblazed on the panelling of the doors. It was beautiful though they could not see it clearly. Two more platforms were placed in the corridor and that took them all the way to the doors. They were amazing, it was a depiction of Alexander cutting the Gordian knot, and an old riddle that was set by King Gordius of the ancient Kingdom Phrygia, he who could untie the knot would win all of Persia. The knot was used to bind a chariot axle Alexander looked at it smiled and drew his sword and simply chopped it open, an easy conclusion to a difficult puzzle. On the other panel was Alexander around a table giving orders to his generals before the battle of Gaugamela, holding a dagger in one hand pointing into the table and he was going over what looked like orders for his army, it was something that Kevin had never seen before .

Standing at the corridor side of the double golden doors the three men pushed with all their might. The doors opened this time with a little more ease; they were swung back against the inner walls of the next chamber. Taking a large flash light they saw what had not been seen for two hundred years. It was magnificent, almost like one of the old roman coliseums they had in towns and cities for their barbaric form of entertainment. The r o v was sent off around on a mission to scan for pressure pads and booby traps. It did a complete sweep of the area and came back clear for traps. Alex said in a confident tone, "This area is safe."

Jack said, "How do you know with that?" Alex strode out into the middle of the large complex and said, "Safe I believe."

Michelle went next walking over towards Alex; she looked into the middle of the arena and screamed. Everybody ran towards her and Jack was there first, with her head slumped into Jacks chest and her arm outstretched and pointing towards the middle of the arena Jack looked over and saw what had made her scream, hundreds of skeletons heaped on top of each other with arrows protruding from their corpses it looked like slaughter on a large scale. Nicolas looked over and said, "Ladies and gentlemen this is the price that was paid for the secrecy of this tomb, for which I who am related to this man by blood who ordered this atrocity am eternally sorry." Jack turned to Nicolas and said, "Nicolas this is not your fault." Kevin walked over and put his hand on his shoulder and said, "As I have said before, General Aloun was a battle hardened soldier who followed orders to the letter, you are not to blame for what happened here and for what I can make out he regretted doing this for many reasons, in his letters he confides in his wife that he was ordered to do a terrible deed for which he would never be forgiven in the after life but as the man said he probably had no choice." Heir Straus walked in at that moment looked into the pit and said, "I've seen this kind of thing before they have been slain in open ground then dragged in and thrown in to the pit. You see there are arrow shafts broken off which most likely happened when they were dragged into the pit from outside, my god what a way to die," nodding his head from side to side he said, "We can at least give these people a decent burial." Everybody went outside again to catch a little air and the digger set about its solemn and grim task digging graves for the lost souls inside the tomb.

Parking the car and setting off to find tracks, they had looked all day when suddenly Bob found a foot print. It was heading into the mountains, "A sheep herder," he said to himself. Looking down he saw what seemed to be tyre prints on the desert floor, he shouted at Joe who nodded and motioned to say he understood walking over to the tracks Joe said, "They're two or three days old, we're not that far behind them, we will rest here tonight and continue in the morning."

In the morning Heir Strauss' teams had completed their solemn task, a trench about fifty feet long and all the skeletons lined side by side, a few words were spoken and then the internment began. Everyone had gotten a good night's sleep before going into the tomb the next morning. The inner chamber looked larger without the skeletons in the room, the men had fitted the place with lights and the beauty of it started to emerge. Like the first chamber it had a pillared surround at the top of the arena, at the bottom of the pit there was an altar and in front of the altar was a statue of Alexander. Kevin had never seen anything like it before all the other likeness of Alexander had been weathered by time but this one was crisp like it had been carved yesterday. On his knee was a baby boy, it looked the picture of happiness and in front of the arena was a set of stairs that led to two sets of double doors. At the top of the stairs there were two statues, one of the God Zeus and the other of Alexander. They were beautifully carved, looking at them he thought, who ever carved these knew what he was doing a master perhaps that time has forgot one thing is for sure what ever is on the other side of that door will change our lives forever. Jack and Michelle stepped side by side towards the doors, "Which one?" asked Jack, Michelle then said, "Why don't we trust my great ancestor." She took out her book and began to read from it as they walked up the stairs, "Believe it or not they actually tossed a coin to choose." Laughing behind them Richard said, "Typical soldiers." Looking at Richard Jack said, "Indeed, typical soldiers." The minute he said that Richard was flipping a coin and it landed on heads, "Yep," he said, "Just as I thought, the right door when you're ready." Just then Jack stopped them; he saw what seemed to be a small marble nozzle sticking out of the side of the door frame, with that he called Alex, "Get your ass up here."

"Sorry boss haven't cleared that area yet."

"Ok then," said Jack, "Next time tape it off with a plastic cordon," throwing him a roll of the cordon tape which read with big red words 'stay clear'.

"Well the floor is clear that I can tell you," looking up he saw the tell tale signs, "Oh no, not again."

"What is it this time?"

"Look above you, it's the spear holes again but this time it's the door that acts as the trigger...Wait one minute, there may be a way around this. If I can get some thing that can keep it stationary while we open the door, let me see, there are two on each side." He walked over to his tool box and pulled out two strips of the aluminium that had been cut from the platforms, he took a hammer from the box and began to hammer the metal in to a triangle shape, he then cut the bottom out of it and walked over to the door and slipped the piece of aluminium over the piece of marble that was sticking out, he then screwed the piece of metal to the side of the door frame and said, "There that should hold it for an hour or two." he then repeated the operation on the other side then he looked at Jack and Richard and said, "On the count of three pull... one, two, three..." They pulled with all their might, the hinges screamed on their axes; eventually they got the doors open. Alex said, "Right, we don't have much time, screw the other side into the flush side of the frame quick." He threw Richard the extra drill and they worked franticly until the danger had passed. What lay in front of them was another corridor this time they could not see the end of it. Jack looked at Alex and at the same time they said, "Distance laser should tell us how long the bloody thing is." Alex scrambled down to get the delicate piece of apparatus, he stood it up-right on its tripod and hooked up the laptop, set it on automatic and hit enter. "If the shaft isn't too dusty or corrupted with something we should get a reading almost immediately," just as he said that the voice mode switched on and said in a computerised voice, "1.609 kilometres," "One mile precisely, these things are built with the precision of the pyramids, one mile exactly and riddled with traps no doubt." Jack looked at Michelle and asked, "What did your diary say about this corridor?"

"Nothing, it was the other door they opened, they did open this door but triggered a trap and the engineer saved their asses."

"Yes," the Professor said, "I can see traces of glass here."

"Right what this means is that the next door is the throne room," and checking it out very closely Alex said in a confident tone, "it's clear." He walked over to them and started to pull at them, the rest of the men got in on the act and when they had opened the doors what lay before them was unbelievable. The glitter of the gold was everywhere, Jack noticed the same data railing running around the room, he lifted his hand and dipped it into the space behind the data railing, he took it down and smelt it and laughed," Richard give me your Zippo." Richard threw the lighter over to Jack and he walked over to where the data railing was and dipped into a tray at waist height he clicked it open and sparks flew everywhere, he then threw it into the tray and he heard a woof. The tray ignited and spread around the whole tomb, in a matter of thirty seconds the whole complex had been lit and you could see everything. "Clever people," said Jack.

Michelle said, "That could have been a booby trap!"

"No, you see it's too obvious for that, all the traps we have encountered have been hidden, elaborate in their nature."

She stood and looked around her in awe; the walls were covered in beautiful carvings, even more beautiful than the others outside. Like the other chamber this had it's similarities but at the same time it was so different, much more opulent, more luxuries for the eye. The walls were covered in gold and gold dust was everywhere, it was on our clothes, it was floating in the air like glitter. The throne was exactly where the journal said it was and at the centre of the chamber was the sarcophagus, it was made of a strange metal that we had never seen, it was like platinum but so much purer. It was covered in what we thought was glass but turned out to be a polished crystal, it was beautiful and inside was the young Greek officer Excios. On seeing him Nicolas' emotions got the better of him and he collapsed and fainted. The Greek who was in his uniform, what ever liquid he was submerged in preserved everything to the last detail. Kevin looked at him with a holy awe and said, "Well he belongs to a wealthy house." Jack asked, "How do you know that?"

"Look at his armour, it's elaborate, look at his greaves they are gold plated as well as his shield," his spear lay at his side on the other side was his helmet with its brightly and beautifully decorated crest, his cuirass lay strapped on to his chest, beside his helmet lay his sword, it was studded with jewels and was also gold plated, beside the sarcophagus was a small granite box with stone tablets inside. Kevin looked at them and closed the box, Jack wondered why he did not even translate them, "I would old boy but I am afraid they're addressed to the young man inside the sarcophagus and I don't feel right reading them, they were marked private for the attention of shield commander excios. Well now I know his rank, it would be the equivalent of major or captain in a modern army."

Richard looked at him and said, "Huh! He out ranks the both of us and he's only a strap of a lad."

"Perhaps Richard, in the Macedonian army, rank was based on performance as well as social status. This young man may have been from a wealthy family or even an aristocratic background but I can assure you of one thing, he earned the rank that he was assigned with."

The lid of the sarcophagus was attached with four pins that were made from the same strange metal as the sarcophagus the Professor pulled out one of these and the men pulled out the rest. Unlike the traditional Egyptian sarcophagus which would take about nine men, three hours to remove, the lid of this sarcophagus was feather light and Jack and Richard lifted it and set it against the throne with ease. The Professor took off his shirt and said, "I will start with his weapons." Jack said, "How do you know that stuff won't do you any harm."

"Oh," he said "as they say, this is my bat." With that he ran his finger on the top of the liquid surface and held it up at Jack, "Well I'm still alive so here goes."

Before he began, he mentioned that the strange liquid had the same consistence of honey, he then drove both arms into the strange concoction and he grabbed the helmet by the crest and pulled it out of the sarcophagus. As he pulled it out the liquid that was on it trickled back into the sarcophagus until it was completely dry. "I've never seen any thing like this," the very bristles that were hanging off the crest were dry and so were his hands. He ran his hands over the bristles and it was like they had been made yesterday, the helmet shone with such brightness like it was new. Alex took a sample of the strange material and scrutinised it under a microscope, he came back in from the command chamber and said, "You're not going to believe this. I think it has been bioengineered to preserve solid mater as well as living mater." They went over to the sarcophagus and looked in at the young man it was almost like he was asleep, then Michelle caught something out of the corner of her eye, "His wrists, they have been cut!" and there were flakes of blood around that area. Kevin turned to Michelle, "You can't be serious. He's been in that thing for thousands of years."

"Professor what you have to remember is that this is not our technology. It's alien to us, if by some reason we get him resuscitated can you communicate with him?"

Kevin couldn't believe what he was hearing, "Just think, you get to speak to a veteran of Gaugamela and some of the Alexandrine campaigns."

The young man had long blond hair, he was very good looking and muscular. He did not seem to have an ounce of fat on him, the rest of his weapons were removed and stored until it was the turn of the Greek soldier himself at that minute a medical team was on standby and ready beside the sarcophagus to receive the wounded young man if god willed it. Jack stood beside Michelle and said, "Time to see how good their technology is!"

Alex stood out in front of the crowd and said, "If this works, the last thing he will remember is being put into the sarcophagus by his comrades so don't worry if he seems a little confused. That is why we disarmed him first."

They had a metal stretcher at the ready, when he was lifted above the sarcophagus they would slide it underneath the man and it would take his weight while the liquid poured back in to the sarcophagus. The four men, Jack and Richard on one side and Alex and the Professor on the other had to wear goggles to go in. At that level they would be submerged for a while, they grabbed a side of the Greek and they all lifted at the same time and out of the goo like substance came the young man. The stretcher was slid underneath him and his weight was taken, the liquid all drained off into the sarcophagus. At that moment they thought they had failed but just then his body came alive. It was like he had been hit with lightning, his head turned to one side and he then vomited more of the liquid. Suddenly his wrists started to bleed out of control, just then the medical team moved in. Barely awake the young soldier reached for his sword but it was not there. Kevin started to speak in Greek, "They are physicians... They are not going to harm you..." Nicolas looked at him and the Greek looked back with a strange familiarity, almost as if he knew him. He looked at Kevin and said, "Tell him that Ammon is with him. That should calm him down a little and tell him who I am." Kevin relayed to him what Nicolas had said and in a weak voice he said, "He looks like General Aloun." With that he allowed the doctors to slowly patch him up. The head doctor came out of the make shift cubicle and said, "A blood transfusion and a few days rest and he will be as right as rain. And let me say he's in really good physical condition, he's really fit. They had to remove his cuirass with care, the rest they removed and burned, not before taking photos of the garment and the designs of course."

A day passed and Kevin went to see the patient, "How are you keeping?"

"Well enough old man, well enough."

"Were you at Gaugamela?"

"Yes, I served with distinction on the battle field that day and was rewarded by Alexander with my gold armour. The sword is the one used by him in that very battle."

"Tell me what Alexander was like?"

"His majesty was a man of the people. He conquered the hearts of those who tried to help him who were helped by him in return. If you opposed him he put his soul into destroying you. He is a remarkable man. Tell me my good man when was the last time you saw him? He is obviously a little older..."

"Ooh you can kind of say that..."

Looking at Kevin he said with a puzzled look, "How long was I in that sarcophagus?"

"What year did Alexander send you here?"

"About a year after Gaugamela, I was posted in Babylon shortly afterwards until I was summoned into his presence and tasked with this mission so my friend is he an old man or perhaps he's dead?"

"Yes my young friend, he is dead. That audience you had with Alexander was held over two thousand three hundred and thirty two years ago. After the opening of the gate your comrades put you into the sarcophagus that was built by the people of the light."

"People of the light?" looking at Kevin with a vex look, "Oh I see now, we have different names for them, you obviously call them the people of the light we call them the Kasoriens," said Exios.

"I've never heard of them...

"Anyway, after they put you into the sarcophagus what they neglected to tell you was the sarcophagus is in fact of kasorien design. It was their technology that saved you. For some reason they cannot bring their technology through the gate so the only thing that would save you my friend is the passage of time in this land. You were lucky, had anyone found you, they would have lifted you out of that sarcophagus and without the proper medical technology you would have lost that much blood you would have died for sure. It was the only way that your friends had of saving you, so don't go hard on their memory."

"Yes, my friend I understand, please tell Nicolas to come and see me. Would you mind translating?"

"No not at all," looking at the young Greek soldier with a lost sense of awe he turned to walk over to where Nicolas was. "Nicolas, Excios would like to talk to you. I will translate"

"Very well," getting out of his chair he walked over to the bed and sat on it. He smiled at the ancient Greek and looking across at Excios he began the introduction, "I am Nicolas, the descendant of Aloun the Greek."

"Yes I know," nodding to Kevin to translate. On receiving the news Nicolas smiled and pulled out a old piece of parchment and handed it to Excios and he explained to Kevin, "It was written by the general before he died and was instructed to give it to him on the occasion of his awakening," he handed it to excios and said, "it had been in his family for thousands of years."

The Greek said to Kevin, "Unfortunately I am a soldier, not a scholar and never learned to read." The distinct echo of shame radiated from him, "In my time this was frowned upon, as is probably the case now."

Looking down at the Greek Kevin said in a caring tone, "I will teach you to read and write but perhaps now it would be better done in a different language."

"What is this strange tongue called?"

"It's called English dear boy, English. I will read you your letter and let you rest for the night."

Exios my dear friend by the time you read this its likely that I'm in the after world playing a game of up or down with Anubis... he burst out laughing, "same old general joking to the end."

My friend if we had not have laid you in the sarcophagus it is certain you would have bled to death in doing so I condemned you to a life of informality and uncertainty of a life of loneliness with strangers who know you not, he who gave you this letter is of the house of Ammon and can be trusted at his word the gold and jewels in the throne room are yours. With these you can at least have a good life. My friend, please understand that there was no other way. We had not the technology to heal you. There was no other way either the sarcophagus or the kasoriens on the other side of the portal who have the medical technology to save you and as for your wishes, we obeyed them, you were unconscious when I reached the portal room and it was I who carried you to the sarcophagus and your comrades who laid you to your sleep. Remember who your King is and was as Philip of Macedonia was to me and that you are a Greek soldier and have nothing to prove to anybody, remember who your mother was and your brothers and sisters and last of all your father. Goodbye my son for we shall be reunited in the after world were we shall ride across the plains of Greece with the gentle wind blowing on our backs and our King at our side.

Lowering the parchment Kevin placed it on the bed beside Exios and said, "I am very sorry my friend."

"We were not the usual father and son, he was more my commander and my friend than my father I 'will miss him,' the general and now for a short walk," flanked by Kevin on one side and Jack on the other they walked out of the tomb. He was blinded by the sun and nearly fell over on the ground, "Easy there fellow," Jack said offering him his hand. The Greek smiled and accepted it turning to Kevin and saying, "Who is this man?"

"He's a soldier called Jack Toner."

Looking at Jack he said, "He is a man of honour this Jack?"

"Yes," said Kevin, "I believe he is."

"Exios, come with me one minute I have something that will allow you to understand what everybody is saying," Kevin took him over to a computer and for one hour explained what it did. The Greek was standing watching in disbelief now this necklace was adapted by Alex to translate ancient Greek. "It's connected to a small hard-drive that goes on your belt so you will understand everything that everybody's saying to you and vice versa. It's the latest in technology so I've heard..." Slipping the device around his neck it was squared for a minute until he got it to sit with a level of comfort and he then tried it on Jack... "Morning of the gods my dear fellow"

"And the same to you," they both burst out laughing. It had a computerised voice box built onto it. Jack turned around and said to the Professor, "Works well but he sounds like a robot."

Alex turned to Kevin and said, "Right then lets try this..." he plugged the hard drive into his laptop and began to click into the voice projection program he made a few adjustments and said, "How's this?" Exios started to talk and he sounded like Kermit the frog, roars of laughter erupted from the small crowd.

"Right, right, all right what about this?" he then programmed the voice box to copy his own voice. It sounded just right. Jack turned to Exios and said, "Exios what is the purpose of this complex?"

"It was originally an Egyptian communications temple, with what you call the people of the light. Even in my time it was a thousand years old, a closely guarded secret which only the pharaoh and a small number of priests knew about. Before us, the pharaoh Akhenaton had sent a small delegation of scribes and engineers and a few soldiers through the portal. There was no communication after that and the chamber was disguised as a tomb of a low ranking official. When Alexander came to Egypt he was offered the Kingdom, which he accepted, he duly became pharaoh and when he did the secrets of Egypt were made clear to him including this one. After Gaugamela we were sent to the oracle at Siwa where we picked up a priest. We were not allowed to communicate with him, our job was to protect him and make sure we got here with the supplies. General Aloun had already travelled here and had started construction of the complex you see now..."

Kevin said, "He did some hell of a job."

"Yes," said Exios, "He would have needed to have had some of the greatest craftsmen in Greece and painters too. Alexander even sent Aristotle to ensure the inscriptions were right."

"Did you say Aristotle?" Kevin asked, "You saw Aristotle with your own eyes?"

"Yes, he's quite the teacher don't you think?"

"Is he what? He is a legend in our time."

"You don't say. I never thought he would be that big."

Kevin nervously laughing said, "You have no idea."

Jack said, "What about the skeletons in the chamber?"

"Oh yes them. They were criminals condemned to death who built the complex. We had to maintain secrecy so after they had finished we executed them outside and dragged them inside and put their bodies in the chamber. We had no choice. If this place was to lay undiscovered they had to die."

Jack said, "What about the others, the painters and engineers, they went through the portal to the other land along with a few selected soldiers."

Kevin looked at him and said, "I've been studying the good general's letters He has made reference to a mystery package, a woman and a boy…"

"I was wondering when you would get to that, only the head priest of Siwa knew his real identity. There was speculation that he could have been the son of Alexander by a Macedonian woman which he did not have in my time unless he lied about it for the safety of the pair of them."

Jack asked "What do you mean?"

Kevin interrupted, "If I may, having a male heir with a woman of Macedonian nobility would have been enough to rule this young man the heir to the Macedonian throne."

"Yes," said Exios, "And at that time that would have been a very dangerous position for anybody to be in. Alexander was the object for assassination many times and the male heir would have been the next in line for murder, being the only object in the path of the throne." Looking at Kevin with a teary expression he said, "What became of Alexander?"

"According to scholars he died of fever in Babylon at the age of thirty three. Some say of typhoid…"

"I do not think so," said Exios, "He was murdered in my opinion, probably poisoned. Tell me who succeeded him."

Kevin said, "This is the biggest mystery of all, he never left an heir, he died without one, surrounded by his generals begging him to choose a King but he never did."

Looking startled Exios wandered off alone and sat down on one of the boulders that had been left by the digger. Jack looked at Kevin and said, "What do you think?"

"Well, he's been through a lot. Maybe it's best to leave him alone for a while. He's just lost everything close to him and you could say everything that he believed."

Looking out from behind a boulder the two men saw Heir Strauss' operation. Looking at each other, "What are they up to bob?" looking at Joe he said, "It's some kind of dig."

"Never mind that, look at the security around this place," just as he said that they heard the noise of a short band radio. They looked behind them and saw two guards standing holding their radios "sir, we appear to have visitors."

"Bring them here to me," Jack looked at the hill and saw the two hapless pair being walked at a fast pace, one tripped and fell on the way down, kicking dust and sand everywhere, he picked himself up and dusted himself down and continued to walk towards Jack. Michelle went to see what was going on, "Who are these men Jack?"

"I'll tell you in one minute, just as soon as I ask them."

The men were pushed out in front of Jack who said in an angry tone, "Who are you and were did you come from?"

Stepping out one of the men said, "I am a captain in the Egyptian army, seconded to the department of antiquates this is my subordinate, though he is the same rank as me I have over all command of this operation."

Laughing at him Heir Strauss stepped out and said, "By god I thought I had some pompous officers in the last war but you my friend take the biscuit. Where are the rest of your men?"

"Dead! When a device took out our vehicles and then exploded so it could not be identified some of our ministers thought you could not be trusted and I was ordered to follow you and report back just in case."

Heir Strauss looked at Jack winked and said, "Weapons down. I think I can resolve this peacefully."

Jack turned to his men and said, "At ease gentlemen" The soldiers behind the two walked off and returned to their patrol, "Now follow me please," they walked into the command vehicle and he pointed to the flat screen TV and looked at the two and said, "I believe there's somebody who wants to talk to you."

"We are officers and cannot be blackmailed or bribed..." hearing a voice from the TV they turned around and saw a familiar face, "Mr President!"

"I'm glad to hear it boys you however can be ordered to do something and that something is to assist Heir Strauss in whatever he wishes. Give him your full attention. I am afraid you were led astray by a few rogue ministers following their own agenda. They have been arrested and are being interrogated as we speak. Dismissed gentlemen," with that he looked at Heir Strauss and said, "Well that is that, you can re-arm them now and use them. Joe is the soldier but Bob however is a skilful archaeologist and may be of help to you in the field," looking at the screen Heir Strauss said, "Thank you Mr President."

"Good evening Heir Strauss and the conversation was terminated.

Jack and Michelle had just walked into the command vehicle when she caught sight of Bob, "My god Bob, how did you get here? The last time we were talking you were going into the army. How are you?

"As things go, not too bad Michelle. What are you doing here?" pulling Michelle aside Jack said, "How do you know him?"

"We were on digs together. I know him very well, he's an excellent archaeologist and very good in middle Kingdom Egyptology."

"Can he be trusted?"

"Yes, without a doubt."

"Ok then Bob, go with Michelle and she will introduce you to the rest of the team."

"Ok and you are?"

"My name is Jack, 'Jack Toner,'" with that Jack turned to Joe and said, "You can join the rest of the security details," handing him back his gun and saying how risky his tactics were on the hill. He simply replied that he had not enough men to cover his back on that position and he was left with no choice.

"Fair enough," said Jack, "This is Richard, he will assign you a new task," nodding and walking off towards Richard.

In the tomb complex Nicolas was having a conversation with Exios he asked, "Who was at the head of the house of Ammon?" Nicolas replied, "He is simply called the chairman."

"Well this chairman will probably know who was brought through the portal. I know of this new god they speak of, does the Ammon order still have its priests?"

"Yes we pray every second day as required."

"Good I worship Ammon myself, the priest will also know. By the way, where are they?"

"On they're way I believe," leaving he said, "Oh yea, the Professor and Alex are going to attempt to walk down the long corridor."

"When are they to do this?" shouted Exios

"Why now of course," taking to his feet Exios ran as fast as his legs would carry him into the second arena and up the steps where he nearly fell. They were fifteen feet in when he got to the doorway, "Stop!" shouted Exios, "Stop now!"

"Why?" shouted Jack.

"Come back and I will show you."

The two retreated out of the shaft and faced Exios, he nodded, "By the gods that was close..." he walked over to a statue of Alexander and reached for his sword and grabbed the hilt of the sword and turned it counter clockwise. They all heard a loud thud followed by a clank they heard a sliding noise and looked back into the shaft he quickly said, "Before it disarms it fires off a volley, it's the way the traps are set looking down into the shaft." They saw about one hundred glass spears slide out of their holes this time they were set differently into the edged of the roof with a strip of thin plaster covering them. "My god," said Kevin, "We would have all died. Thank you Exios, thank you." Simply nodding in appreciation the Greek said, "From this point there will be no traps." Looking down the shaft they witnessed what could have been a slaughter. The ground was almost burnt by the acid. The Greek said, "It will take a good couple of hours to let the acid burn itself out, well that's what Aristotle said when he designed them." Looking at the pair he had just saved he said, "Just another one of his talents," walking away saying to himself "yes remarkable man, a remarkable man indeed." Jack looked at Kevin and said, "He's something else isn't he?"

CHAPTER 8.

"Jack, I am getting stronger now, I will need my armour and weapons," Jack walked over to a cage that had been erected in the command centre of the complex and produced a key that unlocked it. He watched as Exios put on his cuirass and strapped on his greaves, he lifted his sword and attached it to his waist; he lifted the shield and slid it up to his arm so that he could carry the spear in the same hand. Finally he lifted his helmet and placed it under his other arm and walked into the next chamber containing the arena. This is where he started to practise spear drill, it was the same thing that Kevin had read about in Aloun's officer drill parchment. Just then he had an idea, he ran into his desk in the command centre and lifted the old documents, he ran into the next room where Exios was training and handed them to the Greek. Looking at them he said, "These are mine."

"They were with the general's stuff."

"That would make sense since it was he that gave me them. They are training papers that every officer owns thank you Kevin but I do not need them I know the drill of by heart. Please, you keep them. Come Nicolas, you too Jack, train with me." The three men stood in the middle of the arena, Exios began with spear practice that was skilfully executed. His spear was razor sharp and Jack and Nicolas tried to keep up with him, they found two old swords in the throne room and they were not making a bad attempt as they parried and ducted. They finally had something that resembled a spear drill but watching Exios put them to shame. All three men were in shorts and tee shirts the sweat started to run as they switched to swords. Exios started with a simple routine, walking forward with the sword and thrusting it, the shield was in the other hand and was used with a thrusting movement that mirrored a defensive weapon as well. The drill finally finished with physical training that involved wrestling, Jack and Exios paired off and began, they were throwing each other on the floor like rag dolls, Exios used the skilful practice of the unbalanced and tried to catch Jack off guard but Jack was ready for him with an over the body throw ending with the Greek laying on the floor. Exios said, "I've never seen that before!"

"Yes I know, it's called judo and it's from the Far East."

"You will have to teach me this judo Jack Toner."

"Yes, but in return you will tell me of Gaugamela."

"Agreed friend."

The men indulged in a conversation while a few of the female staff had converged on the arena to watch the Greek train, all three were dripping with sweat and were the best looking of any typical male, muscular and lean. The girls were giggling and going red with embarrassment as the Greek looked up at them, 'look yonder maidens, and how would one of you like to know me for a night?'

Nicolas and Jack looked at each other and said, "He isn't half shy is he." Jack said, "You don't think that will actually work do you?"

Just as he finished the sentence one of the girls poked her head through the door and into the arena, looked at Exios, smiled and said, "Hi I am Helen, come get me when you need me," with that she walked into the other group of giggling girls. Jack and Nicolas looked at each other bewildered and Jack said in a comical tone, "That's the breaks eh."

Through the night as the teams worked away doing an archaeological census on the throne room. Out in Exios' sleeping quarters the young nurse was groaning and screaming with pleasure as the Greek took his sexual frustration out on her. Nicolas and Jack were walking past and Jack mentioned the fact, "It probably was ok to do those things back in ancient Greece but in this day and age he's going to have a lot of sexual harassment cases to deal with."

"Well that's if the women don't find him attractive," laughing, the pair walked of is search of their mystery guest who had summoned them to the command vehicle. As they walked over to the vehicle Nicolas spotted a helicopter, "That's the chairman's private helicopter." They both walked over to the door and walked in, where they were greeted by the Chairman and Heir Strauss.

"Welcome gentlemen," said the chairman, "So far you have done a wonderful job in security and finding the tomb." Standing behind him was an old priest of Ammon, Jack looked at him strangely as if he did not belong to this time, it was like going back in time to the court of some long forgotten pharaoh. When Nicolas saw him he bowed and said, "Hello," replying the priest said, "Hello Nicolas I haven't seen you in a while..."

"Oh you know, busy in the field how are you keeping?"

"Not so bad and you? "

"Ok, we must pray before l leave."

Nicolas said, "I would like that..."

"As I was saying..." the chairman interrupted, "I have here with me one of only four priests of Ammon in the world, this is the head priest of the four, the only person that knows the reason behind the building of the tomb complex and the people involved." Walking over to the chair in the middle of the floor the priest sat down and began to speak;

"This complex was built as a negotiation centre for Alexander to accommodate the wishes of the kasorien Kingdom and was used as a conference venue you could say. You see, the only way for the portal to be opened as you know, was the device in front of the portal. The device and the portal is of kasorien technology, the rest of the room is the original tomb, built by the Egyptians mainly pharaoh Akhenaten. The device works in principle on the civilisation that comes across it at the time, the code is activated on the top of the module and here comes the second part and the most interesting; the only thing that can open it is human blood. Whenever the code is initiated on top of the device there are two handles set into the middle of the device to open the door, when you turn the handles your wrists are clamped and two blades appear and as you turn the handles your wrists are slit simultaneously. Your blood then travels down into the heart of the device that starts a chain reaction which in turn starts the activation process of the gate. This is as much as I know about the gate."

Jack then asked about the woman and child that was travelling with General Aloun, "Yes," said the priest, "I was getting to that. You see the talks were about one thing and one thing only. Alexander couldn't take on the kasoriens military; they were far too technologically advanced for Alexander. He understood this when he first opened the gate so he was relived to hear that they were not a war like people but very peaceful and intelligent. He agreed to send some of the greatest minds in his country through the portal including his son, where he and his mother would be safe. At the time it was a state secret, nobody even knew he had a son at that time, it was far to dangerous as they would surely have been assassinated by some power hungry general after Alexander's empire. So Alexander got his way, through the negotiation table his heir was safe and his prodigy would live on in him."

Jack said, "You mean that somewhere out there could be an unbroken bloodline to Alexander the great?"

"Yes and to our religion a living god,"

Just then Nicolas said to the chairman, "Would you like me to go and get Exios and inform him of what is going on?"

"Ah, the Greek, yes, go and I will speak with him. This will be interesting, I've never had a conversation with somebody that's two thousand years old before," smiling at Heir Strauss, the German just laughed and said, "It will be memorable. He is quite the Romeo and sword and sandals type."

Nicolas walked into the area where Exios had his quarters and shouted, "Exios my friend"

"Come in Nicolas," he was getting dressed, at the side of the bed and exhausted lying on the other side was the young nurse Helen covered in sweat and the smile on her face was from ear to ear. Slipping into his shoes, he turned to the girl on the bed and kissed her on the head and said, "Sleep, I will see you again my beautiful swan," with that he threw the covers over the girl and followed Nicolas to the command tent where he first caught sight of the priest. He bowed and reached into his pocket and pulled out a gold coin and said, "An offering to the gods Ammon and Isis," the priest bowed in return and performed the rights and blessed Exios and said, "I haven't done that one in a while, how goes all with the son of General Aloun?"

All is well old man, as well as can be, I seem to be out of my time," laughing at Exios the priest said, "So am I."

"So are you going to open the gate again?" asked Exios

"Yes," said the chairman, "It is time."

"And who may I ask is blessed with the task of opening the gate?"

The German looked at Exios and said, "It will not be you this time my friend, you have done enough and would be to much a demand on your body." Jack will do it this time."

"Ok, he is a good man and has honour."

"At the moment he is the strongest of us all, our medical teams will stand by."

Heir Straus asked the priest "I know the reason of this complex but not completely of the device. I don't understand it fully?"

"The device is in place to ensure two things, one, whoever opens the gate must have courage because knowing how to do so would most likely be the death of anyone attempting it and the second, is the wounding of the person opening it. They built a fail safe into it you must have the medical technology to heal the person. Without so the person who opened the gate would die. That is what the sarcophagus is for, whenever we can treat the person who opens the gate and as a result he lives they will know we have a level of technology that can be taken seriously as a people of intelligence and peace, then again they may have evolved violently and now be an imperial power, one thing is for certain, we have to investigate the possibility that they are still a civilised race."

"Well gentleman, what have we got to lose?"

Standing at the back Jack said, "Everything, if this goes pear shaped."
"Pear shaped?" said the Greek

Nicolas said, "It's a slang word for going wrong…"

"Ah I see."

"And what do we know about this code?"

"Very little," replied Heir Straus "Priest, what can you tell us about the code…" asked the puzzled German.

"It is a picture code and only I have the key that unlocks it. It is an old ancient Egyptian code that is only known to our priesthood," replied the old man.

The chairman looked at the old priest and said, "And you will open it for us?"

"Yes I believe the time is right for the unlocking of the portal."

"Have you gained entrance to the old chamber yet?"

Jack said, "Michelle is about to venture down there with Exios anytime now so I suggest that we make our way down now."

They all exited the command vehicle and started the descent down the shaft with Exios leading the way; he lifted an old torch and lit another lighting mechanism just on the other side of the door. This door was different than the others, it had another theme, it was Egyptian in origin with the Pharaoh Akhenaten sitting on his throne with his recognisable long thin limbs which Michelle made apparent was some kind of genetic disorder. Exios said "that is one strange looking fellow. He is almost woman-like. These doors will be harder to move than the others."

"Why?" asked Jack.

"Because, they are made of solid gold"

The crowd started to look more closely at them. The doors were slightly brown in colour and had a thick layer of dust on them. One of the team said mockingly, "that isn't gold." Exios turned to Jack and asked, "I need to borrow something friend."

"Yes of course Exios." He reached to Jacks munitions belt and pulled out Jacks hunting knife, thinking that he was going to kill the person that just mocked him Jack said, "hold it Exios, don't worry the idiot is safe enough." With that he turned to the doors and ran the knife down one side cutting a slither of the precious metal he then spun the knife in one hand and returned it to Jacks holster in one fluid movement.

He handed the slither of gold to the man that had just mocked him, "yes my friend it is solid gold and it also weighs about a tonne."

Jack, Exios and Nicolas pulled at the door and the familiar squealing of the hinges almost took the fillings out of their heads and one of the team had to walk away while the doors were being opened. Finally the doors gave way and the high pitch sound became more intense.

Exios said, "I don't know why they did not have that sound as a booby trap, it would have scared away all intruders."

Finally Exios looked with apprehension on the last and final chamber, the memories flooded back; the last time he was in this room he lost his father and his life. Thinking back to that day over two thousand years ago, they had been out riding that morning, they did it every morning, they always travelled light in this heat and his sandals clamping the horses side and his father encouraging him to ride faster than he was they rode back to the complex and strolled in. The head engineer walked to him and said, 'General Aloun the ritual is complete all that remains is for the sacrifice of a willing servant of the King. Our men of science do not think they will be able to save who so ever chooses to open the portal.' The general put his hand on the young mans shoulder and said; 'now Exios we have spoken of this. I will go and do this thing for you are young and besides who would look after my wife and family.' Exios was determined to allow his father to see the rest of his life out with his mother. It was the general who was supposed to go in the sarcophagus after the ritual but he simply loved the old man too much to do that. He knew that in doing so he was risking everything including the fact that the tomb may never be found for few hundred years. But even after two thousand years he could still feel the influence of his father on the back of his neck; it was like a shiver running into the room, "The general found me on the ground here with the floor covered in my blood. I can vaguely remember him lifting me and carrying me to the throne room and whispering in my ear how much he loved me as they lowered me in to the sarcophagus. And here I see the instrument of all my troubles and pain and I can see my father looking at me again standing in front of the gateway ready to carry me off again into the abyss. There was something about this room that did not bode well with me." Looking around he saw Nicolas standing on one side of him and on the other was Jack and the Professor, behind him a strange trio the gods had sent him, "now it's Jacks turn for bloodletting and I will try to make him aware of what it is to play with the serpent with the bite that's never felt until it's too late. Given that I will have at least gone someway to preparing him for this hard task that lies in store."

Turning to his right, Exios saw Jack standing in front of the gateway, a roll of ember shade off the oil lighting system ran across his face. The last chamber was like a standard Egyptian burial chamber without the usual treasure store or annex. It would have at one point had just one shaft running from it, the centre of the room had the granite slab where once the sarcophagus had laid. The walls were decorated with paintings that were not unlike the wall paintings in Tutankhamen's tomb, the chronicled workings of the afterlife. One wall it had the god Osiris, on the other, Anubis, who were all helping the lost souls to the after-world. In the middle it also had a pillared surround that once surrounded the sarcophagus, the gate itself was made of an unknown metal that was not like the material that the sarcophagus was made from, it was more like mercury in appearance that seemed to very hard. Exios saw a team of workmen walk into the chamber and they started to assemble equipment. They began with a high powered drill, looking at Jack he said, "Are they trying to gain entry?"

"Yes," replied Jack, "This should do the trick."

"Don't count on it," said Exios, "My father tried something similar, he had groups of men work at it with picks and other tools, twenty-four hours a day for a month they did not make a scratch, not one scratch."

"Whatever it is, it's hard," just then Jack heard the familiar sound of the drill powering up; he turned to the gate and watched in vain as the drill bit just snapped in front of him. Next they tried Heir Straus' new toy, his new laser that he had flown in from Germany for the occasion. Heir Strauss said he would try everything to avoid Jack going up against the device; his scientists were looking over the gate and device and from what they saw it was a new technology that was thousands of years more advanced than anything we had. It worked off some kind of liquid crystal technology, the crystal being the circuit and the liquid being the power source, it appeared to be alive right down to a microscopic level. Looking up from his microscope Alex said, "Oh shit! These suckers have cracked nanotechnology..." Just as he was speaking the laser overheated and the result had been the same as the drill, no joy.

"As I was saying before I was interrupted, you see your blood is being checked to see if it's fresh and if it's human, only then shall it open the gate Jack. Whoever built this knew what they were doing. This level of technology could scan for even specific types, like DNA or blood types, I am sure of it. Just to let you know, whenever we open this door we're walking into a world of extreme possibilities..."

"Of that I am aware..." behind him he saw the old priest of Ammon gaze at the old tomb, "Look at the beautiful paintings, middle Kingdom, this man would have been of great importance that was laid here for the journey to the after life but sadly his sarcophagus is gone."

"Priest remember that this is a mock tomb built by Akhenaten to fool the tomb robbers..."

Laughing the priest said, "The first thing to scare the tomb robbers would have been the desert and heat."

The medical team had been properly set up and all they needed was the patient with a severe blood loss problem, stepping up to the device Exios walked over to Jack and said, "The only advice I can give you is, be brave and stay awake as long as you can." Standing by, was the team with their IV drips and a fresh blood supplies for Jack when he needed them. He stepped up to the machine and he looked at the code, it was a large triangle and was blue in colour, it had about ten pieces to it and depending on what way you set the pieces in the device activated and the handles lifted up to waist height. The triangle was complete already and first he took the right and left hand pieces and folded them in on themselves he then lifted the top piece of the pyramid and placed it below the triangle, the piece clicked into place and the device started to glow. From the centre of the machine the two arms came out and he placed his arms into the catches and grabbed the handles sliding the device in. He began to turn the strange key when all of a sudden the mountain started to shake and shudder, the device suddenly released Jack and he pulled himself out and checked himself for cuts. He caught the sight of blood oozing from his arms and he then felt weak and collapsed back into the assembled medical team that had been standing behind him. While they were working on him something had happened the gate, it had folded back into a hallway and you could see the other side. The nanobots must have activated the mercury like metal and walking through the corridor Nicolas and Exios were the first ones through the gate. Running through they looked out into a beautiful landscape with strange kinds of trees and on hearing a voice they both jumped and turned;

Chapter 9.

"Hail to you envois of Macedonia," before them stood a sentry who was strangely dressed as well as strangely armed but most strange of all was the fact he was speaking to us in English. "Has your gate keeper received medical attention yet?"

Nicolas replied, "He is getting sorted out now."

"I see," said the guard walking back with them, he was wearing metal strips on his hands. He walked over to Jack and said, "Do not be afraid." He grabbed his wrists and pulled them in front of his chest which was clad in some kind of armour, a scanning light came from the Brest plate of the guard, he looked at Jack and said, "It will take a moment for your energy to return but for now you are out of danger my friend."

Jack looked down at his wrists and saw that the damage had been repaired, the cut tissue had somehow knitted together and he could once again feel the blood run through his veins. He looked up in appreciation at the strange person that had saved him weeks of recovering in bed; the guard looked at him and said, "No problem." The guard then had time to reflect on his surroundings he looked around the small chamber and when he saw the priest he dropped to his knees and said, "Forgive me priest. I saw you not." The priest of Ammon casually walked over to him and said, "Do not worry, you were busy executing your duty young man, rise," the large guard lifted himself up and continued to look around the chamber. "So this is the legendary gate room our King came through."

"King?" said the Professor

"Yes our King Philip, the son of Alexander over two thousand years ago."

"If it is not too intrusive, who's in charge now?"

"We are ruled by our Empress Queen Olympia."

"Where are we at now in your land?"

"You are on the border of our empire."

Kevin looked at the fellow and said, "Tell me, what the name of this empire is?"

The guard looked at him with an air of sincerity and proudly said, "The Kasorien Empire. Come, we are a days ride from the nearest village then we can travel to our capital and to Queen Olympia's court. We are given orders to escort anyone who comes through the gate of their own free will and present them to her majesty. Those of you, who wish to come, do so now," with that the guard walked through the corridor and waited for the chosen to walk through. Heir Straus was the first to go through; he called for supplies to be brought through after him. Jack followed closely behind the German and Jack turned to his team and said, "What are you waiting for? Come on lets go, adventure awaits." Nicolas and Exios escorted the old priest and Michelle followed behind Jack. Richard and the security squad followed by a few medical personnel and walked until they reached the gate at the far side where the guard was standing.

"Everyone through?" he asked.

Heir Straus replied, "Yes," the chairman nodded in agreement.

They looked at their surroundings and found them to be beautiful; the entire empire was one very large cavern below the earth's surface that had never been discovered. A strange aluminous discharge gave off day light that was thousands of feet high, another guard walked over and said, "So my friend, it has happened to us. Of all the guards over the centuries it is us."

"Yes my friend. In our regiment there's a tradition, whoever is on watch when the visitors come through are made wealthy by the Queen. Come, we have horses waiting and in the next village we will get transport to the capital, it is called Castorian. It is our great city founded by a King called Kasor, hence, where the word Kasorien comes from. He was the last ruler of the old Egyptian cast and was much loved."

Kevin asked, "What about the people of the light, the original habitants of this land?"

"They live beyond our borders, there is not much contact between our two races," at that his comrade came around from old looking stables built into the side of the mountain which contained the gate. He was leading a pack of horses and said, "Ok, everybody mount up," and we did as he asked. What a strange looking bunch we were, Heir Straus said, "Is there not another available mode of transport?"

"Yes," replied the guard, "But you are not ready for that yet." They started their descent down a steep hill and it finally levelled off. They looked back up and saw how high up they were, at least two thousand feet below the gate.

The guard had said that is was 2010 feet.

"How do you measure it?"

"All the appropriate devices are built into my armour," with that he lifted his arm and hit a button, a screen opened out of his side armour, it had strange looking writing across the screen and then it folded back into his armour again. They soon saw what looked like an old ancient Egyptian town, laid out like they had been on the archaeological digs in the delta. Michelle was intoxicated by what she was seeing, the people were all wearing period dress and speaking a language they could not understand. She could only guess it was ancient Egyptian, the women were beautifully attired with makeup and long linen dresses plated and folded the same as you would see in a tomb painting. The women looked at them with a wonderful cursory and even came up and touched them and spoke to them in the strange tongue they were unaccustomed to. The men stayed at arms length, watching their women and children, they were dressed more in the Greek tradition and they were playing board games of some kind and going through what looked like a physical fitness routine. It was like something from a scene from Athens long ago; the children were running beside the team, teasing and shouting with excitement. Michelle thought that it was kind of nice to see children with a lovely sense of innocence. Riding beside the guard she asked him how he came to speak such good English, he said, "Sometimes you can pick up radio and what you call television signals. We started picking them up around fifty years ago and from the English programmes we were able to translate most of your language and culture. It's interesting to say the least, all the border guards can speak English, and it is one of the requirements of our detachment." They turned a corner and saw what appeared to be some kind of conveyance, the guard walked over to it, held his hand out and the door appeared from the side. It appeared to be made of the same material as the gate and it was in the shape of the octagon with slanted roof steps that materialised from the mercury coloured octagon. The interior was made of glass, even the seats and the most remarkable of all so was the floor, they could see the ground below them and to some it was rather unnerving. Michelle turned to Jack and whispered in his ear, "Cool isn't it."

"Yes," he replied while taking note of the landscape below. It was beautiful there were orchards of oranges and what appeared to be olive trees as well as apples. The guard looked over and commented, "I see you've seen the famous orchard of Alexander, and he sent all the small trees and seeds to start our relationship with fruit. They are not the original fruit trees of course; they are the off shots of the originals he brought through as a result the countryside is peppered with orchards like these. Over there is where the temple of Ammon is. We are dropping the priest off there now."

The large ship landed in the courtyard and the priest asked, "How do I get out of this thing?"

The guard replied, "Just stand in the middle of the floor."

The priest walked over and stood as required, the guard said, "The floor will open for you and you will drop about an inch onto the ground and it will close once the craft has cleared your head."

"Will I not be hurt by the propulsion blast?"

"You would if there was one. This craft is powered by, ah, what is the word, yes, magnetism."

So the priest walked over to the middle of the floor, the guard pressed one of the controls on the console on board the strange vehicle and the glass floor below him opened in the form of a square and he dropped down about an inch. The craft then took off and once he had cleared the craft the floor closed over and all we could see was the old priest waving in the distance. Jack looked at the guard and said, "Our next stop is?" "Castorian city," replied the guard.

"By the way, what is your name?"

"My name is Ottilin, and yours is?"

"Jack, Jack Toner."

"Well Jack Toner, it is nice to meet you."

As they flew silently the craft came into sight of their mighty city, it was massive and around it was what appeared to be a massive defence built wall with towers and battlements on them. The city was lined with streets and pathways and in the centre, exactly in the centre, was the imperial palace. Everyone gasped when they saw its beauty; it was something straight out of a fairytale book. At the front, it had twelve rows of steps that led onto an open court; the main palace was round in shape with beautiful carved doors inlayed with the same material as the sarcophagus. In front were rows upon rows of soldiers all dressed in full uniform with shields and swords. Just after they landed, the guard Ottilin said, "The Empress is waiting, and so my friends is your guard of honour." Jack turned to Richard and asked, "Rough count, how many is there out there?" Richard paused in concentration then replied, "Rough count I'd say about sixty thousand." Her majesty's royal guard said, "Sixty thousand, yes, and on the parade ground here another forty on royal duty."

Jack turned to the assembled crowd and said, "Jesus Christ, she has a personal bodyguard of one hundred thousand."

A tall man approached the small band of explorers; he was at least fifty five and had an eye patch. He was wearing a different uniform and his armour was different, Richard thought out loud, "A higher rank perhaps?"

"Yes," replied Ottilin, "He is general Lieysin, the head of the Kasorien guard, as you would say their commanding officer." As he continued to walk in their direction they noticed that he did so with a limp and had many scars on his face and arms. He marched straight up to Jack and Heir Strauss and the chairman; he looked at Jack and said with a distinguished voice, "Her imperial majesty is now ready to grant you an audience. Please follow me," with that he proceeded up the channel that had been made by the Kasorien guard right the way up to the gates of the palace. He stepped into the palace and into a main state room that was finished off by a beautiful staircase that started at the top and curved off in two different directions at the bottom. From beneath the stairs appeared court officials and soldiers, they were all dressed in period togas and had a Devine air of wisdom about them, as though they had served a long time in this court. Horns sounded and all of a sudden there she was at the top of the stairway, she had beautiful long blond hair and had narrow features, her body was slender and she wore a bejewelled necklace that sparkled in the light of the great hall. Her arms were covered in lace that were studded in diamonds, her white flowing dress fluttered in the light gentile breeze and from the split in her dress one could see her beautiful slender legs. Never before had any of them seen such beauty in a woman, she wore an emerald, ruby and diamond tiara that had a strange fringe to it and tied off behind her ears. As she walked down the soldiers all knelt including Nicolas and as she ascended to her throne she lent back and with a gentle voice said, "Welcome to our Kingdom envois of Macedonia and hail to your sovereign whoever he or she may be. I trust your journey here has been a comfortable one?" Stepping out Heir Strauss knelt and started to explain "Oh great Queen, I bring sad news; the Macedonian empire no longer exists. Alexander died a young man in Babylon and left no heir to his throne. His lieutenants split his empire and so doing destroyed the one thing that kept it together, cohesion, but please take solace in the fact that Alexander is still revered in our world and is thought of as one of the greatest leaders of the ancient world. Many have sometimes wrongfully tried to emulate his glory but have failed miserably. Personally I think they had everything except one factor, Alexander's heart."

"Thank you for your explanation of the downfall of the Alexandrian empire. I will mourn my great ancestor in the temple of Zeus in my great city and thank him for your safe arrival. So if you are not of Macedonia who are you?"

Standing out and bowing Heir Straus said, "We are a selection of scholars, soldiers and scientists." The old general looked at Jack and said, "You're a soldier. I would bet my life on it and with what army may I ask?"

"The foreign legion," replied Jack.

"Never heard of them my lad, never heard of them at all."

The Queen looked at Exios and asked, "Who are you?"

"I am Exios and I am the son of the great General Aloun."

"You were in the sarcophagus weren't you?"

"Yes my Queen."

"There is a legend about you that you probably aren't aware of... that you saved your fathers life by opening the gate instead of him. It is so very good to see you standing before me. I am glad you are ok, what you did is one of the noblest things in the reordered history of my people," the Queen looked at her minister and ordered him to arrange a feast in honour of their guests. They were all taken to different apartments were they bathed and got ready for the night. Michelle looked at Jack and said, "Well, what do you think of our host then?" in a jealous tone. "Well, she is the descendant of Alexander the great and for all we know has his sense of humour," he took a moment and looked around, the whole apartment was finished in marble and the floors were polished granite. The bed was also marble, a four-poster, looking at it Jack reminded Michelle of how sexy she was by slowly undressing her by the bed and making frenzied love to her before going to the massive marble bath were they finished off their antics in an explosion of lust, her long black Hair lapping over the side of the bath and Jack gently caressing her neck with his lips, she then brought a good question to Jacks attention, "If the old general Lieysinhad has so many wounds in which battle did he acquire them? I thought this place was war free or perhaps there was a feud years ago one thing for sure something is going on something bad"

The Professor was changing into his three piece suit, he always liked to be properly attired for such things and he loved the stigma attached to tradition and order, with that he fixed his dickey bow and headed for the great dinning hall. They all congregated in the hall way outside the apartments in excited anticipation of the meal to come. A royal envoy appeared out of one of the corridors and said, "The Empress expects you for dinner, please follow me." Following the well dressed servant they made their way along an open gallery that led out on to a open courtyard, it was surrounded by statues fashioned after the Greek style, they contained all the greats from Hercules to Atlas, another one of Zeus himself, looking around Kevin was like a child in a candy shop, he was totally involved and fascinated, Michelle laughed and said to Jack, "I haven't seen him this happy for years."

"You two are close." replied Jack.

"Yes, he's more of a father than a friend; he's always looked after my back."

"That's good to know," said Jack, "That makes two of us now."

They were led across the open courtyard and into an other building that led into the great hall; the servant turned around and motioned for them to be seated and said, "Her imperial majesty, Queen Olympia." This time she walked in wearing a black dress that from head to foot was studded with diamonds and rubies, it looked amazing. Richard turned to Jack and said, "She's wearing the price of a small African country," in a comical tone. Across the table were the countries elite, they were a strange looking crowd, some of them were dressed in the ancient Egyptian fashion and even had on wigs, the men of Greek influence wore togas the only thing they had in common were the small breast plates they all had that was about four inches across and three long and all had the coat of arms of the Empress, it was a sun disk with spears overlapping it and had the rays of the sun reflecting around it. The breast plate was secured around the upper chest and tied at the back; it appeared to be some kind of dress armour for ceremonial purpose. As the Empress sat down she started her dinner speech, "Welcome to our feast my friends. I believe an introduction is in order, to my right you know general Lieysin, to my left is my notary Tybar and the rest are military officers and members of the peoples council of Kasorien, how do you say…politicians? So tell me Nicolas, how were your rooms?"

Nicolas stood up and said, "Better than anything I have ever seen and your palace is even more beautiful than Alexander's in Babylon."

"Thank you, I have heard much of Babylon from our historians, the hanging gardens..." and she pointed to a painting hanging on the wall she remarked that it had came through with the Greeks the last time the gate was opened.

Kevin addressed her and said, "You mean this is a real representation of the hanging gardens? None exists in our world; this painting would be historically of great importance. May I make a copy your majesty?"

"Yes of course. I will summon the court artist in the morning."

"Thank you your majesty."

Chapter 10.

First came the starter, two giant soup caldrons carried by four men each. "May I enquire general, what kind of soup this is? Asked Michelle. "Horned viper," replied the general licking his lips, "My favourite, here it is a great delicacy. I've only had it twice before, if it's not cooked right it can kill you," laughed the general.

"He reminds me of my old CO," said Richard, "He's a right character." Jack looked up at the Empress and said, "Just think about it, she is the last physical link with Alexander."

Richard agreed, "Yes, look at her long blond hair."

"She's also very clever," said the general, "She speaks all four of the empires languages including yours. She has a fascination for your culture and language."

She began to ask Heir Straus, "What was this world war two?

"Your majesty it was a conflict that happened about sixty years ago, on one side you had the axis powers and on the other you had the allies, the axis powers were evil and had to be stopped."

"Did you fight in this war Mr Straus?"

"Yes your majesty, I was a junior officer in the Africa corps in the German army that was on the side of the axis."

"I see were there many killed?"

"Yes millions were killed," her eyes took a different direction as he answered, she then controlled her emotion and turned and said to Strauss, "Again you are glad you survived this world war?"

"Yes, many of my friends did not and all for the ramblings of a mad man."

"Hitler?"

"Yes," said Heir Strauss, "How did you know?"

"We sometimes pick up what you call television, observe…" pointing to the middle of the table she picked up a controller of some kind, she then ran her hand over it and a hologram appeared, it was one of the old documentaries about the second world war. General Lieysin then began a conversation with Richard, "I see you are still using firearms, apparently lead projectiles of some kind?"

"Yes, what do you use?"

"We have a new weapon called the peltas rifle. It operates on a controlled air operating valve, I believe you call it compressed air and it is very powerful. I noticed when you arrived you were carrying two of such weapons."

"Yes the heckler and cock and glock 9mm. would you like an opportunity to fire them?"

"Yes that would be a dream come true for me to fire off an antique weapon."

"Oh general I don't think it's too old yet."

"Yes of course, you will understand when I show you the peltas rifle."

There in the middle of the room was Hitler in all his glory before the war at the Nuremberg rallies, "He looks like a mesmerising character.

"Yes," Heir Strauss replied, "I can remember seeing him when I was a young boy he had this hypnotic..."

"Hypnotic?" asked the Queen. The general Lieysin turned to the Queen and said another word in her language, "ah yes I understand now hypnotic."

"And did you know he held Alexander in high esteem as well as Julius Caesar?"

"Who was this Julius Caesar?"

"He was a great roman general your majesty," she looked at Lieysin and said, "You mean the roman tribe that lived in Italy?"

"Yes your majesty it appears they made a bid for world domination and did quite well and it lasted for hundreds of years so Richard has told me."

"Yes and also our language and literature are of Latin influence which originates from the Roman as well as their architecture and are responsible for the first drainage system. Unfittingly their work force was all slave labour. The first King of Macedonian blood, Philip, outlawed it, it was one of the first decrees he gave and remains the greatest monarch we ever had. You see gentlemen, there are three civilisations in existence here in the Kasorien Empire; the ancient Egyptians, the Macedonians and the ones you call the people of the light, where we know them as the Kitni. They are the people who first introduced us to their technology and as a result there is no hunger, no disease and most importantly no famine."

"And why did the old Kingdom take a stranger to the throne?" asked Jack.

"Alexander had secret talks with them and in a deal to preserve his family he made a great sacrifice. The old King was dying of old age and he had no successors so in secret, an exchange was done through the priesthood of Ammon who were the only people who were, contrary to the fact this land existed, and Alexander could live his life out in his land and his son in his own domain safe from the hands of the greedy humanity who wanted him dead for their own good. And in this treaty if Alexander died without an heir, his empire would become the property of the Kasorien Empire."

The Professor thought about it for a while and in the end said, "My god that means that you would own about one eights of the surface of the world and with your technology nobody could stop you from taking it either," laughed the Professor in a joking manner.

"Yes," laughed the Queen.

"If I may enquire how old is her majesty?"

"Next month I shall be in my one hundredth and forty second year," clattering cutlery fell onto the table and everyone looked at her. Jack said, "But you look about twenty one?"

"In my world we age a lot slower."

"General may I ask what age are you?"

"Next fall I will be three hundred and ninety five."

"My god when you were born in our world the armada was happening. You see if we are lucky we make it to one hundred."

"Yes I know," answered the Queen, "So my historians tell me and here nobody gets sick, of course we still see death, in the Kasorien Empire there was fifty deaths out of a population of fifty million last year. Those of course are those who died of natural causes though we have lost thousands from battle and war."

"You are at war?"

"Yes against an ancient enemy called the Cast. They like the Kitni are indigenous to this land and live on the islands of Philios in the great sea of Osiris. They are called the Asronas, they are a highly aggressive people and live in fortified cities on their islands and when they feel they are being threatened they march out an army and cause a great deal of trouble and havoc. However they are not like us, they are not humanoid as you would put it they are more beast than man. Their islands are mountainous and are hilly, their feet and legs resemble that of a bears and their upper bodies are hairy and muscular. They have dark blue eyes and wear heavy armour. At the moment we are in negotiations with them for a peace accord but it doesn't look to promising. Their King is a stubborn entity called Riceos and is not keen on conversation, just war."

"May I ask, what do the people of Kitni think of this up coming war?"

"They view it with an adherence of stupidly and pride which to them is a deadly sin because of the taking of life. They are a peaceful people and hate to see those around them fight. In situations like this, instead of taking sides, they sit at the side just like a spectator watching a wrestling match to see who will come out the winner. I suppose when you look at from their point of view there is a strange common sense to what they are doing. We have been at war with the Asronas for three hundred years and yet we are so close to getting peace. King Riceos is a soldier by profession and is not a good politician."

"General Lieysin, what is your opinion of him?"

"Well for a start he is a good soldier. Damn fine infantry commander and inventive. The first time I encountered him he was a prince under his fathers command and even then he had an ability to set up traps with ease. In one case we thought we had him cornered but it turned out to be the other way around. When we thought we had him cornered he had secretly, the night before, mined the area behind us so all he had to do was activate the mines when we had marched over them so there was no way out. I lost three quarters of my men that day, even with our technology they still could find chinks in our armour, the rest of the survivors of my old regiment had to be air lifted out before they were slaughtered. When we returned with air ships with fire capability they had disappeared into the hillside."

Richard looked at the general and said, "That my friend is called guerrilla warfare."

"Gorilla warfare," replied the general

"Yes that's when an opposing force is under manned, it is more mobile, you are slower and they can melt away when they attack it's an old tactic that can sometimes work. Its designed to wear you down and cause the withdrawal of your troops,"

"Huh, it worked, thinking at the time it was what they wanted, we had to make concessions on land and evacuated a border village."

Tucking into their horned viper soup Michelle said, "This is not too bad at all, it's like Scotch broth." Jack and Richard laughed. The Queen lent forward and asked, "What is scotch broth?"

"It is a soup from where we come from."

"Oh I see."

Following the soup, the main course was brought out and laid in the middle of the table in very large containers that were made of silver. The Professor said, "My goodness, I know what they are. I've seen them in carvings and reliefs. The ancient Greeks used them for serving game," just as he said that two chains were lowered from the ceiling and attached by hooks and then they were lifted by the chains into the next floor were you could see the servants pull the large silver containers on to the specially made ledges and then they disappeared. Looking down they saw a mouth watering sight, Heir Strauss lowered his glasses and said, "Ah deer, venison, magnificent."

General Lieysin stood up and said, "Your imperial majesty," removing his chair and then we watched the servants move a stairway into position, she then stood up and the general took her by the hand and helped her walk up the stairway and over towards the deer. The general then opened a box in front of him and lifted out a dagger beautifully studded with rubies and diamonds, unsheathed it and then handed it to the Empress, her beautiful form moved gracefully along the table without hitting a plate or moving cutlery. She then lifted Exios plate and carved a piece of meat of the roasted beast and presented it to the Greek soldier and said to him, "In my country when this happens it's a great honour," smiling at Exios, her eyes sparkling with anticipation and before she walked off the table she turned to Exios and said, "Perhaps you will walk with me tonight?"

"It would be my honour your majesty," with that she smiled and walked off the table and took her seat. The general looked at Jack and said, "It's a very old tradition and I've never seen her play it out before. She must favour the young man."

"Is she married?"

"No she has never taken a husband. I suppose nobody ever caught her eye before. Don't get me wrong, there have been men before but she's never stayed interested and I have never seen her do that before. Well I suppose Exios is a legend, a person who saved somebody he loved by putting his own life in danger to ensure his fathers survival. She has been told this story since she was a small girl and it has always fascinated her. She's bound to have built up an attraction for him over the years. To us, he is all that is pure and true, our legend."

They tucked into their meal and it was delicious. Richard turned to Jack and commented, "You couldn't get better in the Ritz in London."

"It's very good isn't It." replied Jack. After the meal they adjourned to a hall beside the feasting hall that had pillows all around it and tables set out in the shape of an open toped square. They sat down while dancers entertained them but in the back of Jack's mind he couldn't forget how beautiful the Empress was. She had a glow about her and the way her guards treated her you would know they would all die before anything happened to her. Looking at her he dropped his eye line and noticed that she was wearing high heel, a corruption of my world, he thought, the influence of TV no doubt, strangely enough they suited her. All the men couldn't take there eyes of her and sometimes it caused irritation with the few females within the group, one girl said, "It wasn't right that anybody should be that good looking."

After the entertainment the Queen stood up and announced, "It is my wish that you should see more of the empire. We are currently engaged in negotiations with the Kingdom of Asronas and you should be witness to such to make the proceedings legal and if we fail its up to our generals and the persuasion of their armies. They are a beaten people and have retreated to their fortress city of Philios on the island of Philios in the sea of Osiris in the north of our empire and you will leave tomorrow that is if you please."

"Of course your majesty," replied Heir Strauss, "As you wish." Jack turned to Richard and said "What the hell is he getting us into Richard?" just finishing lighting a cigarette he looked at Jack and just said, "Adventure dear boy adventure."

"Yes Richard, I will remind you that you said that later on," laughing the two friends drank up and headed back to their apartments. Exios however, stayed with the Queen and walked with her through the flood lit gardens. Strange lights came through the ground, the paths were all lit like this, and they walked until they came to a lemon tree where there was waiting a tumbler of water and two glasses. She picked one of the lemons from the tree and produced a knife and cut it in two, she then cut it into smaller peaces and dropped two pieces into his glass and poured the freezing cold water into his glass and then handed it to Exios.

"Tell me, what was Alexander like?"

"My Queen, he was very like you, he was irresistible even his own sex found him attractive. He had his weak side too, he could be ruthless when called upon as you probably already know he had entire cities raised to the ground and the population massacred. He could also be capable of great kindness and love. Your majesty if I may ask no contact has been raised with the outside world?"

"No there hasn't, many of our counsellors on the government argue the fact that you are not ready as a people yet and will take another thousand years. There are others that think that now is the time, I happen to agree with them. They have so much to offer the Kasorien people as well as benefiting from our technology it would be a great alliance. I see that they have fitted you with a communications device to translate, rather a clumsy looking chunk of metal. Here take it off for me," a guard approached carrying a tray and the Empress ran both hands through his hair. For a moment Exios welcomed the tenderness that surrounded that magical moment, her hands felt like a cool breeze filtering through his hair, she continued to reach around his neck and pulled in close to his face, she looked deep into his eyes and said, "Exios, do not be afraid of me," with that she unhooked the collar from his neck and did the same to the small hard drive on his belt and placed them on the tray that the servant had just brought her. Exios then motioned to her that he could not communicate with her; she turned around and said in Greek, "We have something similar, a lot smaller and less cumbersome," she produced a box and opened it. There was what appeared to be a diamond in it and so she lifted it and placed it into Exios mouth and sealed it with a kiss, "A gift from a grateful Empress." She walked off in the direction of the palace and smiled behind her and waved goodnight. Exios then swallowed the pill and suddenly he could speak English and understand everything that he could not before. He headed back to his apartments and closed the door behind him, he then started to wonder how Jack and the rest were doing, as he walked over to the door he heard a beep and saw a flashing light and he walked over to it and swiped the light because he had seen one of the servants do it on his way back suddenly he saw a screen appear out of the wall and there was Professor Kevin on the picture.

"Hello Exios, this is some communications device. We're a couple of doors down from you, come on down."

"Ok Kevin, I'll be down in a moment," he opened his door and looked out to see if there were any servants or guards about but there were none so he walked down to the second door and pushed it open. There inside was everybody having a drink and those who smoked had a cigarette. Most of them were around the table, discussing the day ahead when Jack noticed that Exios was not wearing his communications device and he motioned to him thinking he did not understand him. Exios looked at him and said, "its ok my friend, she gave me a tablet that contained the technology to enable me to understand your language." Alex thought for a moment then said, "Biological NANO technology! My god they can programme the brain to understand English and speak it?"

"Yes, I can also read and write in your language for which I will be eternally grateful."

Jack looked at Richard and said, "What do you think of this peace treaty tomorrow?"

"I don't know Jack. They could be trying to make a point, to show us how powerful they are."

"What do you mean?"

"If these peace talks fall through they will have an excuse to wipe out the Asronas as a threat and consolidate their empire for the better. So my friend, we will see in the morning what the empire has in mind for us. I suggest a good night's sleep for everybody."

"Agreed," said Exios, "That sounds like a great idea."

At that, everyone returned to their apartments for a good nights sleep. They were all up early the next morning and the same servant arrived to show them to their breakfast. They all followed the slender looking man who was very polite and was called Thar. He led them to the feasting hall for breakfast and to their surprise it was a fry-up. They were met by General Lieysin who apologised for the Empress who was engaged in matters of state and would see them before they set off. As they sat there they saw a familiar sight, sausages and bacon and different types of breads. The General mentioned that they had also picked up a lot of cooking programs and tried them out for themselves.

Jack said, "That's all and well General, but there is one thing you don't have…" He then pulled out a bottle of brown sauce and the room exploded with laughter. The general looked at the bottle with curiosity and Jack reached the bottle to him and he opened it and said, "That smells very nice. Can I have some?"

"Yes," said Jack and he poured out a small amount and began to tuck into his breakfast. The General said smiling, "That's very good I must have it replicated."

"Yes, it is very nice," said Jack, "I never leave home without it."

When they had finished they were escorted to a landing pad and met by the Empress who said, "This is a great day. We may have peace today and if not, war. One or the other, general please ensure the safety of our guests." She walked over to Exios and said, "How's the English doing?"

"Very well your majesty. Thanks to you I can now understand my comrades."

"Indeed, the gift that I gave you is in this land worth a fortune," taking his hand she said her goodbyes and then dismissed herself walking off into the palace. The general then turned to Heir Strauss and said, "When you came here it was in civilian transport. Today, we will be travelling in a war ship, we call them battle transports they are not as comfortable as the civilian transports and are designed for battle and defensive reasons."

A massive ship appeared; it was the colour of steel and was about two hundred feet long. It had a block affect and was stepped from the bottom upwards and had different levels on it. At the top it had battlements that according to the general, gave the soldiers great cover during battles. They were good for providing cover for ground forces before a major offensive, it pulled up beside them and unlike the other transport it opened at the front and two guards stepped out and saluted the general. The guards took their positions at the entrance of the battle transport and said, "Battle transport ready for inspection general."

"Very good soldier, very good," walking into the transport he motioned the group to follow. The bottom deck seemed to be sleeping quarters, the second was for ship command, the controls etc. The third level was for infantry firing positions and the top level was some kind of observation platform that according to the general was a good place on a good day for a picnic.

Richard looked at him oddly and said, "What about an attack?"

"We don't have to worry about that. This battle ship has shields and a new innovation which is, individual body shielding for our troops it gives the infantry soldier a new level of protection against most of the weapons belonging to the people of the Asronas."

"May I ask, what is the general field equipment of the soldier in your army?"

The old general looked back and said, "Certainly, they are all equipped with a peltas rifle, a side arm and body shielding. Only the elite regiments still carry swords because they are so difficult to use and the members of the houses of nobility of both traditions as tradition dictates of course."

He then held up his weapon and said, "Do you fancy squeezing of a few rounds as I promised?"

"Yes of course, I nearly forgot."

"Let us go up to the observation deck," so they walked over to a number of lifts, they were designed for two at a time and they got off at the fourth floor. The general walked over to a control panel and said, "I would like you all to put your hands on the scanner, you see the peltas rifle has a security fitting. Anybody that is not cleared to use one is disabled by the surge running the opposite way rather than out of the barrel." Putting all their hands on the scanner the general then put his hands on the control panel and said, "Authorisation level one, General Lieysin," at that moment the panel turned the colour green and replied, "Authorisation accepted General Lieysin," he than turned and walked over to the gun rack and lifted a rifle, headed to the battlements and shouted over at the soldier to launch training targets. Out came two targets in the shape of a square with a dot in the middle, "Fair enough," said Richard, as he knocked his safety off and took aim and fired his weapon in short bursts. He then put the safety on and handed it to the General; he disengaged the safety and fired of a few rounds and then turned to a monitor and instructed it to magnify, as it did, he saw two neat groups of holes in the target. He looked at Richard and said "Impressive."

"Is that all it can do?" asked Richard.

He started to describe what its capabilities were, he began with the first setting, "This pretty much does what yours can do," he lifted the weapon to his shoulder and took aim and fired the gun made a thudding sound and put two holes about an inch in diameter the second setting had the power of a rocket launcher the third and final setting was simply called spread. When asked why it was called spread, the general said, "It was mostly used by ground troops for large bodies of infantry." He set it to the spread setting and shouted an order at the soldier, he fired out ten of the targets and all of a sudden he fired. The shock wave cut them all in two and they broke up and shattered as they hit against the hull of the battle transport, with that the general handed the weapon to Richard and said, "Enjoy. I have some business to attend to. I will see you all later," with that he stepped onto one of the lifts and vanished below probably to the command centre of the vehicle to relay or receive orders for the day. As they were in flight Michelle felt the craft lift into the sky with a magnificent power. They must have been ten thousand feet up as she looked out over the landscape she watched as the lush green fields slowly give way to the barren desert. One of the guards explained that it was the desert of Kala and was one of the biggest in the Kasorien Empire, "In a couple of hours we will reach the sea of Osiris then, onto the islands of Philios where the fortress city of the Asronas and the King Kasor holds his court for the summer months."

"What is he like?" asked Jack.

"Well I have only met him once and was lucky enough to survive the experience, thus the scar on my left shoulder," pulling aside his armour they saw the claw mark on his shoulder. Adjusting his armour again he asked Jack, "What is your land like? They say that one hundred is the longest that you can live there, that is very undesirable."

"Yes it is a draw back but you get used to it."

"I wouldn't! I am ninety-four," laughed the guard, "And I am regarded as a young man in this land."

Travelling along at great speed Michelle saw what seemed to be a base, there were millions of troops getting ready to embark onto larger ships than ours. The guard said, "That is one of our frontal assault bases, just in case the peace talks go the wrong way, it's never a mistake to be prepared for the future."

"Are there many bases like this one?"

"Yes, the desert is full of them. You see everyone has to do military service in this land, it entitles you to citizenship and other perks. You can't vote if you have not done military service of some sort or another. The ships they are getting into are called cruisers and are capable of carrying fifty thousand troops at one time. They're also fully armed." Then the desert faded away into sea. It was deep and very blue and the shore line had green lines of shallowness that shaded into the deep blue. The further into the sea we got, the choppier it became and the sky started to darken and the lightning started to become very violent. As we went on slowly we eventually came out of it. The guard explained, "That's because there is no atmosphere here, the lighting storms are more violent here and could happen anywhere."

As she looked down she saw something in the water that was very large, it was about one hundred feet long and had two long tusks and was bobbing in and out of the water. She asked the guard what it was and he replied, "In our language, it is called the bobbing tusk whale. It is a friendly creature and does not harm us so we leave it alone."

"Are there any sharks?"

"Yes there are a number of different species. There is only one dangerous one that we need to worry about. It is called the razor point shark and they are highly aggressive and attack with no mercy."

Looking down Heir Strauss said "This land must have evolved differently from ours. As a result there are different species to our own. The guard did mention that the sea was filled with fish and wild life." Jack looked at Heir Straus and said, "I need to go and have a conversation with the General," with that he took the lift and went down to the command level and walked into the nerve centre.

"This King Kasor, what are we in for General?" asked Jack.

The general walked over to a monitor and swiped it with his hand and then scrolled through images of King Kasor and his family.

"Here is Kasor himself."

As he looked at the monitor in disbelief, the General said, "He is more human than you think. It appears that they evolved from early humans and were accorded the correct physiology for there terrain." He had strong muscular feet with claws and hairy legs, his chest was hairy and his face was different from anything I had ever seen. It was human with a human expression; he was dressed in armour and surrounded by members of his family including his son who was rumoured to be his greatest treasure in his life. He loved his son dearly, just as any father loved his son. The women of their species were a lot more feminine. They were much like our own and only had the feet and claws of their race but had a womanly shape and were surprisingly attractive. The woman was in a chain that was leached around her neck, the general said, and "They are very protective of their women." Looking at him Jack said, "Well she isn't going anywhere that's for sure."

"Yes," said the general, "Their women do not by law have any rights although this does not deter them from being extremely loyal to their men. Slavery is a big factor in their everyday life and their whole civilisation, even domestic life, is based on slavery. Their mighty cities were built by slaves and they were waited on hand and foot by slaves and this through the years had turned to a type of accepted ownership and the slaves were treated by their masters as friends, even as family members. A lot of slaves had went into the army with the blessing of their masters to obtain their freedom and had won it back in the early days but now all it is, is a death sentence. Mostly they are not well enough armed or well enough trained and it often turns into a bloodbath. Jack, if we can't stop them they will be wiped out as a species and that, nobody wants on their conscience. Me most of all because if they don't accept the peace deal I will be ordered to defend the empire and in order to do that we will have to kill them all and I will be remembered as the person who wiped out an entire people and that I do not want. I have not been able to sleep as well as I used to, also, I worry about the Empress too much. Hopefully Exios will take over my job soon."

"As her advisor?" asked Jack.

Laughing he said, "No as her husband, it's obvious that she is in love with him. I suppose she always has been."

"I can tell you general that he's quite taken with her also. He's been quiet all morning and almost in a daydream, who could blame him she one of the most beautiful women I have ever seen in my life."

A soldier walked over to the general and said, "We will be there in five minutes sir," nodding his head with approval he looked at Jack and said, "Come friend and look at their fortress city," and they both headed up to the observation deck and walked over to the battlements. Before them lay the islands of Philios. On the first one there was a series of mountains and on top of the summit was the city of the Asronas it was like something out of a medieval storybook. It had walls thirty feet thick and there were battlements and towers all along it. The battlements were manned with soldiers in full armour, they carried spears and had other strange looking weapons that were much like ours but a little more advanced. Flags fluttered from every tower with the royal emblem, which was a couple of crossed spears with a sword in the middle of the spears and on the other end of the flag was what appeared to be the mountains they so loved. It was breath taking, the top of the mountains were caped in snow and had a strange glow, and the lower lands were lush farmland with all sorts of vegetable and fruits growing there. As we ascended the climb to the fortress city, at the very top was the palace of the King of Asronas, it was crude in shape with spires and balconies protruding from the spires. In front was a courtyard which Jack assumed they were going to land in. As they approached there was some kind of canon trained on them but it was disengaged with the growling order of one of the guards. They landed and saw they had an honour guard waiting for them.

"Oh no," said the general, "They're for our protection." Jack gave a large gulp and they made their way to the front of the ship for disembarkation. They were met by an old looking general who said, "General Lieysin, I trust your journey was a comfortable one?"

"Yes," replied the general, "I have brought guests to bring wisdom to the proceeding. They are from the outside world and have just arrived." "Excellent," said the Asronas general, "The King is expecting you. Please follow me."

They were led through a great gateway into a hall where the architecture was much different than the Kasorien style. It was almost gothic in origin, instead of a large space there was a big hall but the floor dropped about forty feet on all sides and in the middle of it was a table and at the head of the table was the King. In front of him on the table was a sword and on the other side was a pen. Around him was his council of elders and there were seats reserved for us. The King was strange looking, he was six foot tall and his whole body was covered in hair even his face. "Welcome to the fortress city General Lieysin. I believe we have met before."

"Yes, at the battle of Breakspear Mountain."

Sitting down the King said, "That was not yesterday general, I believe were getting old."

"As all people do your majesty," replied Lieysin.

"Who are your strangely dressed friends?" asked the King.

"They are strangers seeking adventure. They are from the world above."

The King laughed, "Then they shall get their fill of adventure here, make no mistake. What are their names?"

"Your majesty may I present Heir Strauss, this is Jack and Michelle and these two are Richard and Exios and the man over there is Professor Kevin o Dougherty."

"Exios, I have heard of you in myth. It's a pleasure to meet you."

"And you your majesty," replied Exios.

At that moment his wife, the Queen, walked out and sat beside him and he introduced her as "Shirm". She had the collar and chains befitting any Asronas wife except hers were made of gold and studded with jewels. She was very attractive; she looked curiously at Michelle and asked, "Is that what women wear in your country?"

Michelle nervously replied, "Not all of them. I am dressed for field work rather than a social event."

"Oh I see, the women in your world, they work?"

"Yes, women have careers in my land."

"My goodness we are not allowed to work. We are busy bringing up children and keeping our husbands happy," smiling and turning to her husband. The men in the group could not believe their ears; Richard leaned into Jack and said, "You have got to be kidding me. These women seem to have been brainwashed." Overhearing the conversation the Queen replied, "Young man you misinterpreted my comment. We enjoy being good to our men for they are good to us and our link is very strong." Richard then apologised and sat down.   The King then said, "We shall start our business tomorrow morning. Tonight we will feast and get to know each other and have a few drinks, as the custom dictates in our Kingdom. So men, to the dinning room," as the King stood up they all followed him out of the commerce hall and into the main dinning hall where they were seated and prepared for the up coming meal.

Suddenly the doors opposite them flung open and servants walked out with pigs that had been spit roasted, eight of them, they were laid on racks in front of them and more men came out and stood on either side of the roasted beasts with carving knives held aloft and the King stood up and gave thanks to their god Belock who was half human and half goat. There were statues of him everywhere; Richard was getting nervous looking at the men with the carving knives. Jack put his hand on his shoulder and said, "Don't worry, if they wanted us dead they could have hit us with that cannon outside."

"Yes I suppose so," replied Richard.

The men standing ready to carve were ordered by the King to begin, they walked around the beasts once and then began carving, as that happened music began and there were dancers. Richard looked over at General Lieysin and said, "I hate to say this but they know how to have a better time than the Empress," to which they both burst out laughing. Jack mentioned to Michelle that it looked like something out of King Arthur's court in medieval times, "Yes," she replied, "I wonder did she mean what she meant when she said the women were happy here with their men?" Overhearing their conversation the general replied, "More than likely Michelle, you see there's something on this side that makes the female more open to suggestion. Our scientists believe it's something to do with the snow that falls here in winter time and has the characteristics of a genetic hypnotic agent that only works on the female of the spices." Michelle looked at the general and said, "What you're trying to say is that these women are constantly at their masters beckon call for anything?"

"Yes they do anything that they are told and are fiercely loyal to their men yet they have no appearance of being hypnotised and some even go to fight alongside their men, rather touching, I always thought."

There was a candle lit chandelier and it swayed side to side in the energetic breeze that fluttered in through many of the open windows that flattered the side of this particular spire. Below were open doors leading onto one of the many balconies, but this one was different unlike the standard balcony, this one swung around the spire and connected with the next level that had identical doors. The windows almost ringed the hall that they were in and from them windows drop diagonally into the next level where the same process of wind and mountain air would start again. It had a beautiful symmetry about the place which forgave the instant thought that they had a Spartan style of architecture. On closer inspection it was a lot more complex than she originally thought before. On the same level that tethered off the rope that held the chandelier, there were two guard platforms which allowed two sets of guards to stand and watch over the King and his guests while staying out of sight. It was rather a clever idea that is what the climbing balcony was for, the quick access of the royal guard. The King was sitting on his throne it was made of timber and beautifully decorated and strangely, for its modesty, it was studded with emeralds and rubies. The King himself had bracelets that more resembled a soldier's wrist guard and the crest on his crown was shaped like a pyramid with the two bottom points turned inward and the top point turned outward. It would have almost reminded you of the crown of Egypt with the cobra faithfully watching over pharaoh. He had his armour on a stand behind him, his helmet was the first thing that caught her attention, it was larger than what she normally had seen, for all the extra hair and had five plums running of the crest his breast plate which was exactly the same as the guards were wearing. His greaves and foot armour were a little different but basically the only thing that separated him from his men was his helmet. As they continued with dinner they discovered the meat was very nice and was covered in some kind of pepper that gave it a bit of a kick. Bread was then set on the table and the King followed by dipping his bread in the peppered sauce that remained from the meal and he slurped it down. This was followed by an exotic wine that had a tinge of mint; surprisingly it was rather good also. King Riceos turned to his wife and said, "Are you not eating my dear?"

"No, my husband, I am keeping my figure in shape for your pleasure." The women looked at her as if she were mad, she than smiled lovingly at her husband and dismissed herself and left the chamber. The drinking continued into the night and the antics got very drunken and macho. Firstly with the General Lieysin making a toast to the Empress and the empire followed by Riceos long life to the people of Asronas which nearly degenerated into a fight where Riceos' brother Karos nearly had to separate them and keep them from fighting. With the old general being carried back to his seat the night had finally come to an end and they were all escorted to their rooms for the night. Before she went to bed Michelle took a look from the balcony and noticed the sun was coming up and again saw the Asronas home landscape from were she was. The mountain dropped sharply and into a beautiful valley, its lush green fields were just about visible and a vale of mist was lifting giving the illusion that this land was haunted and the souls of the dead were going back to the underworld. She saw the first signs of life shortly afterwards, a farmer out checking his livestock and taking a head count, his wife faithfully standing beside him. The landscape was covered in trees and they even went up the mountain until it was not possible for them to grow in that atmosphere as only certain kinds of moss and little grass were allowed to grow there. There were a lot of goats in this land and they were well suited to this kind of terrain they were all over and were even standing on what seemed to be cliff edges, they were walking around them as if they were on flat ground and appeared at home on the cliffs.

She returned into her room and closed the doors and got into bed which appeared to be sheeted in the goat hides that had obviously been treated with something to give them a feeling that was soft as fur.

Jack was thinking of Michelle that night before he fell asleep. She was in a different room to him. It seemed their protocol was a lot different than the palace at Castorian city. Suddenly he heard the door unbolt, he reached for his weapon but remembered it was onboard the ship. He turned the light on and to his surprise it was Michelle, she opened the door and walked in, not before giggling and thanking somebody behind the door. She then bolted the door and walked over to his bed but before getting into bed she dropped her dressing gown around her feet and jumped in. She then said, "That was the Kings wife; she thought it was a pity we were not in the same room."

"How did she know?"

"She said it was the way we were looking at each other and she thought it was a pity for us to spend the night in different rooms. She is a very nice woman, if not a bit dippy, one thing is for sure she's in tune with her surroundings and is very sexual you can almost feel it when you stand close to her. I don't know Jack what's going on here; these people don't appear aggressive whatsoever,"

"Michelle what you have to remember is that we have only known them for a day. Tomorrows peace talks should prove interesting, we should get an idea of what's going on in this place. I don't know why but I've a feeling both sides are being played against each other, but the question is by whom. That will have to wait till later because I have something else in mind at the moment."

Michelle replied, "Is that right is it Mr Toner?"

"Yes that's right Miss Fordix," with that he kissed her and turned of the light on the bedside.

CHAPTER 11.

They woke late that next morning to the sound of a palace in the thrusts of morning, the scurry of servants cleaning the room next to theirs. Jack woke up and said, "My god we're late for the talks," he jumped out of bed and started to dress until they got a knock on the door, it was Nicolas saying, "Don't worry, it's one hour to business time my friends." With that they relaxed and got dressed and then proceeded to get their breakfast in the same hall as they left the night before. They got their breakfast and then hurried into the next room where the King was waiting. The General appeared in his best armour and the talks began;

"Hail to you from Queen Olympia's the Empress of the kasorien empire King Riceos and to your royal wife also greetings. I hope you are in good health and are open to these peace negotiations for the good of both our races. I have entrusted the great General Lieysin to over see the talks in which their may be peace..." the message then cut off and the hologram disintegrated in to a mist that seemed to vaporise into the floor at that moment a visitor arrived, General Lieysin looked at the man with a familiar eye, it was one of the men at the banquet held by the Empress. The general announced him "Your majesty, I have the honour of introducing the council elect chairman, his Excellency Lord Vistock," Lord Vistock then bowed in front of King Riceos and said, "I am here to represent the people of the Kasorien Empire and to show our goodwill to the people of Asronas."

"That gesture is deeply appreciated Lord Vistock thank you for coming." The King rose out of his throne and put a more deadly tinged atmosphere to the assembled crowd of dignitaries, "Let me remind you, if we don't find a way out of this mess gentlemen, and it is a mess, we will end up slaughtering each other. At worst one of us will end up being wiped out as a species and this is what I seek to prevent." The

King looked at General Lieysin and said, "How in your mind did this conflict begin?" "One of our marine vessels was attacked and the crew wiped out. When we found their bodies and what was left of their ships we also found an Asronas weapon on board so we suspected there was a fire fight and one of your soldiers either got killed or injured in the crossfire and dropped his weapon or misplaced it."

The King replied, "I see general, what you are saying to the sober mind makes sense but there is a problem with your version of events."

"May I ask you what it is?"

"Certainly, it's called a weapon restraint bolt," he then motioned for somebody to be brought in. It was a soldier from one of his infantry regiments, "Gentlemen here you see the lowest rank in my army, a hesp, and he is armed with the standard field kit, one of these being a restraining bolt for his weapon. Each weapon he has is connected by a magnetic retrieval unit, please observe," he looked at the hesp and began, "Boy, unhook your side arm and hand it to the Kasorien General standing beside you," the young soldier did as he was ordered and handed the weapon to the general and stood back. "Now general, throw it as far as you can," the general turned and threw it to the other side of the hall, the general turned and nodded to the King that he had done so the King then said to the boy, "Activate retrieval unit!" which he did, he pushed a button on the side of his holster and the weapon flew back to him and stopped about a foot from him and dropped to the ground. He then bent over and picked it up and put it back into the holster and saluted the King and left the room. "So you see, it could not have been any of the Asronas soldiers because all that so called soldier had to do was push a button on his holster and it would have returned to his person right away and it works up to two hundred miles of range."

"I see," replied the general, "This is a matter I must put to the Queen right away, your majesty by your leave?" The King nodded in approval and he walked off towards the transport and disappeared into it. Jack asked the King, "Why did nobody talk after this happened?" The King looked at him and replied, "We are both proud people and in those days my father was King. He thought the Kasoriens were trying to insult us so after the treaty of Osiris we stopped talking and started fighting and my father could not face dialog with someone who was trying to insult us so he ordered the regiments into battle. Three hundred years my friend, that's how long ago this happened," looking outward towards his mountains he said "Finally a chance of peace."

"Yes your majesty, apparently their soldiers have been wearing these for four hundred years and are part of their standard field kit."

"I see, this new development must be followed up, I will send you the weapon in question and their craftsmen can look at it to see if it is one of theirs. You have done well general, keep it up."

"My instincts are telling me there's something much larger at work here." The general returned and told the King of his conversation and the weapon and he was delighted and said, "Good, we will put it to the test to see if it is Asronas technology. There are many ways to see if it's real or it's fake. The first is to stand on it; if it breaks it is fake and if it doesn't it is real. Each of our weapons is marked with a microscopic number that can only be identified by our scientists. General Lieysin, how long will it take for the weapon to be shipped here?"

"About nine hours your majesty."

"Ok then, that means we have some time to burn off. I suggest a hunt on our islands. There are beasts called Rinedo, it is a large animal that has tusks and eats roots and grass higher up in the mountains and can only by law be hunted in this season."

The general said that he had heard of these creatures, "They are very similar to your boar pig that is hunted in your lands but these are larger, about the size of a horse and are very dangerous."

"Your majesty, I believe many people have been killed in these hunts."
"Yes general, but as you well know, that is part of the attraction connected with the hunt. To us it is simply a risk you have to take in order to kill the beast, to our young men it becomes a right of passage, afterwards they are allowed to marry and become the head of the house-hold."

Jack stood forward and asked, "With what will we hunt them with?" The King fixed Jack with a smile and replied, "On horseback with spears." Jack felt the chill run down his back to his soaking shirt at the bottom of his back, it was not fear but sweat, sweat at the anticipation of the up and coming hunt. As a child in Ireland his father had taken him on hunts up into the mountains not far from his home, in the Sperrin Mountains in Northern Ireland. They would have started out at dawn and walked up the mountain until they saw their prey, if lucky a pheasant or a rabbit, they would sit out on the mountain for most of the day and return before the light would disappear. Standing in the royal hallway he thought to himself that gone are those days that seemed so long away and if they were lucky they got a lift down again on a neighbours fordson standard tractor who had been up the mountain cutting turf that same day. One thing for sure he never hunted on horseback before and the challenge ate into his cool professional exterior and he finally relented. He turned to King Riceos and said, "Count me in."

"Very well Jack, you are on."

Exios also joined the hunt as did the general while Michelle worried about Jack. She relayed her fears to Jack about him taking unnecessary risks, he pulled her to one side and said, "Don't worry darling, I was born for this kind of thing, besides, where else do I get to do this?"

The King said in a daring voice, "Come men, if you dare, follow me, the hunt will take place in an hour and you must be kitted up in armour. I kid you not; the rinedo has the capability of taking your arm off with a tusk that is razor sharp. It then by habit drives both tusks into you and the shaking and friction is enough to tear any man apart. Thus gentlemen the armour is required."

They were taken down towards a pair of lifts that were powered from the same power source that powered the Kasorien transport that took them there. There were no sides just a glass floor that was a little bit uneasy to ride on. They got a good look at the fortress palace as the lift dropped below the spires and headed for what looked like the stables and hunt Tec room. The roof opened up with a kaleidoscope motion and as they passed it on the lift, it closed again; they finally descended and were met by the Kings Hunt team. They were all taken to the prep room were they were suited up in armour and suitably armed. The spear was about fourteen feet long and had a bar protruding out of the shaft of the spear. They asked the King what it was for and his reply made their blood run cold. Apparently it prevented the beast from running up the spear shaft when you had speared him and taking a chunk out of you it was the most common way that most young Asronas were killed and did not see it coming as the bottom of the spear was counter weighted with a piece of bone polished and ringed with gold to assure the spear was not too heavy and could be handled easily. It was a piece of art on its own apparently from the spear point to the bar was the correct length to pierce the large rinedos heart. The King was called away on a matter of state for twenty minutes, he returned and apologised for being late. They were then shown the stables, Jack was expecting the horses they have on earth but their horses were different. They seemed to be wider and more muscle, their coats were more like a zebras and their ears sloped down towards the earth. General Lieysin said, "These are not anything like the horses we have, they are supposed to be a lot more aggressive and more powerful. To be honest with you I've been waiting for this for a long time. So remember, hold on tight because they are as fast as hell and respond to the slightest tug of the reigns."

The King turned around and said, "In case any of you get into trouble I am having you issued with side arms." They then started to ride out into the Asronas landscape, the King took point and as he was late coming back he strapped his breastplate on whilst on horseback. When he had finished he shouted at full gallop towards the mountain, "FORWARD!" The horses responded to his command like a machine, they were very well trained and like General Lieysin said, powerful. They galloped through the beautiful countryside, the smell of spring sticking to their nostrils. Green everywhere and the smell of pine rose as they rode through meadows that beckoned you for a sleep. As they rode through, the most beautiful smell was there in this magical place. As they continued they at last saw the side of the mountain that was ready for our ascent. Even here there were trees and remote patches of snow until the trees faded away into the landscape and the terrain started to take on a different personality. It was mountainous and barren and had very little vegetation on it, suddenly the scouts ahead of the King gave the sign to halt and the column came to a gradual stop. The King announced, "They have found the track of the rinedo and are preparing to track it. We may have to do this on foot for a while until the beast has been sighted." From then on they dismounted and made their way on foot and to their surprise it was not as cold as they had imagined. "That will change soon enough," shouted the King, "Another hundred foot and we will reach the first Plateau and the home ground of the rinedo so we have to be quiet from here on up." They walked with their horses for fifteen minutes up and up the mountain they went, in some ways it was like the steps of a small stair case and in some cases these could be ten miles across each Plateau. Just as they were at the half way point they got their first view of the rinedo. The beast was about the size of a large horse and looked very agitated, it knew it was being tracked and had a habit of turning as to make aware anything behind him that he had picked up his sent and was warning them accordingly. It was a strange looking animal; it seemed to be the larger version of the boar that was hunted all over the world but, most of all in the Americas. Its front and hind legs were powerful and lean. It was gnawing at the ground and was excited looking as it had found something. The King told us that he believed that what the beast had found was a very large root and was about to feed on it and now was the time to attack while the creature was distracted. The King jumped onto horseback and set off at a gallop. Across the Plateau they rode, the thunder of the horses and claps of the hoofs serenading the back drop to the mountain, it was nearly too much to believe, Jacks heart was thumping in his chest and he felt old all of a sudden. It was a good mixture of emotions, being with his father, the journey up the mountains of his childhood and the days hunting. He lost his father to an accident and had missed him being there the rest of his childhood but as his father promised he would always be with him. Late at night he would feel his presence or feel his breath on the back of his neck or if he was alone in his car or at the office. He would smell him, he always smelled of oil and hay from the summer harvest and clove rock, that's how you would know he was in the room looking down on you trying most likely to give advice. Pulling himself out of his daydream he lifted his head to see they were closer to the rinedo. It was acting more aggressively and scraping the ground with his hoofs almost like a bull. Its head was swaying from side to side and its eyes were glowing red with anger and its mouth was foaming with rage. Never in all his experience that had taken him all over the world had Jack seen a more aggressive animal. The King looked at him, momentarily and shouted with a happy glee, "What did I tell you Jack, isn't this good sport?" Jack laughed nervously and held his spear aloft and shouted with approval. They then moved in for the kill, the King had his spear drawn to attack, they heard a low sounding thud the Kings spear shattered with the impact the beast took the most of the damage that had obviously been meant for the King. General Lieysin pulled him of his horse and shouted, "Somebody is trying to kill you!" They all ran behind the downed beast for cover, the assassin opened fire again and began to target the beast, the carcass was being blown to bits and they were running out of cover fast. Lieysin turned to the King and said, "If that had been a kasorien sniper we would have been all dead." He then pulled out his side arm and started to return fire, Jack and Exios did the same. One of the Kings royal body guards was killed in the exchange and the other badly inured, the general was hit in the shoulder and collapsed behind the disintegrating corpse of the rinedo, Exios started to get angry and shouted, "Time to end this madness before we all get killed, cover me!" He then jumped on his horse and took off, spear in hand. As required we gave covering fire as he outflanked the assassin, he came even closer as the seconds rushed by, every time the sniper tried to get a shot off he would come under fire from our position just enough to keep Exios safe. He got in close enough and fired the spear straight into the assassins chest, the weight of the spear meant that it went right through the man, the beautiful white snow was sprayed with blood and the man chocked on his own blood and eventually died. We got the all clear from Exios and we made our way over and looked at the lone assassin. He was one of the

Kings royal guards and this is what shocked the King the most. The King had received a wound to his shoulder and was in pain but was shrugging it off; he was more worried about the general. "How are you General Lieysin?"

"I will do for now, but will need treatment shortly," he looked over at Exios and said, "Good job! If it wasn't for your quick thinking we would have all ended up dead. By the way, good piece of riding."

"All it was was a standard flanking drill practiced until it became a reality," King Riceos laughed and said, "Without even blinking, it seems we owe you our lives, now who is our mysterious assassin?" They gathered around the body and looked as his face mask was removed, "Yes," said the King, "I believe his name was Lica, he has been a member of my bodyguards for a hundred years." Something strange was happening to Lica's eyes; the King was the first to see this, he said, "His eyes are changing colour!" At closer inspection they discovered that his eyes were implants, the King got up and looked into the landscape and said, "This can only mean one thing. He's not Asronian, we don't have green eyes, and none of our people have. It's something to do with a genetic defect in our genes; there are even some of our women folk that have purple eyes but no green eyes. The Kitni however have green eyes and are a bit too cold for my liking," the rest of the Kings body guard gathered around and he then ordered them to take the dead man away for tests and to double the guard on his guests. "I insist, it is for your safety and I won't have anybody else being killed on the same day, it's unlucky." Looking over the body of his assassin the King said, "It's especially unlucky for him," with a comic grin. One of the Kings guards shouted, "It's on its way."

Jack turned to the King and said, "May I ask, what is on its way?"

"My royal cruiser is on its way, no need to be nervous the danger is gone and we missed the opportunity to kill the rinedo but we managed to survive this cowardly attack on our persons."

The ship landed on the Plateau and out came the rest of the King's guard; they took the general on board to receive medical treatment and escorted the rest of them onboard. A skeleton team rode the powerful horses down off the Plateau and on towards the meadows and pastures of the lower landscape. They then took off with a frightful speed and headed to the fortress landing pad and they were there in record time, about thirty seconds, giving them a clue of how fast these machines were. They hit the ground hard and the first thing to happen was that the general was escorted into the Kasorien transport where he received emergency treatment by the doctor on board the vessel.

Marching through the wind swept halls of the fortress city the King shouted angrily at his ministers, "What good are you if you don't have any intelligence on this matter? Not only did this assailant try to kill me, but he also had a negligent regard for my guests!"

"Your majesty we have nothing and the tests seem to relay the fears of the court."

"What fears may I ask?" replied the King.

"There were rumours in your royal bodyguard that this man was acting out of character and did not have a lot in common with the rest of the guard. As you know most of your guard is related by blood so this kind of thing does not happen, they drink together and socialise and for the last year there was a constant stream of complaining about him to his superiors, about his personality, that it did not match what the rest of the men remembered. Most of them put it down to stress or problems at home."

"This man was in fact a Kitni!" the hall went eerily cold as the information settled into the consciences, "This is not going to bode well for any of the civilisations in this land."

"A Kitni conspiracy, but they are a peace loving race and hate violence?"

"It appears that they have been trying to engineer a war that would have seen one of us wiped out for sure. After that the winner would have been too weak to stand up to the Kitni and would have been an easy target for them."

Shaking his head the King said, "It cannot be them, it had better not be them! They are the most technologically advanced and the thought of going to war with them is not a nice one. We have to relay the news onto General Lieysin, how is he by the way?"

"Recovering well your majesty," bowed the counsellor Vasta of the Asronas and then he gracefully retreated from the room, according the King the correct royal protocol. The King walked back from his hall into the great courtyard, he then walked over towards the Kasorien ship and stopped at the front opening where he was met by the Generals aide, "Your majesty!"

"How is the general doing?"

"He's awake now and talking."

"Can I see him?"

"Of course your majesty, follow me," so he followed the aide to the generals bedside. Whenever the general saw the King he straightened up and said, "Your majesty, I am improperly dressed and am in no fit shape to receive a King. Please, give me five minutes to dress accordingly." "Very well general, you have it."

General Lieysin appeared from behind a curtain and walked towards the King, "How may I be of service King Riceos?"

The King started to relay his concerns to the old general and advised him to go secretly to the Empress to voice his concerns because the Kitni have the technology to pick up their communication devices and unravel their codes, "It is better that it comes from you back in the imperial palace in Castorian." The general agreed and shook the Kings hand and said, "We will have that little runt that runs the Kitni!" The man to whom he was referring was a man named Risard, the leader of the Kitni and by reputation a very slippery customer and highly intelligent leader who supposedly sat on the bench as the giants slugged it out then when one was defeated and the other weak from battle they would strike. The general greeted the assembled people and said to Jack, "My boy, I will not be back for at least a few days; my senses tell me that you can trust the King. He may be ruthless in battle but he is by reputation an honourable man and every inch a King. So if he moves then so do you and beware for more Kitni assassins. Because of their man being killed they will either think that the masquerade is now at an end or that he was killed before we could discover his identity." At that minute the King walked over towards the group, stood in the corner and said, "I have started a rumour that he was killed by a freak accident on the Plateau, hopefully this will fool their intelligence officers into believing that he was killed by the rinedo before he could strike, thus giving the illusion that the incident did not happen, therefore it is most likely that they will sent a replacement, what they don't know is that I have had all of my royal guards screened for DNA and the first traces of oddness will be treated with suspicion. Anything out of character or perhaps a slip up in memories might give him away; we are wrestling with the idea that there might be a second spy master that accompanied this man. Never the less he was still a brave man and I ordered that he is to be buried with full honours and will receive a decoration from the war commission for his selfless act of fighting to the end. In our culture there is no bigger act of courage than to lay down your life in pursuit of your victory even to an enemy this honour is given." Moving away from the crowd the King walked over towards the general and said, "I will see you soon, I believe that I have made a friend out of you, have I not?"

"Everything is possible," replied the old general as he shook the Kings hand and said, "In two days I will return with the Empresses answer and I am sure it will be a positive response. Until then King Riceos," he bowed and headed for his transport and boarded it which quickly took off and started on its long trip back to Castorian. Michelle looked at Jack and said, "I am sure it will be all right won't it?"

"Yes, everything will be all right," this time Jack had sincerity in his eyes, not the usual cold stone professionalism that normally accompanied the soldier. He was thinking that if things went south what he would do, his intelligence told him that the three great cultures were on a collision course and nothing would stop them from colliding. As it appeared, the cast was set on this story and if anything, it would be a dangerous adventure and if any of them saw the upper world as the Castorian Empress called it, more than luck would be required to save their hides, then again, they were in great company and the King was a great soldier and with the alliance between the Castorian empire and the Kingdom of Asronas they would surely be a good enough match for the forces of the Kitni. He turned to the King and asked him, "What are the Kitni like?"

The King nodded and turned to him and said, "Young man, the Kitni are the oldest of all of us, they are more technologically advanced and are a strange race of individuals. To sum them up, they don't like to tell anybody what they are thinking or what they are doing and they are also infatuated with the idea of a silenced culture, what are the correct words in your language... yes... they are capable of telepathy."

"Telepathy?" said the Professor.

"Yes, as far as I know, but only at short ranges, still, a very good advantage in any situation."

"How many are there?"

"Nobody knows for sure, they say their leader has been in power since the first Macedonians arrived from the upper lands that you yourself come from."

"But that was over two thousand years ago," said the Professor.

"I know," replied the King, "Somehow their long life is extended further than ours. His name is Risard and what I have told you is top secret, so if anyone asks you about anything, you don't know anything. Our intelligence officers are at this moment trying to gain access to the Kitni stronghold of Glazeer in the Kitni foothills near their capital, a magnificent city that was cut out of translucent crystal thousands of years ago and is equipped with the latest Kitni defence technology, it is said to be impenetrable."

"Nothing is impenetrable," said Exios, "With Alexander, we were able to get into any besieged city that defied him."

"Yes," replied the King, "Exios you are also forgetting that Alexander is dead my friend and it would be a different matter. You forget that since your slumber the world has developed more effective weapons for the defence of cities."

Exios nodded in agreement and said, "Yes, I understand that King Riceos, but what I am saying is any fortress is able to be breached regardless of how impressive its defensives are. That is the one thing Alexander did teach us and he was a very good teacher."

As the military transport flew over the great sea of Osiris, the general was tinkering on the edge of mild euphoria thinking to himself, the chance of peace and all it would bring, but first he had to tell the Empress of what he knew and of what the Kitni were capable of. At the end of the first night the lights of the Castorian city were in sight and the landing light on the palace was visible. The craft sent the correct code to the imperial palace and they quickly dropped their defences and the transport came into land. As it touched down the general stepped onto the landing pad and headed towards the apartments of the Empress, he stopped off at his own private rooms to clean up and get into the correct toga of the inner counsel and to imply the correct dress code that applied to royal protocol. After he had bathed and prepared himself he made his way to the Queen's private apartments and there he waited until he smelled the usual rose tinged perfume that accompanied her royal person, she appeared from behind the door of the state rooms, and said "It's Exios, isn't it? Is he all right?"

"He's fine your majesty, believe it or not he actually saved us from impending doom. Your majesty, I believe that the war between us was masterminded by the Kitni."

"How so?" replied the Queen. General Lieysin then started to impart what he knew to the Queen and what fools they had been made to look, the Queen responded by directly ordering the imperil forces to cease their attack on their Asronas objectives. The King responded accordingly and pulled his armies back, he was then formally invited to the imperial palace for talks on how to deal with the Kitni threat.

At the fortress city the group was making sense of what they could, the Kings top advisor kept them informed and imparted the information that they were all going back to Castorian city. Jack took a walk with Richard and asked him what he thought, "Well my old friend, it can go either way. All we can do is ride it out and hope we've backed the right horse."

"Don't say that."

"Why not?" asked Richard

Jack replied, "The last time I backed a grand national horse it fell at the first hurdle. Trust me to back a nag."

Smiling at Jack, Richard said, "I think you got more out of this than you thought. Perhaps a partner for life?"

"Yes, it is going well," said Jack

"Has she asked you why you joined the legion?"

"No not yet but I am preparing myself for it."

As they were talking, a guard came out of the adjoining corridor and said, "We are going to Castorian city to meet the Empress and we leave in the hour. An Asronas battle cruiser will be waiting for you where you landed in the transport that you came in. See you there!" With that he whistled down the hall and into a room that was full of the royal guards.

They collected their belongings and headed towards the landing pad which was inside this rustic but beautiful courtyard. Before Michelle left the rooms she was once again visited by Queen Shirm and she smiled and said, "Be careful and look after Jack, are we not the ones who save our husbands from jeopardy most of the time?"

Michelle replied laughing, "Jack is not my husband."

"No, not yet..." replied the Queen, "But he will," and she kissed Michelle on the forehead and said, "Take care my dear and goodbye."

Never a stranger woman you could have met or a kinder one thought Michelle. She looked on as Shirm disappeared around a corner and deeper into the fortress with only her flowing dress fluttering behind her and leaving the fragrance of a woman who was once there. She tenderly put her arm around Jacks waist and said, "Come on, let's go." As they were heading out of the fortress they overheard the King addressing one of his many commanders, catching our eye he turned and shouted, "Jack, come here I have somebody to introduce to you. This is captain Thrush, he is in charge of my eagle regiments," looking at Jack he tried in vain to get the correct English terminology when the captain intervened, "I believe his majesty is looking for the word airborne infantry, we fly low level craft called darts that fold into our back packs and allow us to engage the enemy on the ground of our choosing or out flank an enemy and cut off his rear. We will have the honour of escorting you back to the capital of the Castorian Empire. If you excuse me I have to go and prepare for the final checks," and with that he disappeared behind one of the many doors that led off the hallway. The King said, "Follow me on to our battle cruiser and we will set for Castorian and the imperial palace. I have never seen it but what I have heard from my father it is supposed to be beautiful."

"It is," replied Jack nodding.

CHAPTER 12.

The King looked at his commander and roared an order at him, the captain bowed with the respect any committed subject shows his monarch and with that the craft lifted of and proceeded along a different route to the one that had landed them there. They flew over the islands of Philios and towards the sea and doing so they picked up speed. They suddenly heard the sound of a beating drum, the King said, "It is a tradition that was kept from the old days when they sailed the seas in large boats not that uncommon to your Greeks." As they flew over the great sea of Osiris, the light reflected off the water, this habitat had no sun, just a shining haze that was created hundreds of thousands of years ago by a natural event that was both strange and alien to them. The Asronian battle craft was a menacing and austere looking vessel, at each corner, it had a gun platform and a golden horn mounted in silver, the state symbol that meant King Riceos was on board and effectively meant that he was in charge of all forces under his command or whatever battle zone he entered, from whatever commander he took command of giving Jack the impression that this man really new what he was doing. All his commanders had given Jack the conclusion that he was respected and revered and had a lot of experience, just like General Lieysin. It struck him that they were both of the same calibre. Suddenly the journey took on a different feeling, an alarm sounded on board and the King shouted at them to get down below. They ran onto one of the many lifts that took them to relative safety for the moment, the deck they were on had a viewing deck and from what they could see there was a strange looking vessel which was black in appearance, it had an almost evil persona. It was much smaller than their craft and they suddenly heard a voice that sounded aggressive, it was in a language none of them recognised. One of the soldiers on board with us translated the mysterious sound and said it was from the Kitni and they were demanding that they hand us over for the pleasure of the Kitni government. The King replied, "I will think it over for a moment." Thirty seconds later the Asronas battle cruiser opened up on the Kitni vessel, the fire coming from the King's ship was devastating. The Kitni ship was peppered in holes and was limping badly, it was swaying from side to side and the King then replied, "I have thought it over and decided that you lot can go to hell. Oh yes and speaking of such..." he looked at his main gunner, who was patiently waiting for the order, then the King lifted his hand up to his chest and then he suddenly dropped it to his side. This was the signal the gunner was waiting for, he then opened fire with the ships main complement of heavy guns. The Kitni ship exploded and debris from the once proud ship fell towards the sea and crashed into it. The King came into us and said, "Nobody, and I mean nobody demands anything from me. Such bad manners, I can not tolerate. This means that they now know what is afoot and are aware that we are on to them. From here on in it will be a dangerous voyage."

Just then Exios stepped forward and said, "There are many soldiers standing beside me and they would be of more use if they helped fight off this threat, it is a possibility that there will be more of them."

The King replied, "If you wish, there are weapons in that locker over there." They all looked over and the locker opened automatically and the complement of Asronas weapons was visible. Jack said, "We will use our own as well."

"Very well," replied the King, "Gentlemen take your positions.

Jack and Richard headed up onto the upper deck and waited for the inevitable. Jack took one of the Asronas rifles and placed it beside him; he then pulled out a sniper rifle and mounted it on the railing that ran around the top deck of the ship. Richard pulled out a heavy calibre machine gun and then he clamped it to the railing and squeezed off a few practice shots. The Asronas soldiers looked at the odd weapon for a while and nodded their approval. The only weapon Exios chose was a small fire arm, he still trusted his sword and shield for close combat and of course repelling boarders which he felt was coming next.

Suddenly they heard the attack alarm once again, the King was looking puzzled and said, "Nobody has ever fought a pitch battle with the Kitni, this of course means that we don't know what they're next move will be, but that wont mean that we will not be ready for them," he then roared another order to the commander of the vessel to contact the eagle regiments which he did quickly. From now on they will be in sight of the ship at all times. Suddenly out of nowhere came their first attack, they were in smaller ships and they were easily landed onto the deck where a battle ensued. They jumped from their transports and onto the battleship; they spread out as if they knew where they were going. Exios was the first to engage the boarders with sword and shield, driving his sword deep into the chest of one of the attacker's, he gave a defiant scream as Exios closed him down with a deeper thrust. Pulling out his sword, he fell to the ground, he was dressed in black from head to bottom and was armed with a sword and side arm of some description which Exios pulled out of the dead Kitni soldiers holster and then started to use on the rest of the boarders. Jack was carefully picking out who was in charge of the commando raiding party but discovered they were communicating telepathy so he started to pick of the lead complement. Richard was concentrating on the landing craft and was knocking off the inhabitants who were getting off the boarding craft; more and more of the small crafts landed on the deck and deposited more men who all had white hair. Their sheer weight of numbers were now taking affect, one of Jacks men was killed out right, taking a direct hit by one of the Kitni weapons. They were all low on ammunition and were about to be over whelmed when out of the sky came captain Thrush. They looked magnificent, their back pack gliders had under wing machine guns which were mounted at the tip of each wing. The main assault of the eagle regiment wiped out half of the Kitni raiding party. When they landed, their wings folded into their back packs, their arms were armoured and an object slid down the eagle soldier's shoulder to his wrists where it opened out into a shield and he pulled out his side arm and began to fight. At this moment the Kitni ship that had sent the boarding parties prepared to open fire on the Kings ship, you could see Kitni personnel running on her deck going about their duties. The ship fired on us doing large damage to the ships engineering department which slowed us down. The King shouted at his commander to finish the Kitni ship off and that he was of to repel boarders on the top deck. On his way up on the lift towards the top deck he heard the sweet sound of his own complement opening fire and as he reached the top he saw the Kitni ship being blown to pieces by his cannons. He then joined in the fight when the raiding party saw what had happened they hesitated and began to fall back into their boarding crafts. The King joined battle and the first one he came across he beheaded with his sword, the second he gutted and then beheaded, one thing is for sure this man loved his carnage, his muscle bound physique impressed on everybody and the skill he showed, fighting to this man came as easy as looking at something and the next thing it would be gone. As they were clearing the deck of enemy dead and their own, they saw the last few Kitni attackers being killed and their boarding crafts were thrown over the side. They were about to continue on their way when a larger and more dangerous ship approached, they made the same terms when all of a sudden the ship exploded in to a thousand bits and behind it there in the flying debris and mist was General Lieysin and the imperial battle cruiser which brought them to the fortress city. It pulled along side and the general stepped on board with the Kings permission, "We were sent just in case this was attempted. Is everyone ok?"

"Yes," replied the King, "Except for a few of my men and Jacks. Your majesty we will escort you into the hill borderlands and then into the capital itself. I believe it's safer that way and they will not attempt that again with the both of us in close proximity."

"Agreed," said King Riceos, "How long to Castorian?"

"Three hours your majesty."

"Three hours," repeated the King, "Well I don't know about the rest of you but that gave me an appetite. I am starving," with that he headed off to the kitchen for a feed.

Richard laughed and said, "Remarkable man isn't he?"

"Yes," said Jack.

"Who did we lose?" asked Richard.

Jack replied, "I am afraid we lost Ned and Darren."

"Ah," replied Richard, "I quite liked them but looking at the peaceful expressions on their faces, they were ready for this and willing to go this far and at that they died protecting the group."

Their bodies were prepared for the after life by the priests of Ammon. When they landed at the palace the Empress was standing out in front of the landing pad and greeted King Riceos herself.

"King Riceos, I pray you peace and understanding in this time of great betrayal and misunderstanding between our great nations. I also heard of the unprovoked attack on your ship by the forces of the Kitni and I am pleased to see you well and unharmed. I see your ship did not escape the assault, it is damaged."

"Not to worry Queen Olympus, I have already sent for a bigger one to collect me afterwards."

"I see," replied the Empress, "Please accept the generosity of my palace."

"Thank you your majesty," with that they walked side by side into the great commerce hall the Queen used for public events. It was packed with the entire inner counsel and leading generals who King Riceos remembered from previous battles. He sat on a throne beside the Empress and she started to address the assembled crowd.

"Here we are gathered to access the legality of the war that both sides have been fighting. Firstly it being instigated and designed by the Kitni so I have sent their leader a summons to attend this meeting for this situation to be amended and positions to be made clear because they stand accused of a crime most heinous for the continued survival of the three great races." As she spoke, the Kitni leader walked into the hall and began to speak, "My name is Risard, the commissioned leader and I am here to give you an ultimatum... either leave with the strangers or face our wrath."

"How dare you!" said King Riceos, "You know we will never accept your demands so what are you waiting for you thug."

"I would be careful with your words," replied the Kitni leader, "As you know we nearly disabled your ship."

"Now let me see," replied King Riceos, "Three against one and we still came out on top..." intervening, the Queen with her common touch and honey like voice, "Why do you want us to leave Risard?"

"Empress, as you know I was here when your ancestor took the throne. Since you have come there has been nothing but fighting and strife and we are sick of it."

The Queen looked frustrated at him and said "I don't know why, you started it"

"Yes," replied the Kitni leader, "We started it to see if you could patch things up and become civilised. We the government of the Kitni declare war on you and will crush your puny armies," after he had said that he turned to walk out throwing the shoal over his shoulder arrogantly. He then attempted to walk out but was stopped by Riceos, "I make you this promise you slimy little bastard, before this is over I will watch your body fall lifeless down the steps of your great capital Glazeer, of course, minus a head." Gripping his sword as he eyed the Kitni leader up, Risard simply laughed at him and replied, "I will believe it when I see it Riceos," with that he walked out of the palace to the awaiting vessel and took off out of sight.

"King Riceos I believe we need to prepare our armies for an impending invasion."

King Riceos thought for a while and said, "The Kitni heart land lays east of your position so my Kingdom is under no immediate threat. With your permission I would like to move the bulk of my infantry regiments into your eastern woods of Pramidia. General Lieysin, how did you like my new eagle regiment?"

"From what I saw, very effective."

"Good because I am giving you one."

"What?" replied the general?

"General Lieysin, now that we are allies and have an understanding of each other our main objective is the defeat of the Kitni military and their government structures. This will take our forces combined."

"Agreed," replied general Lieysin, "and it will also take a miracle to beat them but we will overcome their onslaught."

The general looked at the King and said, "Gentlemen, we will have victory!" Roars went up amongst his generals and the air was deep with the thoughts of up and coming battles and victories. Even there the confidence of steel ruled the day, one sentry broke ranks and began to pull the sword out of his scabbard and drop it down on the hilt as to cerate a metallic clash, the young man saw the glare of general Lieysin burn into him, fearing the discipline that usually accompanied the general the generals glare turned to a softer one and he in turn started to do the same with his sword. Clash went the swords and by this stage even the King was playing to this orchestra of testosterone driven euphoria.

After the meeting most of the soldiers returned to their rooms, as did Exios, he was getting his wound dressed. During the battle he had received a small wound from small arms fire and had taken a graze for his efforts. The doctor said, "Now Exios, hold still, this wont take long," as the doctor was cleaning his cut, he felt a warm but slender hand on his shoulder, he turned around to find that it was the Empress. Before he could automatically revert to the protocol he was used to, she put her finger over his lips so he couldn't talk and nodded for him to leave silently the doctor quickly left by the side entrance that the Queen had just entered. As she tended to Exios' wound he said, "Is there much damage physician?" The Queen replied, "Not much. You will live." He jumped up and sat down on the table the doctor had examined him on, "How long have you been there your majesty?"

"Long enough Exios," and then she kissed him, it was long and lingering and sweet as a fresh rose. Pulling away from each other the Queen confessed to him that she had been in love with him since she heard the legend as a little girl of the Greek warrior who sacrificed himself to save his fathers life. Exios gently lifted her hand and kissed it he said, "You are the most beautiful woman I have ever looked upon and ever will and this promise I make to you now. As long as I live I will love no other. But will you promise me something..."

"Yes darling anything."

"After this war is over, we will marry," looking at him with a smile the Empress replied, "Yes," kissing him on the forehead. She laughed as she said, "Of course it does not mean that you can't have your wedding rights before hand."

He jumped off the table and lifted the Queen onto his bed, the room was magnificent, marble polished floors and a marble four poster bed, he looked deep into her eyes and pulled her hair pin out to reveal long blond hair, just like Alexander's, she herself was as beautiful. As he unclipped her dress, it fell to the ground, she had tanned features and full breasts, not an ounce of fat anywhere, and her arms were marked with a strange kind of tattoo from the temple of Ammon when she was young. All she remembered was it being very sore and unpleasant, she brought his head to her neck and there he started to tenderly kiss her it was like a religious experience, she was wearing her most expensive perfume for him, it was intoxicating and almost rendered Exios unconscious he then unclipped her necklace which was a present from Alexander to the dying King all those years ago and had naturally came to her through the crown. She loved wearing it but this time she threw it on the bed and there she allowed Exios to take her. As the hours rolled by the couple enjoyed each others company, as she listened to Exios' childhood stories she laughed and giggled with excitement.

King Asronas and general Lieysin were discussing the battle tactics after the Empress had given her explicit permission to allow King Asronas' infantry regiments into the Pramidian forests. These were great forests, mostly uncharted and alien to human eyes. The only people who had a good understanding of its outlay were the woodsmen who inhabited the woods and forests of Pramidia. They were subjects of the Empress and always kept a respectable distance between the imperial court and themselves. General Lieysin said, "I have sent for a representative of the woodsmen of Pramidia. He will be a few days getting here. Your majesty may I suggest that you move the infantry forces into our forward control barracks so they are not open for attack."

"Yes general, that is a good piece of advice. What do you call this woodsman?"

"His name is Eileion, the leader of the woodsman conglomerate and an old war companion. He retired last year and did so gracefully with the intention of tending his garden and his woods and also his family who are still of a young age. He was also one of my top commanders so his tactical skills will come in handy for all of us."

"Yes," replied the King, "He will know exactly where the regiments can be placed and how much cover there is going to be and how far the Kitni border is from our position."

The light was falling in the sky and the city took on a different personality, it had almost an orange glow that was lit by the street lamps. The magnificence of the imperial city was breath taking; the citizens went about their lives oblivious to the danger that was represented by the Kitni threat. The Professor went with Richard and Jack to view some of its wonders. Out before the palace was a huge statue of the Kasorien King Kasor in an Egyptian style garb. He was dressed as a pharaoh sitting on his throne and directly behind him was a obelisk bedecked in strange hieroglyphs that Bob was able to translate: "you who gaze upon this statue know that it is King Kasor you serve and if my time is at an end and I am in the underworld, stay true to your Kasorien blood and give thanks to the great lord Ammon and also my mortuary temple in the mountains beyond this great city and to the people of the light who gave to us this sanctuary of peace and tranquillity."

Looking at it in a more concentrate mode Bob said, "It says here that it was erected in the first year of his reign. It also says..." looking in disbelief, "no it can't be..." The Professor said, "What is it bob?" Standing with both hands on his head, "My god," replied Bob, "It says that King Kasor is the son of the pharaoh Akhenaten. This gentlemen, also means that there is a possibility he was a half brother or full brother of Tutankhamen, the boy pharaoh buried in the valley of the Kings in Egypt as we know but the thing I would like to know is, is it possible to live that long? Over one thousand years he lived, over one thousand years."

Walking away in disbelief the Professor turned to Bob and said, "How is all this possible?"

"It's their technology," replied Bob, "Remember when the Empress said they normally lived to the ripe old age of five hundred?"

"Yes."

"Well what she did not tell us is that is those before her lived a lot longer."

Richard said, "Perhaps the physiology of the Castorian's is starting to reject their technology and resort back to their human boundaries. What ever is happening, they are holding their cards tight to their chests. If I was in their position I would do the same."

They the continued their walk around the city, they were given a body guard who also acted as guide. It was Ottilin, the border guard we met at the start of our encounter, now he was Infantry Master Ottilin, he had been promoted to the third highest rank and been given land and riches by the Empress. They asked where the mortuary temple of King Kasor was and he replied, "It is known only to the Empress and her close counsel and was considered a state secret."

"I see replied," the young Egyptologist, "The ancient Egyptians had the same mentality, except the state secret was the tomb of the King in question."

"Ah," replied Ottilin, "That explains it; you see the tomb is buried below the mortuary complex, making it known only to the head priest of Ammon and the Empress. The mortuary temple also contains the temple of Zeus that the Empress visits every other day for prayers and offerings."

"What other wonders does this city contain?" replied the Professor.

"Well now let me see, there's the mount of the gods, it's an architectural wonder or so I am told. It is down this way..."

They walked for fifteen minutes; they passed small alleys and could see people standing outside their houses. They even saw a restaurant that had just opened for business. Ottilin asked, "Anybody hungry?"

Heir Straus replied, "Yes and I am paying."

"Fair enough," said the guard.

On entering the establishment, it was like any other eating house; they were seated and presented with a menu which they left Ottilin to decipher.

After the meal Heir Strauss asked for the bill, the lady approached him and pulled down the blind and she then hit a button on the table and the price appeared on the blind on the bottom corner. It came to the princely sum of 4 talons, Jack looked at him and said, "Heir Strauss, don't you only carry American green back abroad."

"Yes Jack, but this time I brought something else," he pulled his belt out from around his waist and inside were gold coins that were blank but weighed approximately three grams each. "I see," said Ottilin, "She will need one of them." The poor waitress looked at the gold coin with a reverence and Heir Straus gave her another for good service and the woman dropped and kissed his leg uncontrollably. As they were leaving the woman waved them off into the distance. Once they were near the mount of the gods, Jack asked ottilin, "What had happened to the woman in the restaurant?" Ottilin laughed and replied, "The majority of the cities people are poor but looked after well, you have just made that woman very rich and she was overcome with joy. She has probably bought the restaurant by now," and the crowd exploded with laughter. When the laughter had subsided they caught sight of the mount of the gods. Standing two hundred feet high was the statue of the King of the gods, Zeus, made of the finest pink granite, According to Ottilin the empire was full of the granite, which had a glow to it, and next to him was the Egyptian god Horus and on the other side of Zeus was the god Seth. They were all placed at the top of the mound and over looked the exercise fields that local citizens used every day to exercise at sun-up. Walking down from the mound they looked at Ottilin, he looked different in his normal everyday garb and when asked what age he was he replied, "I am one hundred and eighty five years old." Even this amount of exposure to their ways they could not but hold with awe to the grace with which these people lived their lives. With that they headed back to the palace for a nights sleep and contemplation on the evenings events.

Meanwhile, back in the gate room of the tomb which they had come through, the skeleton crew that Heir Strauss had ordered to leave behind were taking their time and in the last weeks had become lax and mostly bored, getting fat and laying around. They were taking soundings from the wall of steel that the rest of them had opened to allow the rest through. Joe was walking around and as every day went past he became more stressed, "I have been fucking left here to rot, no one has made contact," turning to one of Heir Straus officials he simply replied, "They will be here when they're here Joe, take it easy and relax."

"Relax! How can I relax! They have been nearly gone two weeks and you want me to relax," all he could do while sorting out security for the site was clean his weapon and read reports. With all his short comings he was still a professional soldier and he was a good one. He liked the nights, they were a break from the unbearable heat and he was mostly calm at this time of day, the sun had dropped below the Egyptian sky and the cold stuck to your bones like glue but it was a relief in short doses. "Sir, I have a report for you," handing him the fax sheet that had just been faxed from Cairo. It was from the president and the head of military security, it read 'attack imminent from unknown force. Approximately two hundred strong. Fully armed. Will see about reinforcements later. For now you will have to hold them off. Stop.' Fluttering, the report fax slipped from his hands and settled on the floor, he waited in the limbo for a while, almost an eternity, as the cold hard truth hit him. If he did not hold this position they would all certainly die. He lifted his radio and called a security meeting with all the men to see what position would be taken, "As you know Egypt and Heir Strauss are very close allies, all I know is that this tomb must not fall into enemy hands at any cost. The enemy is two hundred strong, there are fifteen of us and the odds get worse, we're low on ammunition, so gentlemen make every round count," with that Joe headed to the command vehicle and ordered the technician to activate the device that Jack had told him about. Again the eye in the sky was to be used, except this time, for their survival. The technician typed the password into the laptop and the device activated with a thud, the eye was fired up into the sky about one hundred feet, it then started its motor and the blades started perfectly. The eye was sent up to fifteen hundred feet and the night mode selected so they could make out the shapes of men jumping out of trucks and starting their four mile hike on foot. The Tech said, "We have about one hour to prepare for them."

"Is that so." replied Joe, "We will be ready. They don't know who there fucking with now." Joe looked at the rest of the men assembled, giving his orders, "and here is a shipment of claymores, please do something wonderful with them," pointing at the screen with a sense of urgency Joe said again, "We must hold our position or the others will not get out alive. We must either bloody their noses that they don't come back or we will have to kill all of them." A big American looked at him with an unbelievable sense of confidence and said, "Well boys, we better go and earn our pay," and they trooped out of the command vehicle and dispersed into pairs. Some pulled out sniper rifles and the rest were armed with heavy calibre machine guns and side arms. By this stage they had turned the tomb and surrounding valley into a death trap for anybody with ideas about pillage and murder and the hills had been saturated with landmines and machine gun bunkers and automated machine gun positions, a new inspiration from Heir Strauss laboratories in Germany. As Joe watched the up coming enemy troops advancing he sat with a cup of tea and concentrated as a bead of sweat dripped down his face. He put the V R glasses on and watched the men climb over the rough terrain; it was like watching an ant hill explode and all the ants tripling down the hill. He could make out the different kinds of weapons RPG's and AK's, they seemed to be well enough trained and were breaking off and teaming into groups of two and heading in his very direction, almost as if they knew were they were going. Looking over at the direction of the Tech he said, "In coming message sir," and the monitor in front of him activated, there was the president, he looked sternly at Joe and said, "I take it you have been told of the situation and know what is going on." "Yes sir," replied Joe.

"Right then, these guys are a breakaway faction of the brotherhood of Ammon that split in the thirteenth century, and they are hell bent on getting into that tomb for some reason or another. The only thing I know is that we are five hours from any hope of reinforcing you and they are twenty minutes away. Hold them off as long as you can and hope that it is long enough," giving Joe a reassuring look he logged of and the screen went black.

Chapter 13.

Back in Castorian city, Jack was taking a specialist arms training course for the non military in his party, which strangely enough was in the exercise grounds of the mount of the god's. Exios looked at Jack and said, "My friend we have powerful beings watching over us," looking at the colossal statue of Zeus he spoke the words, "Oh great Zeus, father of your children who shape our world and play with mankind as if it were a piece in a board game. What destiny do you hold for these humble pieces gathered here today? Smite thy enemy and make ours a destiny, that is one of victory."

"Well said Exios," replied Kevin who was watching with eagerness. Suddenly a landing craft landed on the exercise grounds and one of the generals aides ran out and over to us and said, "Come, their plans are nearly at a stage of readiness and your company is required at the palace." So they all boarded the landing craft and it headed for the imperial palace, flying over the streets that we had walked on the night before, below us we also saw the statue of the first King Castor and into the grounds of the palace. They were met by Ottilin who said, "Come this way, we are nearly ready to march out," he looked excited but calm. Twenty thousand of the Empresses personal guard had been assigned for front line duty because they were the best regiment in the army and they were eager. Walking into the great hall the Empress welcomed us with a smile and the King with a nod, Jack spoke first, "I take it their weapons are more powerful than ours?"

"Yes," replied King Riceos, "But now we have the advantage of numbers." Michelle looked at them and said, "Isn't there anything that can defeat their technology?"

"Yes," replied the Empress, "The power staff of castor, but unfittingly it is entombed with him."

"Your majesty," said Heir Strauss, "What is the power of this staff?"

She replied, "When the Egyptians first came, the Kitni leadership made Castor the King, their leader was a good man called Alto who in a sign of goodwill gave him his power staff that had the power to switch off Kitni technology, but as you know, that was along time ago."

The King intervened, "From what we know, in that time they only updated their systems once. There is a slim chance that it may work and the Kitni believe we won't go near it because it's buried with a King. The tomb is riddled with booby traps of great cunning."

The Empress turned and looked at him and said, "How did you know that?"

Smiling at her he replied, "Good intelligence Empress, good inelegance." Almost embarrassed the Empress turned and said, "Will you do it? You had to break into a well defended tomb to get here and you seem to have the most experience in this vicinity."

"Yes," replied Jack.

Richard looked sternly at Jack and rolled his eyes in annoyance thinking, 'good one, Jack volunteered us for another low risk operation, ha, some chance.'

The Empress looked at the assembled squad and said, "If we cannot beat them militarily, the power staff will be the only thing that can save us". "In the mean time, I have an army to march into Pramidia and air borne units to activate," lifting his goblet and toasting the Empress with the chilling, "Victory or death I will see you all on the battlefield my friends, Jack good luck in your endeavour, from what I here about the tomb you will need it," with that he marched out of the hall and onto an awaiting Asronas military transport where he was taken to a forward command post to await his troops. As he walked onto the craft, the doors sealed behind him and the ship took off and made its way to the secret location. Jack however would be escorted by the Empress herself and the general would command the imperial armies of the empire. In her heart the Empress believed this was the right place to be and she would be close to Exios as well. That evening they boarded a transport and headed to the temple of Zeus deep in the hills of Castorian. They lifted off and moved towards the mountains, the snow caped peeks reminded them of the mountains outside the fortress island of Philios. They were still miles off and would be about half an hour getting there; they flew deep into the forests on the outskirts of Castorian city. There were massive trees, as tall as the ones you would find in the rain forests of Brazil, all strange kinds of life lived here from monkeys to the most poisonous snakes, wild cats to their own variety of lion, which the locals called the razor cat. It was then when it dawned on Jack that during the apocalypse that supposedly wiped out the dinosaurs, this could have been part of the earths surface that dropped in on itself and was sealed over thousands of feet below the earths crust. As they went further into the forest they saw a large mountain with water falls flowing from the side, they suddenly dropped and headed straight for one of the water falls. Jack thought the pilot had went mad but when he saw the Empress was calm, he knew there was nothing to fear. They flew straight into the water fall which was part of the masquerade that hid the tomb and mortuary complex that also hid the temple of Zeus. It was beautiful, it had rows of columns coming from either side and came together in the middle and formed a landing pad. In front were steps that lead to a temple that mimicked the acropolis and Parthenon in Athens. They dismounted the craft and headed towards the stairs which sharply rose in the direction of the opening of the temple. They then started to ascend, there were statues on either side of the steps, in the world up top, these minor deities had all but been forgotten with the emergence of the faiths of the world today, but in this lost world they were as real to these people as you could possibly believe. They laid tributes to each day, each household had their own special deities which were locked away at night and produced in the morning. They could be made of any material, stone, wood or metal. As they made their way to the summit, they walked into the temple. It was huge, it reminded them of a medieval cathedral, and it was rowed with six lines of columns that supported the roof of this mega building. They headed towards where the altar had presented itself and behind was the man himself, one hundred feet high, the Queen said, "He was made of granite and over laid with tons of gold. It nearly bankrupted the state the year that he died but it was completed and to think nobody but me and a few aides have ever seen the temple. It is a shame but it is the law."

"I see," replied Heir Straus, "And that is the only way into the complex?"

"Yes," replied the Queen, "The water pressure is such that if you tried to enter on foot you would drown. There is no other way in."

Jack took a moment to take in the scenery and atmosphere of the mountain. Zeus was looking down and you would have thought he was looking straight at you with those large eyes that were made of polished marble and around the pupil was studied with ornate uncut diamonds. The iris had been studded with blue uncut diamonds, the entire complex was lighted just like the tomb with a rim running around the top of the columns and around the sides the diamonds caught the glare of the light and energetically sparkled in the gaze of the Empress which was devout and humble in this her time of need. The walls were decked with swords and shields and were crossed with two spears. Kevin walked over towards the shield and pulled out his glasses, he placed them on his face and began to scrutinise the shield, he stood back and said, "This is the Aegean star, if you please Alexander the great's coat of arms, his calling card?"

"That is correct," replied the Empress, "They were a gift to his son and were placed here according too his will. They formally hung on the walls of the imperial palace and were transported here on the event of his death, to where they remain today."

After standing and watching the Empress saying a prayer they moved into the right hand wing of the temple and saw an amazing sight. A massive lions head carved into the rock foundation and they went into its mouth, the teeth made of solid gold. They started their decent down into the bowels of the complex and it was then that they saw the start of the pharaoh's mortuary temple. Michelle took the lead and thought out loud, "Ah now, we're in my part of the woods. The entrance was of ancient Egyptian architecture, papyrus stemmed columns and the cartouche of castor flanked by wings of that of an eagle. It was much simpler in design but never the less as beautiful as I have ever seen it." They walked into the mortuary temple and a different atmosphere took shape, now they were out of their comfort zone, and they knew it. They walked towards a beautiful statue of the King himself, at first inspection he had all the recognisable physical associations that his brother had, Akhenaten, though his facial features were more defined there seemed to be radical chiselled characteristics. He appeared more regal and had an air of greatness about him, one thing was for sure who ever gazed upon this representation of the King, walked away convinced that he was a great man.

Out of the corner of his eye, Jack could see a figure cloaked in a mist of incense, the man walked over and as he came into sight he could clearly see that he was a priest of Ammon. As he got closer they discovered that he was in fact the old priest of Ammon that had accompanied them into the cavern and had been dropped off at the temple of Ammon some distance outside the city of Castorian. Nicolas was ecstatic to see him again, as was the chairman of the secret order of Ammon, they both embraced him like he was a lost family member, "good too see you old man," keeping an air of respectability and reverence and simply bowing he turned and bowed to the Empress and said, "The brotherhood of Ammon welcomes you, your majesty and also thanks you for your hospitality and kindness. I am truly blessed that we are allowed to see this wonder with our eyes."

The Empress replied, "It is my duty to treat all fairly and just according to the rules of Maat."

"Of which I am glad to hear, your majesty, the priest of Ammon is here in order to help you in your task in retrieving King Castor's staff of power."

"Exios, promise me something. Treat his body with respect if you get there," kissing him gently and pulling back and said in a stern voice, "I will lead you to the entrance of the tomb, this is the only part of the complex that has no lighting. When Castor built it he made it clear that no lighting systems would be installed in the tomb or in the attached entrances." She walked behind the large statue of the dead King and reached for the scarab built in to the Kings armour, she pushed both wings in until they heard a click, followed by a motorised sound and the wall opened in front to show the entrance to the tomb. Her guards went on first with lighting devices attached to their armour, the rest of the group followed the Empress and the tunnel stopped about half a mile into the rock. As they accustomed themselves to the new atmosphere they noticed the walls were glittering. Michelle broke ranks and walked over to them and shone her flash light at the glittering objects, "Oh my god! They're 'diamonds."

"Yes," said the Empress, "when they were building the tomb they came across a small amount of the valuable stones which, believe it or not, paid for the rest of the construction of the tomb." They walked on in awe of the mineral wealth of this land. They walked until they came to a flight of stairs that took them down into the base of the entrance to the tomb itself. As the Queens guards lit the beakers around the entrance a pattern started to emerge, a double set of stairs leading down into this crypt of forgotten mysteries. In the middle of the steps was a flat surface that had decorations carved into the rock. It was like this until the steps stopped at what appeared to be one hundred feet; it took on a different personality from there on in. It was decked out in granite and polished, smooth to the touch. They started the descent down; being careful not to lose their footing they reached the threshold of the tomb. It was magnificent, gilded statues of the gods Anubis and Osiris. "They are the main gods of the underworld, all except Seth who murdered his brother Osiris. Seth has sometimes been singled out as the modern counterpart of the devil and this interpretation has seemed to be carried out here as well," said Michelle. At his name the old priest became uneasy and walked over to Michelle and placed his hand over her mouth, "Please young lady do not mention his name in case he is listening." He then removed his hand and put it on her shoulder and smiled, "Thank you, May Horus be your guide in the after-world."

The Empress walked over to Jack and presented him with a strange looking key, shaped in the old Egyptian ankh style, "It is the key to the tomb entrance of King Castor, and it is the only door that this key will open." Accepting the key Jack nodded at her and replied, "We will do our best and god willing shall retrieve the staff of power." Looking at Jack she said, "Two of my best soldiers will accompany you into the tomb, you may need their strength and help." Jack nodded in agreement and the Empress gave a subtle nod and two of her imperial guard broke ranks and joined the hapless squad of men at the base of the entrance.

Standing in the balcony, Risard stood facing the tens of thousands of soldiers standing in line attentively listening to his tales of deceit and poisonous spite. "They want to destroy us and steal our technology," raising one hand in the air he twisted his face and shouted, "They even want to kill us!" But in his mind the true motivations were floating about, in his greed propelled state of self it was want, the want to destroy the other races and when he was finished he would declare himself ruler of all the empire of the Kitni people and their subordinate slave population. The only thing that was stopping him was the far flung ranting of one of the Kitni senate who was constantly reminding him that they were not a war-like people, but a civilised intelligent race who fix things instead of breaking them. Walking up to him an aide spoke into his ear, cruelly relayed the news that the old man had been assassinated on his orders. He looked at his troops and ordered them to deploy on the borders of the forests of Pramidia and to await further orders. The amassed broke into lines and started to board massive ships bound for Pramidia. As Risard watched this spectacle unfold he turned to his commander, a dark skinned man called Hesser. He had started off thousands of years ago when the other civilisations weren't even heard of. This man had the air of total war about him, he had fought through the primal wars before the Kitni became a Kingdom and he believed in the dominance of the Kitni people and the purity of there race and was a fanatical follower of Risard. "Soon my lord, we shall have dominance of the other races and they will be our slaves or our cannon fodder for the up and coming assault on the humans in the upper world. But for the weak leadership that brought this situation about and gave sanctuary to these genetically weaker humans, as you know we are the first of their kind and are the strongest, thus we will prevail." He looked deep into Risards eyes and said, "But first we must slaughter their populous and bring them into line, so that they may know who is in charge."

After accepting the key from the Empress, Jack turned to the entrance of King Castors tomb and walked up to the two massive gilded doors. On one of them was the keyhole, shaped in the form of a pyramid with a single hieroglyph at each point. The priest looked at it carefully and said, "It is a code," he took the key from Jack and pushed it into the key hole, the key had two layers of prongs but for what purpose they were not sure. The old priest pushed hard and turned clockwise. He in turn said a prayer then he pulled it out and turned it anti-clockwise. The priest stood back and said, "Behold the last resting place of the great King Castor." The doors made that all too familiar sound again, squealing on the hinges and slowly they moved back into the fully opened position and locked tight with counter weights. They looked into the dark abyss and found only the first thing to hit them was the smell. It was damp and they could almost smell a perfume of some kind, it was weak but could still be made out as a fragrance. The two guards lit the torches and proceeded forward, lighting up the first passage. They walked down it for a quarter of a mile, then the passage took a sharp right, walking out ahead was one of the guards who was quietly conversing with the other, when suddenly the ground fell away from him and he dropped into a shaft cut into the floor. He managed to cling on to the edge, but before they got to him he slipped into the shaft, and then came the screams and the deafening sound of a horrible death. The poor soul stepped into a spear pit. Looking down in disbelief at the young impaled soldier's body draped lifelessly into the spears, the other guard was badly shaken but quickly gained his composure. At closer inspection the floor was made of the same material but had been as thin as a quarter of an inch, basically candy coated with the same material, but sprayed with some concoction to give it durability through the years. Looking down at the ghastly sight that confronted us, his blood was slowly starting to drip down the spear shafts and pool on the floor. The priest walked over to the other surviving guard and said, "Grieve not, he is in a better place and his body will be retrieved and shall receive a graceful departure into the after life, but now dear boy we must continue," the guard looked at the priest and nodded. He turned to the group and said, "We must be careful from here on in." He took the peltas rifle off his shoulder and set it on low discharge, he then pointed to the floor and opened fire hitting panel by panel until the second spear pit was revealed. Turning to the old priest he said, "And this one could have gracefully seen me into the afterlife." They continued into the massive labyrinth that awaited them, coming to a stairway that descended about fifty feet and into the main chamber and already they were one down. As they entered the main chamber it took on the ancient Egyptian persona, wall paintings and relief carvings of the after life. The priest was enthralled looking at the craftsmanship of the work. In the mean time the soldier was scanning the floor with an x-ray device built into his armour, he looked at the walls then scanned them, the air was deep with the stench of danger and anticipation. He suddenly picked up something on his scanner, he turned quickly to Jack and said, "Arm yourselves, the walls, look to the walls," the guard pulled back. They heard a clank then a sliding sound, the wall panels were opening on each side of the corridor. They then heard a growling sound followed by a roar. Then it appeared, a mass of fur and teeth, it was the beast of the forests that we had heard of. The razor cat had an uncanny resemblance to the extinct sabre tooth, its roar was deafening and its appearance was also frightening, its two long sabre teeth were shining as bright as ivory that had been polished. Then another one came at us from behind us. The guard shouted, "We must act now!" With that they huddled into a compact unit and it was enough to allow the two cats to sense each others presence and the first cat walked past us and started to size up his opposition. With that the guard ran out into the middle of the corridor and held out his arm sideways and out of his armour came a metal screen that extended telescopically with a sharp position and jammed itself to the wall. He detached the device and said, "We don't have a lot of time, it won't hold them for long." With that Jack ordered all the men to put as much fire power into the beasts as possible. He pulled out his glock 9mm pistol and started to fire. The beasts roared in protest as the slaughter began, putting two bullets into the first creature's head he watched as the animal slid and pawed the ground. As it fell over the other beast looked us in the eye and paused for a while, it had a strange look of distance and former recall. The beast seemed to be going through its instinct to survive, it was bigger than the first beast and obviously was the male of the species and for a moment you could cut the atmosphere with a knife. The tense abandonment of this miscalculated moment that was leading up to was what everybody was trying to figure out, and then suddenly the beast pounced with all its might. Its eyes were filled with hate and its only remaining instinct was to kill us all; with this Richard pulled out his general purpose tsar heavy machine gun and pushed the barrel into the groves of the protective screen and began to fire, the beast was running when the deadly hail caught him off guard. He roared in pain as he flipped over, the amount of firepower that was bearing down on him was final. As the beast came to a stop at the front of the screen, he let a growl out of his lungs and then died. The guard walked over to the screen and reconnected it to his armour, looking at Jack he remarked, "This has saved my skin once before and is worth its weight in gold." The device then refolded itself into his armour and they stood and looked at the terrible sight which greeted them. Behind the screen, the blood drenched bodies of the once magnificent animals lay on the floor with no dignity.

The guard stressed that they had no time to waste and must continue. They headed on down the main passage, to the beginning of what appeared to be the ant-chamber. The guard stopped dead and looked at his instruments on his computerised console on his arm; he looked at us and shouted, "Back, back now!" They ran back about twenty feet where he said, "If you have breathing gear put it on now," the guard placed a small object in his mouth and started to breathe. The rest of them were struggling with their army issue respirators. Jack and Richard and the rest of the security squad, being former soldiers, got theirs on quickly and began to help the rest of the team, amazingly, Heir Strauss had his on. Sometimes the team forgot that the old man was once a soldier. Just then a sliding sound filled the passage and crystal vials of what appeared to be poison, yellow in appearance, they stopped once they reached the ceiling. There were six in all, then all at once they dropped onto the floor and smashed, the gas started to lace the interior of the passage and was deadly to all that came in contact with the yellow mist, a veil of death. Looking at Jack the guard said, "From my readings, it will take a few minutes to redirect the poison gas." After three minutes the sound of a mechanical device was heard behind one of the walls, it was some kind of back up generator attached to a fan that cleared the tomb passage, the gas exiting the same way the beasts had entered, through the panels on the wall. The guard turned and removed the breathing device that he was wearing, "its ok, the chamber is clear of all gasses." Jack looked at Heir Straus as he pulled off his respirator, the old man said, "Jack I am almost one hundred percent sure that was mustard gas, my god they had access to that kind of weapon over two thousand years ago... no wonder Alexander backed off." Turning their attention towards the sealed entrance that lay before them, it was quite clear that it was the entrance to the anti chamber. Before them lay two massive doors that were made of gold, carved on the panels attached to the doors were the images of the pharaoh seated on his throne and in front of the door was a puzzle. The priest stepped forward and gazed at it for some length, "Yes, this is a mystery, a mystery indeed," the priest stepped back and looked at the relief's on the wall not far from the doors. It was of the Kings crook and flail, the signature of power in ancient Egypt and of monarchy, the picture was of the King sitting on the throne but instead of having the crook and flail crossed over his chest they were set into the throne arms, shaped as lions heads, the crook went into the lions head on the left and the flail went into the lions head on the right, the pharaohs hands were extended onto each one of the instruments and in a downwards motion the relief of the pharaoh almost seemed to be pushing the crook and flail downwards. Michelle was mesmerised standing beside the old priest she looked back at the doors and noticed that on the door was, two lions heads inlayed on either side of the throne. The lions were opened mouthed and almost awaiting the slender throat of a distant enemy, the craftsmanship was unbelievable, the quality of the gold was much better than the other tomb, it had a shine which sparked of the age old saying; all that glitters is not gold. No matter how many times she thought that to herself, in here it would do no good because everything was made of gold. The priest walked over to the puzzle once again and looked at it hard, it was not that dissimilar from the key stand in the gate room except this time there were no holes to put your hands in, just the puzzle. Looking at the inscription, the priest read out aloud, "To enter the Kings hall you must master the mystery of air and light." At the side of the marble stand was a small console that allowed one to open the top of the device, as it opened the priest looked inside and to his amazement there were two lights on the bottom of the stand and on top there was nothing, just air. He then placed his hands into the opening of the stand and found that by moving his hands in the compressed air the lights took the same projection. So basically he controlled the lights but the question was, what does he do with them? The priest said, "The answer is normally the simplest thing, in here is a broken circle so I will realign the circle and the cycle of life will be restored once again," with that the old man skilfully manoeuvred the lines of light into the unfinished circle and finally he completed his task. The crook and flail came out of the front of the stand in a different section, the priest took the crook and flail and walked over to the door. First, he took the lions head and turned it half a turn, this left the teeth turned to the side just enough to slide the crook into the left lions mouth and the flail into the right lions mouth which he did simultaneously. He counted to three and let them go, they slid into the hilt of the lions mouth on each side, we heard a click and the lions heads automatically reversed into their original position, the glint of the gold and the stripes of lapis luzai blue, the top and bottom of each of the instruments were carnelian, a red semi precious stone, they were a work of art on their own. The crook and flail touched when they turned and the locks all around were unlocked and the two doors opened. We walked in awe of what our eyes were presented with, a massive temple that was lit up by the guards lighting devices that he threw out in intervals, slowly lighting up the architecture. It was set out in columns and on the sides of the tomb were the treasury and annex rooms, everything the King would need for his after life. On the far side were two large boats to carry the King's soul across the sky, at the extreme gable of the tomb was a simple opening into the burial chamber. They looked around the annex and everything you could think of was available, the treasuries were closed by iron gates and we could see inside the amount of gold and jewels were beyond belief. Michelle estimated, "There must be at least thirty or forty times more than was in Tutankhamen's tomb."

Standing behind her Richard remarked, "Man it looks like his brother got a raw deal as far as gold is concerned." In one of the treasure rooms there was a mountain of gold stacked on top of each other, about six metres high and twelve metres wide. One of the Americans soldiers said, "I can tell you right now, there's more gold in this place than Fort Knox, and I should know I used to guard it." Heir Strauss stepped in front and addressed the group, "In this place, you no doubt have noticed that there are enough riches to make all of you very wealthy. This is true but think of the people of the respective territories who will end up being slaughtered by the armies of darkness, so I appeal to you, think not of the wonders in this great tomb but of a great nation who will be very grateful for helping destroy its greatest enemy. This much I can tell you, I once served an evil and this one by comparison is much greater and must be stopped," turning in the direction of the burial chamber the German turned once more to us and said, "Lets go say hello to Castor and deprive him of his power staff." Walking thought the pillared hall the tinge of orange glistened off the guards light, one felt as you were being called for an audience with the King, such were the surroundings, the walls were adjourned with the history of the Kings battles and to him, obviously peace treaties were more important. The relief carvings were mounted in gold and built into the walls of the tomb, around each one was carved marble cartouches of the King, further into the tomb we progressed until we saw the steps that descended into the burial chamber that were built around what appeared to be the sarcophagus. "It was a large golden volt that had been sealed by his vizier," the guard said, "There was a legend that his devoted servant took his own life after his master was laid in the sarcophagus." Jack illuminated the room with his torch and in the corner bench was the remains of the vizier on the ground. Kicking a bottle Jack said, "Poison, he took poison," turning the torch back again to the large vault he noticed the royal seal that locked the entrance of the sarcophagus. It was made of simple dried clay that was hard, the guard stepped up to the seal and said, "Jack I am afraid we are running out of time, I have just received a message from one of the other royal guards, the Kitni army has just engaged King Riceos in the forests of Pramidia. We are now up against the clock."

Looking at the guard Jack said, "The seal?"

The guard replied, "Stand back," the guard flicked his cloak behind his left side and unsheathed his sword and in one movement he cut through the seal. The cut was clean and the seal hung in two pieces swinging from side from side. Returning his sword to his scabbard the guard said, "Lets get going," they started to lift the heavy shrine screens over to the wall and one by one set them down carefully, the roof section was the most difficult piece to move down and required the strength of all of the men in the room, slowly the outline of the sarcophagus began to appear, it was carved out of one piece of yellow quartzite and on the corners, like his brother Tutankhamen, was carved the image of Isis. The humidly in the tomb was getting to a all time high, the rolls of sweat running down faces and onto the floor leaving spots on the floor of dust that had collected over the mists of time. We all took to the lid of the sarcophagus and started to lift, even with the guards strength he could not shift it, so we improvised, we lifted two of the shrine sides into position at either side of the sarcophagus and secured them with parts of the roof section, on the top we placed one of the planks of the ship that was meant to take the King across the sky during the day. The priest was not pleased at this, he was shaking his head and repeating the words; "sacrilege, by the gods what sacrilege."

CHAPTER 14.

Meanwhile back in the forests of Pramidia, King Riceos was at the head of his troops, on horseback, with general Lieysin at his side, "Your majesty what is our defensive stratagem or do, as my experience dictates, we attack?"

"Firstly general we sit and wait to see what kind of tricks the enemy has up its sleeves," at a quick pace they both started to ride in to a large clearing that had been made by the battle cruiser, here the allied Asronas and Castorian armies amassed. The dust rose up into the air as the hundreds of thousands of soldiers marching into the clearing that was to be used as a forward command centre. Three imperial cruisers had been landed in the centre as a defensive perimeter for the troops, they also had the duel purpose as command centre's and supply vessels for the infantry. The two unlikely allies boarded one of the vessels, they went straight to the command centre where the viewing screen was on the King who turned to his second and asked, "Is he in position yet?"

"Nearly, your majesty." On viewer the sight that greeted them was unbelievable, looking at the view on the visor worn by the Valliant young captain Thrush, there amassed were millions of Kitni troops and they were advancing into the forests twenty thousand at a time. Almost carried by the pure awe of the moment the King looked at the general and said, "Just imagine, they engineered this war between us to try and avoid this war. They were going to wait until one or the other was wiped out and then wage war on the victor who would be weak by that time and in no fit state to fight the Kitni. Here's hoping that we are strong enough to counter whatever they are going to throw at us! Come general to where we will do the most damage, at the head of our armies," they walked out and mounted their horses and at a fast gallop headed to their front lines. They rode into the forest where the light was nearly blocked out by the high level canopy of the trees, they passed scores of men who were carrying their kit into battle and were cheered as they rode onwards to the front line. As the King rode hard he roared, "VICTORY!" the troops lifted their arms into the air. They were armed with peltas rifles and the officers wielded their swords returning in kind the word, "victory."

As they rode through the alpine undergrowth, they passed all kinds of strange animal inhabitants; snakes coiled around branches and camouflaged themselves with an uncanny resemblance of the forest itself. Most were deadly and to the careless green recruit could prove deadly, other beasts like the razor cat and more varied types of wildlife, but something else lurked among the darkness watching the King and his allied general. Nearing the front the King stopped dead and almost with a sixth sense he felt a presence, Riceos turned to Lieysin and said, "I do believe old friend, that we are being hunted. Whatever is going to happen is going to happen soon." Looking at General Lieysin he nodded and unhooked his hilt guard on his sword, his gaze ran across the endless trees and darkness that created shadow that allowed this thing or creature to hide affectively. The general said, "I have heard that the Kitni used to assassinate the enemy leaders before a battle to demoralize the army that they led, the assassin was normally a highly experienced man who was garbed in black and carried an array of weapons. The only question I am thinking is, which one shall he use on us?" The King said, "Look up ahead, there is a natural bottle neck, this is where he is most likely to attack." Although no sound could be heard the lone assailant could be felt making his way to the closing. The King's royal guard was at least half a mile from his position, a serious miscalculation of bravado which shortly he would correct, if he managed to survive this encounter. As they neared the bottleneck, the trees on either side exploded, as they fell across the route they exploded again doubling over, thus blocking the road for the two. Suddenly streaks of red light struck the horse under the King, the animal rearing in pain, the action of the horse threw the King across, knocking the general off his horse also. The King lay on the ground watching for the next onslaught when suddenly shadow turned to matter before them they saw a man dressed in black and he was making his way towards them in fast succession. He came towards the corner of the bottle neck and jumped from there, his body flipped whilst flying through the air, before he landed he drew his sword and his side arm, flashes of red light came from this weapon which he had decided he would use on general Lieysin, his sword he would use on King Riceos. Still recovering from the fall, Lieysin was struggling to get to his feet; the deadly fire was plowing into the trees and also the horses that were wreathing in pain, their entrails half hanging out on the ground. King Riceos roared at the killer, "Come on!" With that he drew his sword and started a deadly duel with the assassin, the hooded attacker parried and trusted but with all of his skill he had forgotten the King was a master in the sword skills of his Kingdom, tutored by the best of his countrymen, his sword was heavy and had three metal cutting bars built into his hilt, the slice came through the air and he was able to catch his sword in the cutting straps of the Kings hilt, with a twist of his wrists the sword of the mysterious attacker broke at the hilt, the King followed through with a cut to the back of his leg bringing him down in front of the King. The King was about to finish him off when the general shouted, "Alive, keep him alive for information!" King Riceos was reluctant to agree, stating that this scoundrel would be more likely to resist any form of interrogation and reminded General Lieysin, "His telepathic abilities were more likely to compromise our security and put the lives of our selves and our men at risk! The old general looked at the assassin and pulled out his side arm and with a single shot to the head, killed the attacker, his body slumped into the holes that one of his own explosive devices had made. The duo looked into the hole to see the body of the once great killer, "He won't be targeting anybody ever again. The only problem is; how many of them are there?" The general replied, "Our intelligence indicates that there is a whole sect of these men, they are trained from birth with the one common goal, the assassination of their enemies leaders or officials or even officers in the military. They have even been known to kill their own, who oppose the leadership of their race in the great wars before the creation of the civilizations and the dominance of the Kitni race as the most powerful to inhabit this world. After the wars their government took the steps to ensure that violence would never again be apart of their agenda, the ruling class from that time are all dead or those who have survived have themselves been assassinated. Chancellor Risard and an old Kitni general who from what I have been able to asses is simply called commander Hesser, to the Kitni the rank of commander is reserved only for men of great distinction. I can tell you right now King Riceos, he is not going to be easy to kill."

"How do you know your information is correct?"

General Lieysin replied, "We have for many years had good relations with a man called Counselor Diron, he is a good man who would see the leadership of the Kitni remain as it was, peaceful, but his kind are dying off in a quick manner. He has requested political asylum at a secret level and so has imparted us with some interesting facts and knowledge about Kitni life at the echelons of power." The path was cleared and they were given fresh horses where they continued on there way to the front.

Trumpets sounded as King Riceos and general Lieysin entered the front ranks of the Asronas battle group, General Lieysin rode of to the side of the group to allow the King to address his troops.

"Here is where your unwavering bravery and loyalty have led you. Here is where we will stop the true enemy of our peoples, swords drawn with fire," looking deep into the eyes of his men he shouted, "Only to be extinguished when it has been pulled out of the last fighting foe and returned to its sheath and may the gods hope where it will remain in peace alongside our brothers the Castorian's who are standing beside you. They are now your right arm, so guard it well and if we fail our loved ones will pay the price with forced slavery and summery execution. This I can promise you! We have to stop them here! Here, where this majestic forest cloaks the sun from our faces and darkens the strut of our shadows and at the same time bewilders us with its beauty. We take heart of the one good thing that has come out of this terrible war, our unity to stop, to deny the true rulers of evil the right to descend across our lands like a plague," motioning for general Lieysin to join him the general rode over to the King where he took his place at the head of his troops. "Sire, captain Thrush is reporting movement in the canopy but their visuals are limited, the disturbance was one mile in our direction and coming our way."

"Very well," replied King Riceos. Looking around he said, "What we need is time." The general replied, "Yes, as well as defensive trenches." The King said, "We have so little time,"

The general said move the men back twenty feet, suddenly Castorian engineers moved in and set explosive charges in a straight line in front of the front line, they went off with a deafening bang. "That should suffice for now!" They had used just enough explosive to blow out trenches and make defensive trenching for the oncoming frontal assault. The two dismounted and commanders started battle checks for weapons and made sure their supply route for reinforcements and ammunition was kept clear. The front line jumped into the trench and manned their positions, all went silent for a short while and all that could be heard was the gentle rustle of a low wind. Animals suddenly started to run out of the woods and past our positions, it was then we heard the oncoming army advance. We could just about see the Kitni front rank advance; they had different armor and were armed with strange kinds of weapons. King Riceos looked at the side arm that he had taken off the dead assassin, he pointed in their direction and pulled the trigger, a sharp red light flashed out of the muzzle and it was then that he said, "It's a laser, by the gods, they have laser weapons." The shot he had fired hit its mark with deadly surety, the Kitni soldier fell where he had been killed, and King Riceos comically slid it into his gun belt and remarked that it would come in handy for a pickle. The front line of Kitni was about twenty thousand in strength. A captain emerged from the swell at the back of the Kitni ranks and offered terms for the surrender of the Asronas and Castorian alliance. The King thanked the young man for his offer and then pulled out the side arm that he had taken from the assassin and fired point blank into the captain's body. As he fell the King replied, "There's your answer," turning to the general he said, "Told you it would get me out of a pickle!" General Lieysin burst out laughing and replied, "That's great! Now, what about them?" The Kitni front rank prepared to attack at a slow walk, they started slow, and then turned from a walk to a quick run, they fired, and their first shots which pounded the trench and all within were visibly shaken, but not deterred. King Riceos roared the order, "Open fire!" Equipped with their new peltas rifles, the troops took position and fired. It was strange for a battle, the peltas rifle only made a compressed pinging noise that gave deadly results. The front rank of the Kitni were decimated, limbs flying in the air and the sounds of the injured and dying were heard in the air as the wind carried it towards them. The line behind them stepped in front of their dead comrades and immediately took to their attack formation and the game once again started, "Fire!" roared Riceos. General Lieysins column which had wheeled left to create a left flank was about to be attacked, the general took his leave and headed to his defensive front which had just been created. The Kitni came at them with renewed further, adding to the fear that was building in the line. The Kitni warriors made a screaming noise as they advanced; it chilled them to the bone. From first observation the Kitni soldier was a well trained being, his amour was black in color and had a ringed affect on the breastplate, his sword was curved and was carried hung from his belt, at his back his side arm was carried in a holster and a dagger was hung in an attachment, built on to the holster, which could be reached quickly if needed, indeed the Kitni soldier was something to behold, but what was more important was the ability to destroy them. They were adapting their shields to the configuration of the alliance's weapons. Suddenly King Riceos had an idea, he relayed it to the general who agreed that it was worth a go and began to give orders, "Men, the main thing here is aggression, we have noticed that our weapons are slowly being compromised so we will form an assault line and drive them back. When we have drove them back, lift the weapons of the dead and injured so we have them when we need them. Line Advance!" With that one order they advanced and crashed into the enemy front ranks, this is where the brute strength of the Asronas warrior came to bear, the front ranks of the Kitni line broke and they were drove back to the third line of there defense. King Riceos watched from the front ranks of the assault line and noticed one of the commanders, who was angry at the retreat, ordered his front ranks to open fire on the men running back, thus branding them all deserters. Hate raging from his eyes and pulling out his side arm he shot the first man running towards him, after a while the enemy general commander Hesser had produced himself to his men and assumed command. Looking at a distance, the general commented "It appears the black diamond has arrived."

"Hesser?"

"Yes, King Riceos, Hesser."

This man had all the hallmarks of a seasoned commander, his face was scared with thousands of years of conflict, it was the one thing he could do perfectly, war, and it was his life and his passion. He was a man who lived his life to the extreme and believed in following a code, a dark code, one that held little mercy and had no kindness built into its very existence. He was a man who could not tolerate failure or countenance, the release of a captured foe, once he had taken them prisoner he would kill all of them slowly. The thought of this brought him a strange kind of kick and he would invent strange ways to execute his prisoners and was held in high regard by his men and was feared by others.

Looking across at Hesser, the sight it presented was one of the expression of a stone cold and hard being, all that remained of his persona was just a glance of sickening hate, which on occasions shone like the north star,

"Majesty, our battle cruiser is being hindered by the high canopy of the trees, they cannot see the enemy and fear firing on us."

The King shouted "Men fire above the Kitni heads, aim for the trees!" The men loaded there rifles and took aim, they fired and the canopy exploded into shards of timber, leaves flying everywhere, but it was enough to expose the Kitni front line. When the commander of the battle cruiser saw this he ordered his vessel to open fire, Hesser, seeing this, calmly moved out of the firing line, he knew that his own vessels were on their way and were fully armed and was just a matter of holding out for a short time. The ship opened fire and the Kitni front line was decimated, the firepower being more potent, a roar rang out from the allied front trench. When the smoke had cleared, the men watched to see if any of the enemy were still alive, none they were all dead. The shouting lasted for a few minutes and suddenly the laughter and chatting shut off dead, they heard the familiar sound of enemy infantry marching into position. They stopped just where the last ranks had been, this time the general Hesser walked up with them and looked sadistically at them, as much as to say, 'is all you have got', just at that very moment the battle cruiser came under attack from a Kitni vessel, that no doubt Hesser had called for earlier that day. The battle raged on through the day, the allies were being slowly grinded down, King Riceos looked at general Lieysin with a serious air and said, "We have to pull back or we will lose a great deal of men." The general agreed and he sent a communication to his mobile command that sent two further vessels to aide there retreat. On principal, the King and general were the last men to leave, in a calm manor, the vessels over head gave suppressing fire but still the Kitni gained ground as the tired heroes retreated back to the mobile command centre located in the clearing that had been made especially for this moment with great thought and care being taken for its defensive properties. A new front line was established and the tired soldiers were relieved and got sleep where they could. Back in the cruiser, King Riceos said, "Is there any news of Jack and the Empress?" "Only that they are in the main hall overlooking the burial chamber itself, if Zeus is watching us they will have it soon and this tyranny will be over. I have kept a few royal guards in the loop in order to keep information flowing and to send reports to them and to receive information that will help us all."

Scratching his beard Riceos said, "The only thing I can think of that will be tricky will be the sarcophagus, its heavy, its very heavy, well they normally are."

Back in the tomb the team assembled around the beautiful yellow quartzite sarcophagus, on each corner there was the carved image of Isis out stretched, leaving one to think that she was protecting the dead pharaoh's soul. The middle of the sarcophagus was strapped with some kind of metal, the same one this strange world produces, it shone like it was alive, glowing bright and had the normal mercury effect. Richard noticed that it was connected to the opening of the sarcophagus and was probably linked into some kind of triggering device; the one thing that did worry him was that the metal strip was connected into the ground and ran into each corner of the burial chamber. After it was checked out with great vigor, not wanting a repeat of the traps in the outside corridor, they concluded that it was rigged up to some device of which we had no idea to its purpose. On top of the sarcophagus lay the pinnacle of the metal strap, it was shaped in the guise of the King, he was kneeling on one knee out stretched in his hands was a sword that was pointed down in the same proximity of the strange metal. Beside the strange image of the King was a message written in hieroglyphs, Michelle walked forward and began to translate;

"I, King Castor, being laid in my place of rest, will tolerate no intrusion of my peace and if you have come for riches you will find none on my royal person, take what you want from this place and no harm will come to you, but if you dare open the royal sarcophagus death will follow on all those who participate in this debauchery. Only he who is of good heart may proceed for the right reason and save the people of this great Kingdom."

The guard said, "Back in his day, it was still a Kingdom and not an empire. What worries me is that there may be a protocol for opening his sarcophagus and the wrong move would herald the end of us all. The rest of the traps, as lethal as they were, they were manageable to get through with good odds. This, I feel is different. If we set this baby off in the wrong direction we're all dead." The imperial guards words rang in their ears for a good few moments, then Jack spoke, "Ok then, lets not set this baby off in the wrong direction." The old priest stepped forward and said, "What we know about this is very simple, it is written that by slaying Seth, all will be shown. That is all that has been written about this." Michelle walked over to the sarcophagus and looked over the inscriptions and found nothing, she followed the line of the corners up to the lid of the sarcophagus and onto the lid itself. She gazed at the statue of King Castor with the sword pointed down, she followed the line of the blade right down to the metal seal that had a tiny inscription on it, and she pulled her head up and said, "How could I be so stupid." She turned and said, "The inscription said, Seth the evil one, in Egyptology. The ancient Egyptian people believed if you said somebody's name that was dead they would live forever in the afterworld, so if we drive the sword into the inscription we will be destroying his memory in this life and the one in the here after also. That's it! There must be some way to move the sword." Suddenly the guard that was with them said, "I think I know what to do, the royal guards undergo a ceremony that dates back to the time of Castor. I do believe I know what to do…" Walking forward Jack said, "Are you sure?"

The guard said, "My name is Atlas. Now that you know my name, I am asking you to trust me."

Jack looked him in the eye and saw a man who clearly knew what he was doing. Jack then said, "Atlas be careful please."

The guard nodded in appreciation and walked over to the sarcophagus and looked at the figure of the once great King. He reached out and held the sword, he turned the hilt of the sword towards himself and the sword clicked into place, and he then began to speak, "I, Atlas, pledge to guard the Castorian peoples and their Empress with my dying breath. Into the body of evil I thrust my sword and with the rule of Maat we shall live forever," on saying that he thrust the sword into the seal that contained the inscription of evil, it sliced into the seal and surprisingly the sword went right into the hilt. The metal on the hilt of the sword reacted with the strip of metal and like a fluid movement turned a fiery color, all around they heard the metallic clank of devices activating, suddenly the sarcophagus started to move, the mass of yellow quartzite slid along the metallic strip and revealed the magnificent golden coffin of the King. Next they heard another clank and the coffin was lifted to waist height, it was set on a block of pink polished marble. The coffin was beautiful in its design, he had all the distinguishing features of a pharaoh with his beard finely laid in lapis lazuli, precious stones were inbuilt into his coffin, all over the lid of the coffin were the remains of flowers that were put there by his vizier, no doubt the sweet smell still had a strong aroma. They set about opening the coffin and it was an easy proposition, they lifted the lid and set it over by the back wall. They looked into the coffin and were confronted by the dull sight of a black sheet, it was lovingly placed over his body before he was entombed, and they carefully lifted the sheet with as much respect as could be given. As they lifted the sheet the dust became airborne and a cloud of dust filled the burial chamber. They folded the sheet and waited for the dust to settle, then they looked down and the sight which confronted them was an old man of gentle years as if he had been buried yesterday. They could make out facial aspects, he was clean shaven and had good teeth, which was rare for a person of such importance, in the mist of power they normally had a very sweet diet which ate away the teeth and wore them down badly, as well as the bread that they ate, it had a very thick consistency also like beer this had a bad affect of the poor as well as the rich. His arms were crossed over and in each one was his crook and flail, by his side lay the staff of power, given to him by the Kitni leader all those years ago. Exios stepped forward and reached in and lifted the staff, he held it aloft and gazed upon its beauty. It was encrusted with unknown gems that they could not identify. At the top of the staff there was a clasp and in that clasp was the source of all this mystery and power, a large translucent crystal which caught a little of the light that was available. It shone with the beauty of a diamond. They placed the lid back on top of the coffin and walked away from the pink block of granite which also doubled as the Kings canopic shrine. The guard Atlas walked over to the sarcophagus and asked everybody if they were ready. They all agreed that they were and with that he pulled the sword out of the seal and returned it to its rightful position. They suddenly heard the same events of metallic mechanics that opened the sarcophagus, close it. First the King was lowered back into his resting place and the sarcophagus realigned itself and then covered the Kings resting place where it was destined to be. "Right," shouted Jack, "We're getting out of here right now. Move!" With that everybody retraced their footsteps back along the antechamber and back out onto the main passage. They walked past the beasts they had slain getting into this place, the shattered remains of the shattered crystal that, not so long ago held its arsenal of deadly vaporized gas. They reached the marble steps which took them up on to the same level of the main passage as the spear pit. As they edged their way past the pit, they looked down and gazed in horror at the young guard impaled on the spears. They walked carefully back to the entrance of the tomb where the Empress was waiting. On seeing Exios with the staff she almost broke her composure, at the knowledge that her true love was still alive,

"You have the staff of power; you have all done very well indeed. Come let us hurry, the allied armies are in the greatest danger of being destroyed." Walking up the great stairway the Empress asked, "I believe there were two royal guards, now there is only one?"

"Yes, your majesty," replied the remaining guard, "The other guardsman did not survive the mission, he was killed on the way in." Sparing the Empress the gory details he quieted off into solemn reflection as he respectfully retired to his position at the head of the royal guard. On her way to the top she reflected her emotions in a comment, "Jack, I fear this conflict will claim more young victims before if is finished."

Jack asked the Queen, "What do we know about this staff of power?"

"All that is written about it in the archives is that when held aloft in front of our army it will take affect then, however it did not say anything about the nature of the staff or what it would do. All that we can surmise is that it deactivates their technology in some way or another." Smiling at Exios she said, "If the gods are kind, we will be victorious and the forces of darkness will be defeated and peace will be restored in this land." They retraced their footsteps back into the funerary temple of King Castor and from there into the temple of Zeus where she gave up a short prayer for the lives of all her subjects and for all her soldiers fighting on the newly erected front with King Riceos and general Lieysin. They then hurriedly walked out of the great temple and boarded the same craft which took them there. They lifted off and with a different sense of urgency took off and headed towards the water fall and with a mighty crash they were through the other side heading away from the mountain that mimicked a massive pyramid. They gained height and started off at breakneck speed, the pilot reached the Empress and said, "Your majesty, we are now at top speed, it will take us at least a day and a half to reach the entrenched positions of general Lieysin and King Riceos. I believe they have pulled back to a more promising defensive position." The man who walked back in respective protocol looked like a real veteran of many conflicts and was sharp with his crew, shouting orders and running drills. The ship was awash with water from the water fall and was slip prone in some areas. As he looked off in the viewing platform, Richard approached him and asked, "When it's time we fight?"

"Yes, if that is what the men have decided, yes ,my friend we fight," looking pleased, he stood back and said, "With pleasure sir, I'll start weapons checks now and fire checks later." Looking at Richard, Jack smiled and said, "Very good captain, proceed." With that Richard saluted Jack and headed for the crews quarters and started carrying out those orders, "Men, up now", with that, one of the mercenary vets stood up and shouted, "Hu-rrah! Let's roll." They started striping down their weapons and preparing for what they knew best, war. They had been selected from all over the world; they were the best of all their profession. Jack had under his command, ten of the most highly trained killers in the world beside him and all of them together could fight off a small army.

CHAPTER 15.

Back at the forward command centre King Riceos and Lieysin were concocting a new stratagem. To their immediate front was the Kitni onslaught, to the rear of them was the meadows of outer Pramidia, after those came a baron desert to the east, looking at the map general stopped pacing the room and concentrated on the task ahead. "Our main task is to engage the Kitni and hold them back until Jack gets back with that damn staff. If we can fool them into that were running in a rout, we can head for the desert to the east that should give them enough time to get here and save our necks and also put the Kitni into the dark ages, literally." The general stood back and listened to what the intelligence officer had to say, "General, from what we know the Kitni are preparing another offensive to the east, the bulk of their air fleet has been ordered to that area, that is why we have only ran up against lightly armed ships and their mid range attack vessels which are still dangerous, but still with our numbers we can deal with. However, if we run into the combined Kitni fleet they, without a doubt will destroy our air and ground forces..." The King intervened with a cheerful comment, "What if the entire allied fleet got here at the same time?"

"That would make the difference in life and death, your majesty," replied the intelligence officer.

Turning to his captains he ordered the fleet to leave the small islands surrounding the Philios islands and make its way there. General Lieysin spoke candidly with the King, "You do know if we fail, you will have no way of protecting your people against a Kitni attack?" Looking at the old general he replied, "We have a few measures in place if it all goes wrong, but do not think that any Asronas will surrender. We will all fight on to the end," smiling at his old acquaintance King Riceos said, "Thank you for your concern old friend, the one thing that's true in life my friend, is that we all walk a path, sometimes it can be smooth and sometimes it can be rocky," laughing the King said, "It just depends where that path happens to be." With that he motioned for the general to come over closer, he lifted his finger and pressed it onto the map he then looked up at the general and smiled as he said, "I think I found that path I was talking about." Looking down at the map, general Lieysin noticed that in the desert to the east there was a large cavern, enough room for the armies and air core of the allies to hide until they had a chance to strike back at the Kitni. It was wide looking on the map and was situated at the top of a mountain range and had both defensive and offensive properties. "Just what we were looking for, the Kitni would not know what had hit them. The only thing was their land forces would have more mobility on open ground and would be in their millions and they could also call on there superior technologies to come to bare as well as there air assault regiments." The King looked wearily and said, "Very well, however I can tell you one thing, if Jack doesn't get here on time we are all in a lot of trouble," turning from the table the King commanded "Strike camp and make for the following coordinates…" The allied armies of the Asronas and Castorian's filled into air transports and prepared to take off, as they waited the Kitni launched an attack on the ground forces designed to demoralize the men. They shelled the outlaying positions with high explosive rounds, after the onslaught a massive Kitni control ship circled over head and started to drop something over the side. At first they didn't know what it was, then to their horror they discovered that they were the severed heads of the dead and wounded left behind. The King ran outside and roared at the ship, "You will all pay for this with your lives, do you hear!" Screaming at the ship he made out the shape of a figure laughing on board one of there observation platforms, the general stood beside the King and raised his hand and activated his console on his arm. He used the zoom function and zeroed in on the two Kitni standing on board, he spat with fury and cursed "Risard and his bastard commander Hesser," the King rolled his head to the side and calmly without rendered emotion he spoke only two words, "Open Fire!" "Direct it at the observation deck of that monstrosity." All his gunners' shells hit their mark, but to no avail, the Kitni ship was simply too well shielded to cause them damage. The reflections of the impact of the blasts could be felt from the floor of the woods, a bubble like effect spread over the ship protecting its inhabitants from the fire being taken from the ground. The King looked at the general and said, "If they are over head, how will we retreat?" The general said, "I have taken care of that." Suddenly the Castorian flag ship 'Conquer' made its impressive entrance into the theatre of battle. The generals alert went off in his console, he answered, it was his air commander, General Garrison, "Good afternoon general, I am here to give a rear action so that your men can get away unscathed." General Garrison looked serious and said, "Old friend, go save the army, save the people, save the empire," he smiled and saluted by bringing his fist down hard on his breast plate. He then said in a soldier like tone "permission to open fire on the enemy vessel general?"

"With regret old friend, yes," the communication shut down, the supply transports powered up and started its ascent into the sky. The Conquer opened fire at the Kitni control vessel, unlike the ground bombardment this was more sustained and powerful, their shields started to strain with the pounding that was being given to the Kitni ship. Suddenly cracks started to appear in the shield and as they took off, the couple watching from the observation deck ran into the bowels of the ship for protection. Other Kitni ships quickly appeared on the scene and started to fire on the Conquer. She started to breakup from the deadly assault, the King and general Lieysin stood on deck and watched the commander of the Conquer turn and look at them as he was engulfed in a sea of fire. The general looked down and said, "I am ashamed. I could do nothing…" the King intervened, "Do not worry, he did not die in vain my friend, he has given us the time we need to fix what is broken."

Aboard the imperial transport the news had just been received that the Queens flag ship had just been destroyed by the Kitni. The Empress was furious; she was pacing the deck of the transport in a flurry of emotions, "The captain as well as three hundred of my soldiers in one moment, all gone," slowing down a little she walked towards the railing that lined the deck of the transport. She stood there silent for a moment and turned to her captain and ordered that they be transported on to a military vessel as not to arouse any suspicion. Jacks men had just finished all their weapons checks and were ready for war. Jack himself was armed with the usual tools reserved for the art of warfare his MP5 hung by his shoulder his side arm a glock 9mm was securely fastened to his holster, on his belt diagonally hung was his combat knife, he had designed it himself and fashioned its strangely curved blade, which he primarily had designed for throwing and was handy in close quarters combat. Heir Strauss walked over to Jack and asked him how he felt, "Nervous, but strangely eager to get down to business," replied Jack. Looking at the old man he sensed that he was reminiscing through the mists of time. The German had an MP5 also and said it reminded him of the weapon he had issued to him when he was in the Africa core. Looking at it he said, "This one is lighter," Jack burst out laughing and replied, "Then as now, I have no doubt you will have to use it again." Seeing the irony in what Jack had said, he smiled and replied, "That is most likely how it will come to pass my friend."

The ship had started to come to a halt and the vibrations echoed through the large vessel. One of Jacks men ran down from the observation platform and said, "We're docking with another vessel and this time its one of their military class attack vessels." At that moment Exios ran in and informed us of the Queens plans, "It appears that we are getting onto the other ship for the remainder of the flight. Apparently it's better armed than this one and we will not be as easy to pick out as we will be in disguise until we reach our destination. Hail to our impending battle!" clutching the hilt of his sword he looked at us and spoke the unforgettable words, "it seems we are going to tango with fate and as fortune has it fate will tango with us," smiling he said, "let's go and pick a fight." With that, they all followed Exios onto the military escort; they headed through the side door and onto a floating platform. As they started to walk across they noticed the size of the beast that they were boarding. It was charcoal grey and had two white stripes on the tail of the ship; the decks were all much more heavily armored and everywhere there was firing positions that were reminiscent of the gun loops in a medieval castle in Europe. Castorian troops were everywhere in their heavy armor, up ahead Jack caught sight of the Empress who was conversing with the commander of the vessel as they drew closer they heard the captains apologies for not having the suitable quarters fitting a royal person of her stature. Dismissing this, the Queen reassured him that the quarters of a Castorian soldier held no shame for her and asked him how long they would be until they reached general lieysins position. He replied, "Half a day your majesty," the Queen thoughtfully nodded and ordered the commander to proceed. They heard the clank of the platform retract back into the ship and then they heard the drive mechanism engage. Jack and his men stowed there equipment in their makeshift rooms and proceeded to the observation deck to catch a glimpse of the departing ship they had been on. Suddenly there was an alarm and the captain came onto the intercom and said, "We are going into top speed, so secure your persons accordingly," Jack looked at Richard and said, "In other words, grab on to something and hold tight." The ship then started its acceleration, the other ship just vanished within ten seconds and the landscape was moving very quickly. On the way to the location they picked up two other escorts and amazingly the ships all joined together to make one massive fort like structure. On first appearances they believed that the transformation would slow them down but to their astonishment the craft went faster, the landscape was now moving so fast that first impressions gave one the belief that they were watching a globe being slowly turned on its axis. Onto the deck walked the Empress, she then apprised them of their situation, "King Riceos and general Lieysin are in full retreat. The Kitni army is in its millions and they are heading for a natural cavern in the eastern deserts outside Pramidia. That is where we will make our stand," the Empress said no more but they could all sense her worry. Standing beside her Exios smiled and nodded in a reassuring gesture that comforted the troubled Empress.

On their way towards the cavern the allied army and air core were being harried all the way by Kitni riders. The King said, "Strange the way they send small ships to engage us," the general nodded in agreement and replied, "They are saving their best ships for something, it's like they're nibbling away at us."

On the Kitni command vessel, Risard was laughing with Hesser and complementing him on a job well done. Risard said, "I would like you to if possible, to take alive the King and that old dog Lieysin. We will hold off our best ships until they stop running and then we will finish them in a humiliating last battle," opposing this Commander Hesser replied, "Finish them off now my lord or we will regret it,."

"No Hesser, your finely tuned sense of militarism is not going to spoil my fun," with that commander Hesser complied with risard and then removed himself to his command deck. Walking over to his second in command he gave the usual bland expression that was by now evident that he was not amused by Risards casual outlook towards finishing off his enemy. "That man is going to make a mistake and when he does it will probably be the end of him." Asking his superior, "Commander do you think the castorians will be able to resist us when the time comes?" Looking at the shaking officer Hesser radiated a confident and defiant look, "For a while at first, but as they start to commit reserves that they cant afford to replace, this is what will inevitably defeat them in the end."

"And the staff they talk about in the ranks, does it exist?"

"No it doesn't," dismissing it as, "a fabled myth that was invented by the empire to create worry and panic in our ranks and to make us think twice about attacking." The young officer walked away content in believing everything that Hesser had said. Hesser thought into himself, 'at the moment you need to believe what we need you to, Tomorrow, however may be a different story.'

Chapter 16.

Onboard the Empresses vessel, the team was waiting for their first engagement. Jack and Richard had them out on patrol on every deck along with the other soldiers. Suddenly Jack was reached on his shortwave, it was Richard, and he shouted, "Incoming bogies, twelve o'clock!" As he ran to the deck that Richard was on the general alert went off followed by the voice of the captain, "action stations, this is not a drill. To your battle stations," As we ran to fill in positions that had not been filled already Jack shouted, "There," he mounted the czar general purpose machine gun on the tripod and took aim and waited for the enemy vessel to come in range. Its black menacing shape came into range and from what he could make out from its mannerisms; it was clearing its deck for firing. It was then that they heard the command from the captain who was, by this stage, on site with his men in full battle armor he shouted, "Open fire." Their training took over and they began to engage the enemy vessel. "Our gun battery's opened up," they looked in horror as the ships shielding took the general bombardment and the bubble like effect was at last seen. Jack turned to the captain, "Does he have to drop his shields in order to fire?"

"Yes, as do we."

"Right," replied Jack, he ordered his men to fire on the ship when they were preparing to fire back. Turning back Jack asked the captain, "any weak spots?"

"Yes mid ship is where they store the power supplies for their canon, however there is a problem with this tactic, their shield is invisible except when they receive a hit and you get the crackling bubble effect." Jack turned to the captain and said, "Aim all your guns at the mid ships and wait for my command," the captain looked at the Empress and she nodded at him to comply to Jacks orders, he looked at Jack and said, "as you command." Jack took one of the sniper rifles from his men and looked through the sights, the scene that presented itself was a mass of activity, the crew was running on top deck and a figure of authority was sighted relaying orders to his men. He then scanned the gun decks for movement, they were prepping the guns for range and were preparing to fire. Jack raised his hand and waited for the captain of the black beast to give the order to drop shields, when he saw the man look behind into his command centre and give the nod, he watched as a man walked over to a control centre and started to punch in commands to the terminal. He then waited for his commanders order, suddenly he turned and nodded the man punched the final command for the shields to be turned off. Jack took aim and fired; the commander took a direct hit in the head and dropped. Jack turned and shouted, "Fire," the ships complement opened fire, first with the short range weapons that obliterated the first deck where the commander had been standing. The second, more powerful weapons opened fire and ripped into the shell of the Kitni ship, a deep glow of orange quickly amassed into an uncontrollable fire ball which blew the ship apart. The flying debris clattered against the ship and left its burning mass flying towards the ground. A roar erupted from the soldiers on board and fluctuated from one side of the ship to the other. The Empress walked forward and congratulated Jack on a job well done and by the look of it just in time too. It was then that they noticed they were coming in sight of the secret location where they found a large crescent moon shape naturally eroded out of the landscape. Richard said, "This should be enough to give us adequate protection until King Riceos and general Lieysin arrive." By this time the Empresses vessel had completed its wonderful metamorphose, three more ships had docked with her and it now resembled a mobile fortress. They landed directly behind the unusual formation and immediately began to disembark troops who took up positions on the top of the range. Jack and his men were to be personally addressed by the Empress. She and Exios walked outside and she smiled at those around her, she looked at Heir Straus and said, "We thank you for your gallant efforts, but it has occurred to me that this is not your fight, so I have arranged a small vessel to take you back to the tomb entrance if you so please, and if you choose to, no animosity will be held against you. If you want to stay and fight you are most welcome by our side." The old German spoke back, "Your majesty the men are under my employ so I cannot speak for them. I however will let them do that for themselves." Looking back at the small band of soldiers he said, "What do you think?" One big man moved out of the crowd and said, "We reckoned you would give us a choice, well the guys believe they are ready for what comes," and with that the burly American lit up a cigar, took a few puffs then said, "bring it on." That was the final say and in a way also if they failed there would be no way home because they had just burned their only bridge home.

Jack and Michelle said there goodbyes in the empty corridor "Don't worry, if I don't comeback you will be fine."

"Jack what if the staff doesn't work?" looking her straight in the eye he replied, "after all this hype it would need to," he then kissed her and led his men out into the front lines which had been newly built. Exios took his leave from the Empress, what was said between them no one will ever know. They took an infantry transport to their positions and dug in awaiting their Kitni opponents. Jack pulled out his binoculars and scanned what seemed to be a never ending landscape for enemy activities. Suddenly he heard the distant hum of an engine that sounded like it was in trouble; one of the Castorian soldiers stood up and said, "That's them, that's King Riceos and general Lieysin." They only had three of the five transports left and were in danger of loosing a forth, they were being harried by enemy attack ships, small in design but deadly. Jack and the allied general on the ground agreed that the best way to protect the crippled ships was to pull them in behind our protective fire cover. The general on the ground was called Eiosol, he turned on the console that an engineering crew had brought them and scanned the ships for danger. "Their communications are down and they have hardly any weapons available."

Jack said, "Can we establish a communications link with them?"

"Yes," replied general Eiosol, doing so at the consul he worked at the device pushing buttons and making checks until we heard a welcome voice. It was that of King Riceos, Jack dropped his head in relief and said, "Thank god for that."

"The general is badly injured and will need emergency surgery when we land, Jack did you get it?"

"Yes King Riceos, we got it."

"Thank the gods, it was not all in vain," the general said to the King. "Another half mile and you will be under our protective shield,"

"Copy," replied the King, "on our way." The general turned to Jack and said, "Time to get your men ready," smiling at the general he turned to his men and shouted, "Safeties off!" He turned around again and said, "My men are ready."

"Aim your fire at the smaller attackers, at the moment they're doing the most damage," the general said, "Oh yes; you can't use your weapons…"

"What?" replied Jack, "The peltas rifle has a restraint built into it that only allows you to hit the attacking ships, and it's safer."

Jack turned to his men and gave the order, "Put your weapons beside you and pick up a peltas rifle," after they had been all equipped the general started to count back from ten. Waiting for the last number seemed to last an eternity Jack stretched his neck and took aim until it finally came, 'one, open fire!" screamed the general. Jack squeezed the trigger, he had targeted a small attack class vessel, the first shot hit the winged section of the fighter and it swerved from side to side. The second and third hit the cockpit blowing the glass canopy over the pilot, "Now I have you," shouted Jack and with that he squeezed the trigger once more and the pilot was blown to bits, his ship then lifelessly dropped from the sky and landed in a ball of flames on the desert floor. Jacks men followed his example and used his tactics, aiming for the cockpit, it seemed to be the only Achilles heal the small craft had and they found that out of the control ships range, its shielding was not so effective and was open to manipulation from ground forces. The soldiers took full advantage of this and soon they were dropping out of the sky like flies, but being so numerous, it made little effect on the plight of the remaining ships. Jack shouted at general Eiosol to order the reaming three batteries's to open up. "Yes I know, I was waiting for them to cram in as many attackers as they could and by then it would be too late," with that he pointed at the officer in the second row to open up and the sky was filled with Kitni debris. They were falling out of the sky like leaves in the autumn season, with that the three ships were able to dock safely behind the Empresses command fortress vessel. Kitni aggression for the moment stopped and the remainder of the attackers returned to base.

King Riceos waited until his friend and allied commander was taken to safety, he mounted his horse dressed in fresh armor and shouted a command to his troops to fall in with the rest of the soldiers on the newly built frontier. He rode off in the direction of Jacks men and oncoming danger. As he rode through the ranks of men marching to their positions he shouted words of encouragement and bravery, he rode on until he caught a glimpse of Jack and greeted him with a hearty slap on the back, "You've made it. Good to see you my boy!" Jack smiled and replied, "Good to see you, your majesty," at that moment someone shouted Jacks name, it was one of his men, "More activity sir." Jack and the King ran over to his post and Jack looked through his binoculars and could not believe his eyes, three, no its six the King put his hand on his shoulder and said, "I am afraid it's more," pointing in the other direction. They were black in color and were the size of the Empresses mobile fortress. Jack said, "They're troop transports aren't they?"

"Yes," replied King Riceos, "And each is capable of carrying five hundred thousand enemy infantry." Landing in separate blocks they started to deploy into combat blocks, the first five hundred were assault troops and took up their positions at the front of the army and they were equipped with some kind of shielding that was built onto their armor. The shielding had a green tint to it and the men nick-named them the jelly babies. This aroused great amusement in the camp, Jacks team laughed uncontrollably he turned and saw that the King had one of his puzzled looks and bent down and said to Jack, "Jelly babies?"

"Yes your majesty. Where we come from they are a child's sweet which comes in different colors," the expression on the Kings face changed to amusement and he bellowed out from the bottom of his lungs, "A child's delicacy?" by now the King was unable to stop laughing and it became infectious. The soldiers followed suit and began to laugh which was broken by the movements of the Kitni troop's transports. Six landed to their point and another to the rear. Out of these ships marched entire regiments, it was one of the most wonderful and terrible things Jack have ever seen. Each block of infantry would wait until they were pointed to their appointed position and it was brilliantly conceived and smoothly executed. When all troops were in position the command ship carrying Risard and Commander Hesser moved right above them and then suddenly a small craft left the control ship and landed on the desert floor. It was Commander Hessers personal transport craft, a guard then surrounded the craft and escorted the general to his position. He had chosen, as always, to lead his men into battle. He switched his own personal shield on and then started a communication to Risard. "My lord we are ready to proceed with the air bombardment."

"Very well, good luck Hesser," and the communication was cut.

On the ground in the allied camp the shout went out that an air bombardment was imminent.

"Yes," replied the King, "They're pooling all their cursers in one place." The King borrowed Jacks binoculars and browsed the situation, "They're opening their gun ports, take cover!" The ridge that we were occupying was slowly being pounded to pieces; the King opened a channel to the Empress and asked when it would be ready. The Empress replied, "I am working on that matter now, there seems to be encryption codes on the side of them and I am trying to decode them."

"Good your majesty, please hurry we are being torn to pieces." The bombardment started to take its toll on the soldiers in the frontier positions. Body pieces were flying in the air, the atmosphere was thick with the stench of death, one of Jacks men was blown in half, mounds of earth were scattering across the ridge slowly changing the lay of the landscape. All of a sudden the bombardment stopped, a scurry of activity alerted us to look at the Kitni lines. Kitni commanders were running to their positions and with that the general commander Hesser walked out in front about one hundred feet and with one hand signal the entire Kitni army started its advance. The pounding of the marching feet was like being shook, the ridge moved the loose soil as if it were going through a sieve. Looking down in horror Jack said, "Any word on the staff yet?" "Have faith in the Empress, she will be successful, she needs yet more time." Looking at his men Jack said, "Well then, let's give it to her." Jack lifted his tripod mounted heavy machine gun onto the mound of earth and shouted at Hesser, "You there, with the frown," Jack blew him a kiss then gave him twenty rounds from the weapon. To the surprise of the Kitni, his shield did not save him. He was raked with gunfire right in front of his men. Jack shouted to his men who were preparing mortars "fire!" off went the first the first mortar shell taking a few seconds to find its mark which it done when it took out two of the infantry commanders on the ground. Then went the second which ripped through the Kitni front line but all to no avail the Kitni simply replaced their loses in seconds as if they had never been there. Hesser's dead body lay in a twisted mass, blood flowing from the corpse; it appeared to be blacker than normal. His body was pulled behind the lines and returned to the shuttle that had brought him, the amassed Kitni army then continued its march slow and menacing.

The King contacted his master of horse and ordered him to bring out the best of his stock and any others that he could find. Jack looked at him and said, "You've got to be joking, you're not going to charge that?"

"Indeed," replied the King with a smile on his face, it almost mirrored a kind of weak insanity, "Indeed Jack I am, I am going to ride into the amassed evil and cut out its heart."

"When?"

"In fifteen minutes when I have all I need assembled."

"Fair enough," shouted Jack for they could not hear each other for the marching of the oncoming Kitni army. The King laughed and said, "It's been a pleasure to meet you Jack, just incase this does not go well." Asronas heavy troops and cavalry made their way up to the ridge and prepared for the battle that was about to begin. Jacks men were sniping for members of importance in the Kitni ranks but they had caught on to this and recalled them to the back lines. Looking at the distance we saw something emerge from one of the Kitni ships that had brought their infantry. They were in many respects alike a version of the tank, from the soldier's talk they heard that they were mobile artillery for the support of the infantry and from the green glow all were suitably shielded from attack. The enemies march came to an end and the mobile artillery positioned itself behind the massed formation of Kitni troops.

Back aboard the Empress's mobile fortress, she was trying to decode the hieroglyphs on the side of the power staff her wisest vizier Seliok was appointed the task to decipher them and finally he started to read the translation, "Take this staff aloft where the eagles do soar, on one knee drop and touch the power crystal. When it burns with the fire of the volcano, release, and once more peace will reign in this land he who carries the power staff must be of royal blood, that of Alexander's." Where eagles sore? That I take it is a reference to a high up place, a guard steps forward and said, "Your majesty, may I be permitted to talk?"

"Of course soldier," replied the Empress.

"The highest place is in the observation tower on the mobile fortress, it towers over the desert floor and is about one hundred feet higher than the defensive ridge that King Riceos is fighting on now."

Looking at the guard the Empress replied, "Young man, you may have just saved the day," the young man nodded in agreement and simply stepped back and stood to attention. The Empress made her way to the lift that would bring her and her vizier to the top of the observation tower. It seemed like an eternity getting to the top but eventually they got there.

Jack noticed from his position that he could see the Empress and alerted the King to the development. Just at that moment the console hailed us, it was the Empress, "King Riceos I have found how to work this device, prepare for what ever happens." The Queen dropped down on one knee and placed the power staff on its end, to her amazement the staff opened into a tripod at the end which allowed her to release her grip on the device.

On the Kitni ship, Risard was in a gloomy mood after the untimely demise of Commander Hesser. He noticed however that the Queen was clutching some kind of device, he ordered his men to magnify the image and to his horror, "No, no it can't be, they couldn't have, it's the power staff!" He turned to his second in command and ordered every one back, "My lord I cannot there is not enough time," Risard turned and looked helplessly as the Queen activated the device.

The Empress took hold of the crystal and touched it with her hands, the staff came to life with a glow of deep red radiating within the crystal, and a computerized voice came out of the staff, "scanning for genetic identification," the Queen stood back and allowed the device to scan her genetics. The laser in the device scanned her body and then said "Genetic identification assessed, the Alexandrian gene has been identified. Hail ruler of Castorian," with that the device sent out a blinding light that swept across the desert floor and across the sky. Brilliant white in color and it had a piercing effect almost as if it could sense evil, at that moment the Kitni mobile artillery opened up and started to devastate the ridge Jack and his men were dug in and were taking cover from the onslaught, suddenly the blinding light swept over them and shielded them from further oncoming fire they raised their heads to find that the device was shielding them and was growing in size. It swept by the amassed Kitni troops, the green glow of their body shields dissipated and their weapons would not work. The mobile artillery simply seized and powered down, the operators jumping out in disbelief. Once the artillery had been taken care of the King ordered that they be taken out. The Kings badly shot up vessel opened fire destroying all the mobile artillery units, "Ok Jack, its fun time." King Riceos mounted his horse and offered one to Jack who accepted, jumping up on to his horse he looked at Richard and said, "Look on the bright side, when am I ever going to get to do this again," the King said, "Stay with me Jack, this I believe your new at. Remember draw your sword when only when you need it." Exios mounted at his right and started to laugh, "Heed that lesson well, if you draw your sword too early it can unbalance you and as a result you could fall off. I suggest that you use your side arm until you are in close enough to use the sword."

Jack looked to his right and to his left; all he could see was Asronas and Castorian cavalry, their amour shining against the brilliant light coming off the power staff. The King rode out on point and drew his sword, looking back at his men who were expecting a long speech but to their surprise he smiled and simply said, "For those who have died!" The King then returned his sword to its sheath and began at a slow trot, the rest followed, the horse's mane gently blowing around my wrists; it was a strange felling of pure freedom, if indeed there is such a thing. In that moment he felt it, the King started to gallop and they followed, the ground shaking with the cavalry. The Kitni army was at this time retreating, it's once ranks of disciplined formations breaking and running, turning into a routed rabble that once resembled an army. The front ranks stood fast and waited for the assault of the oncoming allied cavalry led by King Riceos, at a gallop King Riceos rode. As they crossed the last short distance King Riceos drew his sword and screamed, "CHARGE!" The muscles of the horse shined and glistened he watched in disbelief as he rode out in front about twenty yards ahead of his men. He rode right in to the amassed, sword cutting to all sides, the rest then crashed into the front line of the Kitni defense without their shielding and weapons the only thing they could rely on was their swords. It was like something out of a medieval battle, Jack used his side arm until he had no space to use it he then switched to sword and began to slash and cut, he felt a strange connection with his sword as he cut his way deeper into the Kitni ranks. Looking behind him Richard and general Eiosol were bringing up the allied infantry, then Jack dismounted and Richard threw him his czar heavy machine gun. Laughing at Richard he said, "I think I'll stick with this!" He then pointed it in the general direction of Kitni and pulled the trigger. There was so many, how could he miss, zip went the rounds out of Jacks gun as they made a whining sound then a series of meat like thuds. This close the rounds were going through three or four of the Kitni combatants. Suddenly a warrior dressed in black ran out of the masses and cut his weapon in half, he turned and the masked aslant prepared to strike again when suddenly Exios rode past and decapitated the warrior. His headless body slumped to the ground and his head rolled at Jacks feet, unnervingly Jack shivered and laughed it off. Just then Jack remembered, he grabbed Richard and said, "What about the troops at the rear?" Richard replied, "No worries, Ottilin and the imperial guard are taking care of them."

"Ok then, onward."

They fought hard for the most of the day until the Kitni lines began to founder a mass exodus of millions. The battle field was laden with the Kitni dead and our own, a figure emerged from the front and raised his sword aloft and shouted, "We have taken the field." A roar went up from the victorious allies which almost deafened Jack. He relayed his fear to the King about Ottilin; he nodded in agreement and called for horses. He ordered his commanders to secure the field, they mounted the horses that had been brought and started to ride in the direction of the defensive ridge to where they could see the imperial guard with its newly appointed General Ottilin. They were deployed in formations resembling blocks. Although outnumbered by the Kitni, the old general

Lieysin was watching everything from his bedside and was in close contact with Ottilin. Suddenly the fortress opened fire on the massed Kitni formations; the decimation they suffered was unspeakable. Once the bombardment was over, the old general gave his last piece of advice, "General Ottilin, Attack!" then sadly the old man died, sliding back into his bed and closing his eyes. He had a serine smile on his face as he could take solace in the fact that his Empress and empire were safe. At his side the Empress sat in tears as she said goodbye to the man who had been her father figure, teacher and friend. She stood up and said, "We will meet again old friend," she said nothing more and returned to her observation tower to see what progress was being made. The young General Ottilin drew his sword and shouted, "For general Lieysin who has just died. Charge!" The front ranks of the imperial guard marched off behind Ottilin giving a stretched effect that made them look more numerous. He started to run and the rest followed suit, Ottilin ran right up to a commander who was shaking, the commander drew his sword but Ottilin had cut him down before he had a chance to counter his blow. Passion ruled the day and battle got heated, the spray of blood and sinew lay everywhere, decapitated bodies and limbs scattered about the battlefield, it was not long before they broke there formations and scattered to the four winds. Jack and his men were back together on the ridge and Jack turned to Richard and said, "Look there's Risard." Richard said, "We have a few mortar shells left?"

Jack replied, "No good, we're out of range..." King Riceos intervened with a comment, "Yes but my gun ship is not." The King raised his captain with his communications device and ordered him to take out one of his engines to do no more than that to slow him down. The King then said as he smiled at Jack, "It will be a slow journey back to his capital Glazeer and every once in a while I will blow off a portion of his ship to see how he likes it," laughing, they all headed back to the fortress command center they were met by the Empress who looked glum. She looked at us all and said, "I am afraid general Lieysin has died." The King took this news to heart and replied, "The general was a good man and a brave soldier who personified excellence in all those who knew him and I will miss him," the King looked at the Empress and said, "Risard is going to pay for this."

"But first," replied the Empress, "On to glazeer city in the Kitni heartland."

They waited two hours for Risard to build up the general impression that he had successfully escaped, after that they had all their troops on board they took off and followed the spewed wreckage that Risards ship was making, with no shields he could hardly keep the ship together. It was peeling apart like a jig saw. On the forward deck they saw risard and the look that accompanied him was dire. He was in trouble and he knew it, his eyes were watering and he wondered how his own people could betray him. So he started to ponder all the wrong thoughts, 'my forces have disserted me, 'they fled the battlefield. What shall I do? Who can I trust? Treachery everywhere!' Risard started to go into a whirlwind of madness that seemed to be sucking him down into the abyss from were there was no return. All he could do was await his punishment in his city of Glazeer.

Risards control vessel was the only ship that was not disabled in order to chase him back to the Kitni capital and every once in a while King Riceos fired on his ship blowing off a part and rocking it to its core. Risard tumbled from side to side every time the ship was subjected to cannon fire from the Kings vessel. At this stage the King was on deck with a goblet of wine, and every time Risard's ship was hit he laughed and took another sip of his wine. At his side he had chosen his best blacksmith to sharpen his sword on deck in full view of Risard who cowered in anticipated horror. Once the blacksmith had finished his work he handed the sword back to the King who reached into his pocket and paid the man for services well rendered, into the blacksmiths hands fell a menagerie of gold coins, the man looked at the King and said, "sire, this is a Kings ransom. It is too much for the sharpening of only one blade," the King looked at the honest blacksmith and said, "For the work this sword has in store, in my opinion, it is not nearly enough." The King smiled and returned his sword to its sheath, "and there blacksmith we will end our conversation," the man nodded with admiration and backed off towards the door.

Jack and Michelle were once again united and glad to see each other. Then Michelle berated him for taking part in a cavalry charge, answering back in his defense, "I survived didn't I?"

"Just about, please Jack don't do anything so stupid again."

Looking into her beautiful deep blue eyes he said, "Ok I promise darling, besides the Kitni are defeated."

Looking at him scornfully she said, "Ok then," and she smiled and they playfully kissed in Jacks private quarters. At the rear of the Empresses fortress ship, she and Exios went about the sad job of organising General Lieysins funeral and embalming, then eventual entombment. His corpse was carried aboard the Queens private transport, his body was carried on his shield supported by spear carriers at the front. The newly elected general Ottilin escorted the great mans body back to Castorian city, the body was laid out on the command deck of the ship where as custom dictates, four soldiers of ordinary rank stood guard over his body. General Ottilin took personal command of the vessel and ordered it to the capital with all haste, standing at the outer quarters of the command deck the general saw the Queen smile at him and waved goodbye. He returned the smile and waved back; he then stood to attention and slammed his breastplate with his fist, the salute to a commanding officer or in his cases his monarch. The couple watched as the ship passed into a cloud of mist and vanished. Exios put his arm around her and reassured her everything would be all right.

Meanwhile, back at the tomb, Joe was in the mobile command centre and watching the enemy advance the first line of defense where the automatic machine gun positions were which locked onto body heat and opened fire at the direct source of body heat. They were located about half a mile from the second line of defense where all the veteran soldiers were waiting for them. The attackers ran over the hill, they seemed to be carrying a tracking device which was guiding them, all of a sudden the automatic positions opened up, the guy running at point got the brunt of the concentrated fire it, blew him of his feet and he flipped right over, slapping the ground his lifeless body lay peppered in gunfire. At the first sounds of gunfire Joe pulled out his side arm and knocked off the safety and calmly walked over to the detail that were in charge of guarding the tomb. He had a word with them and then he went and joined the troops in their quickly constructed bunkers. By this stage the gunfire was roaring away in the distance and they were counting the body drops on an inferred camera. The large American who was called John turned around and said, "The autos only got around fifty of them," then they heard an explosion, john said, "My god there taking out the auto positions with RPG's, they're wearing some kind of biological suits that don't show up on the heat sensitive sensor, man, they're all gone." Joe looked down at him and said, "It looks like we will have to do this the old fashioned way," knocking the safety off his heckler and cock, "to our positions soldiers," the guy next to him shouted, "hu-rah lets go." Running to the first point of contact Joe saw the first enemy combatant, he squeezed the trigger and the man was hit with the full force of three rounds which went right through him and he dropped dead to the ground, running past one of the men shot the man in the head to make sure. They encountered their first engagement a quarter mile ahead of the main body of enemy, john turned and said, "He must have been scouting out our position and relaying information back to the others, right we wait here and if they succeed we will pull back to the tomb." Over the hill they came in lines of five, the American laughed and said, "I wonder if they would line up." They set off a claymore, the explosion ripped through the first two waves of men leaving only two survivors out of ten. John lifted his rifle and fired twice at two of the stumbling survivors and they fell lifelessly to the ground. John looked at Joe and shouted back to second line after seeing ten more coming over the hill, this time one of them was carrying an RPG rocket launcher, "Take cover," shouted Joe jumping into the ditch, just at that moment there was a loud bang, looking over his shoulder he noticed that they had taken out one of the bunkers that had just been manned on Joes orders. He shouted over to John to take out the guy with the rocket launcher, he shouted back, "Already on it" Looking over he had his light weight sniper rifle on its tripod and with a single shot he took out the trouble maker who dropped dead to the ground and splattered blood dripped from his head onto the ground where it ciphered of into dry granules of desert sand. They got the rest of their guys out of there and proceeded to the next line of resistance. After this one they were in trouble, the only thing left was the tomb, thinking to himself, 'how ironic,' while reloading his weapon he lifted the claymore controls and waited for the first wave of morons to charge and as he waited over came three guys with those cursed rocket launchers and they ran at them and as they did Joe set off the first explosion which ripped through the two of the assassins and John shot the other before he could get squatted and in position. He shouted over, "They will not make that mistake again."

"Agreed, switch to heavy caliber machine guns," and then they came wave after wave and they mowed them down, the sound of bullets ripping through flesh was the order of the night. After killing fifty of the scoundrels his exhausted men backed off to the tomb entrance where the fresh team took over the fighting. There were about seventy five of them left, Joe wondered to himself, 'what is worth the life of so many men, what in the name of god was in that tomb besides the portal, What would make them go so far almost too suicidal proportions? Oh well,' laughing to himself, 'hope it was worth it what ever the hell it was,' "I am a soldier and I have my orders hold or die."

Chapter 17.

On the journey to Glazeer city, they came to the outskirts and saw what seemed to be an area which was awash with poverty. There were people begging on the streets and sickness everywhere. The Empress saw what was happening and remarked, "It seems that Risard has more than we know to answer for." Exios said, "It seams that he has striped the people's wealth to finance the war and left millions hungry." King Riceos landed onboard and was greeted by Jack who asked "have you seen…" "Yes Jack," and they looked at each other and Riceos broke the silence, "what does one do against such a man? Or should I call him a monster? Jack I have ordered my vessel to drop three quarters of our rations over the streets where they need our help most." Looking down they saw old men and children in rags, dirty and even some diseased and lying in the gutter, the stench of death filled the air. The Empress walked in and greeted King Riceos, "Your majesty, I hope I find you in good health?" "Thank you Empress, as you can see I am in a lot better health than those below us."

"Yes Risard has a lot to answer for."

"What do you do with such a man? I thought there would be a quick beheading and it would be all over."

Jack stepped forward and suggested an idea, "Now that we are in the Kitni capital, reinstate the old regime and make Risard face the courts of his own people, manned by his own people and judged by his own people. I would imagine by now he will have no support in any part of Kitni life because of the level of death and disease and starvation he has brought to his own people. The kindest thing he can hope for is a quick death under those circumstances."

The Empress and King Riceos conferred for a few moments and agreed that Jacks idea was the best and would be in everyone's best interests. The Empress admitted that her government had given Zeus' shelter to a few of them, "which I later found out was their version of political asylum"

The party was called out on deck for something, the King walked over, "Risards ship is about to dock at the great hall of Glazeer," gripping the hilt of his sword he said "Come gentlemen we have an insect to deal with." As they looked down at the wondrous sight that awaited them, the whole structure was made of crystal blocks and was breathtaking and had a diamond quality that captured its light and held it within its walls. "You could say, a solitaire of a city," the Empress commented, "No wonder they called it the diamond of the east, I see now."

"Yes," replied King Riceos, "I often heard my father make that remark. Also as a boy he visited this city on a diplomatic errand for his father long ago and always held fond memories of it in his heart. I am glad he is not alive to witness what we have just seen." Shortly after we boarded a small transport after the city hall had been secured by troops the others were sent on a mercy mission to find and feed all those that they could and heal if they deemed necessary, a feeble resistance was put up by Risards personal guard after three of them were killed he was quickly handed over to the allies by senior members of his security detail and in every respect he behaved like a cornered rat, ranting on about the Kitni people building out of the ashes. King Riceos quickly reminded him that he was responsible for much of the anarchy which seemed to reign supreme under his rule as well as the hunger that been generated. On that evening he was hauled before a court of exiled Kitni leaders who opposed his regime. He was escorted into the main audience chamber of the Kitni people, the man in charge named Kosos sat down before him with King Riceos by his side, the old man perched on the edge of the seat and eyed up Risard and then in a sharp tone he said, "Risard you are here to answer charges of high treason and sedition which even in our culture carries the death penalty," shouting at risard he asked the question, "What say you?"

"Not guilty." replied risard in a cocky and arrogant fashion.

"Regardless of what poison comes from your mouth you have been charged and found guilty of high treason and the sentence is what the Kitni people deem it to be."

King Riceos stood up and commanded that the doors be flung open outside where one hundred starved Kitni citizens who were dreadful looking. The King then said, "Risard, you have done us harm, but it is nothing to what you have done to your own people," the new Kitni leader Kosos stood up and said, "Risard, into the hands of the people I resign your fate," the people started to become uneasy, one old woman hobbled over to the brigand, her long white Hair at her waist and screamed, "You!, you took my boy from me and turned him into a killer. I am the only member of my family left alive because they all starved to death with your programs that were designed to feed the army and everybody else was left to rot in your dictator state," the old woman collapsed at his feet and the rest of the crowd started to bay for his blood. Unawares to Risard the old woman had regained some of her composure; she pulled out a crystal bladed knife and plunged it into Risards groin area, driving the knife in so hard it snapped off in the attempt. Looking at the spectacle King Riceos turned to Jack and Richard and commented that was not a bad start at all by any standard. Risard dropped down onto his knees where the rest of the crowd slowly kicked him to death. The populous pulled back and changed their position allowing them to see the terrible sight; Risard was covered by this point in blood and was black from the beating that his own people had given him. They pulled away from the spectacle and watched him die with his broken arms reaching towards the sky in a feeble attempt to justify his actions as Kitni leader. Then his arms dropped and he fell on his side and he died. The victorious King Riceos walked over to his body and knelt by his side and said to the crowd, "You are now free people and can live as such," the King nodded and said, "Peace be upon you." The old woman stood up and brushed herself off and replied, "peace onto you also King Riceos," it was strange to see the King who was normally the professional soldier never showing his emotions, shed a tear and then briskly walk off towards the Asronas landing craft that had brought them. As they left the Kitni capital they wondered if they would ever see it again, on the ground they could see Asronas and Castorian troops serving side by side only a month before this they would be trying to kill each other. Exios and the Empress walked out on to the balcony of the powerful air transport which was by now heading back to Castorian city. The Queen said, "Jack you will never leave our hearts or that of my people, when we get back to castorian city you and your team may return to your world." nodding upwards, "with our blessing," "And mine also…" in barged King Riceos who by this stage was bathed and clean from the enemy blood which had at one point covered his whole body in a horrific sight which even he could not toll. "Jack thank you for your endeavor in the affairs in our world for which we will be forever in your debt," the King and Jack had some light banter on the way home to the impearl city and when the ship was entering the last phase of its journey towards the city they had a sense of lost friendship which had brought them together and in time would make each other stronger. As the ship landed outside the palace everybody went to their rooms for a nights sleep and refreshment, Jack and Michelle bathed and helped each other wash off dirt and blood and sinew which had gathered in dried deposits over Jacks body. After she had made sure he was clean she looked at Jack straight in the eyes and said, "Play time," in her elegant French accent which had a sexual tinge to it. Her jet black hair radiated in the light and even though she had not enough time to wash, it felt like silk flowing through Jacks hands, a beautiful cold feeling ran through Jacks hands as he touched her hair which brought goose bumps to his arms. She ran her hands over the affected areas, his fingertips contracted a little as an electrical surge went through his body spurred on by the adventures which lay ahead but this time there would be no bandits, no deserts, no tombs, no dangerous men, just a beautiful woman laying in his arms. He lifted his arm and gently brought her head back to the side of his neck where he started to caress her neck with loving kisses, he then lifted her hair back around so that he could gain access to the back of her neck where he started to kiss her right down following the line of her spinal column. His hand followed her sleek contours of her side turning on his knee he turned her around facing him and started to kiss from her neck down, his tongue followed the beautiful contours of her breasts and continued right down until he arrived at her navel, which he played with and the delight was apparent to Michelle, she laughed and slithered like a reptile for a minute. Looking at her Jack put his arms around her and lifted her onto the marble surface beside the bathing pool, from this elevated height he would be able to corrupt her body properly, he continued with the same tactic he had employed in the pool and this time he started from her waist and worked down towards her ankle. Her body was by now covered in goose bumps and was still wet from her initial bath, her being was now at a heightened state of pleasure, Jack jumped out of the pool and soaked her as he lay beside her he then started to kiss her and smoothly lift open her leg. He then made love to her, their two bodies sweating and heaving with pleasure as Jack lifted her and flung her down in the bed, her loving expression had turned to that of sexual aggregation, her eyes glistened with the anticipation of what he had in store for her, her mouth was glazed with saliva and her tongue was playing with her lips in a seductive manner, the night hot with the mists of passion, the young lovers continued through the night. The morning came through in a ray of light and the room illuminated with a deep colour of gold which bathed the couple in its rays. Jack turned to Michelle and said, "We will soon be going through the portal back home and then we can look forward to the monotony of our daily lives." Michelle replied, "If that means no more conflict," laughing, "happy days, also the presence of heavily armed men is a sight I will be glad to say good bye to." The pair got up and went and had breakfast, unusually this morning the Empress was not at the head of the table, her servant told us that affairs of state had to be settled and she would see us later. The old German sat down beside us and said, "We will be home in a day or so, I wonder how the rest of my team is getting on in that hot hell hole outside the tomb?" Nicolas was also in attendance that morning and Heir Strauss asked, "How long has the brotherhood of Ammon been in existence?" Nicolas replied, "It began with the meeting with Alexander the great on his death bed so that will give you all food for thought." "Have you ever had any trouble in the order? Asked Heir Straus. Candidly Nicolas nodded and replied, "Yes in the thirteenth century a portion of the members broke away from the main organization over the method of the integration of our plan to find the tomb. When they did they would hold it for as long as possible throughout the ages passing the secret on to one from another, this was deemed to be wrong because the brotherhood of Ammon believed that the tomb would be intertwined in our destiny and at the right time would be shown to us. The other breakaway group is very violent and would do anything to get their hands on the tomb."

Jack asked, "May I ask, what was your major disagreement over Nicolas?"

"Yes," replied Nicolas, "When they discovered the tomb they argued that it would be better to ask for military help from the Castorian's in order to once again secure Alexander's empire which they are bound to do by law. If they are asked of course, if not they will not."

Jack nodded and said, "I see, are they still active?"

"No," replied Nicolas, "As far as I know they were last heard of in the last century, in the eighteen tens, their top man was a priest called James Prinn."

Heir Straus sat uneasy for a moment then said, "I have heard that name before," the look on his face became grave, he turned and pulled out his laptop, he then inputted his password into the computer he then started to go through business records in connection with the Napoleonic officers, scanning he found what he was looking for. He took off his glasses and said, "Oh no."

"What is it?" said Michelle, the old man put on his glasses and began to explain, "I have here an entry from the chapel in England from the restoration job, one of my companies was fixing up, here is the ledger of the priest telling of the treasure and tomb, looking almost sick, his name is father James Prinn. The appetite wore off them when the German replied, "Nicolas they have been tracking us for the last two hundred years," turning to his right he said, "Jack what security have you at the other side of the tomb." Jack replied, "Tight, the best money could buy. Anybody trying to get it there would have to have a death wish. Its utter suicide," a strained concentrated look came over Jacks face then he replied, "If they had the numbers, were well trained and heavily equipped there would be a chance." The team finished their breakfast and returned to their rooms to pack they then went to see the Empress and just before they went Jack said "Remember, don't mention anything about the breakaway fraction and let me do the talking." They were then welcomed into the main audience chamber, sitting in front of them were the two monarchs looking serine and majestic, the Queen stood up and announced that she knew they were about to go, "but before you do," she presented them all with golden bracelets which were inscribed in the Castorian tongue. It read; "from a grateful Queen, to her friends", she herself translated it, turning to Exios she said, "We are to be married in the year and Exios will share my throne and live side by side for a long time." The Empress and Exios walked over to where the team were standing and in a gesture of love and appreciation kissed and hugged everyone. On sitting down again she said, "I do not think general Lieysin would have approved," King Riceos looked at her and said, "on this occasion I don't believe he would have minded that much Empress," standing up, the King of the Asronas walked over to the assembled squad of souls which destiny had flung together and he handed everybody a medal, "from the people I have the pleasure to rule," walking over to Jack he looked him in the eyes and said, "I hear in your land soldiers no longer have need of the sword, you my friend will always need one," the King turned behind him and lifted an object which was covered by a velvet cloth. The glint of gold and silver reflected off the teams faces when suddenly the King produced a sword and presented it to Jack and said, "where I come from we still use these, believe me a man like you will have need of such a weapon, if the warrior cast ever reproduces its self." Jack was nearly overcome with emotion he accepted the sword and bowed in front of the great King. Michelle smiled at the rogue King and said, "Only once in history have I every heard of such a man to equal you, his name was Rameses the great," the King nodded in appreciation and then Jack intervened, "your majesties as you know we have come from the land above and may have made an mistake, there is a band of criminals who may be trying to access the tomb at this very moment from our side." Exios stood up and said, "I will go with you and make sure you reach the other side safely," he turned to the Empress and asked, "May I take a small detachment from your guard," the Empress nodded in agreement and sent for her fastest craft. She and Riceos stood up and retired with out ceremony. Exios and the rest of the team made their way to the ready docked ship with a detachment of guards made up of Ottilin and fifty other men. Jack and Richard looked for the last time as the ship made its way from the imperial palace and flew over the great city that had been so kind to them, Then the ship cracked into its high speed mode and the ground soon became a traveling map until finally they were traveling so fast that there was no point to remain on the viewing platform. The team now had a somber realisation that they would never again see the Castorian Empire. Michelle sat down beside Jack and said, "We will soon be out of the frying pan and into the fire," and then they all laughed. Richard jokingly remarked, "It's a hell of a lot cooler here," and then they passed the temple of Ammon. Jack asked about the priest and Exios replied that he had chosen to stay here and live out his days in the temple in the service of his god. Exios smiled and said, "He sends his love and wishes the best for all of you," Jack responded, "I thought he would pull something like that, best of luck to the guy." Jack walked out to where Heir Strauss and Nicolas were talking. Jack asked, "Is there anything else we need to know about this lot before we encounter them?"

"Yes," replied Nicolas, "They are ruthless and will stop at nothing to achieve their aims. The one thing I can't tell you is who their leader is, we simply don't know."

CHAPTER 18.

They began to realise that they found the landscape familiar, they were flying past the old village that they had rode through at the beginning. They noticed that their men were coming home from the front and were embracing their families. I turned to ottilin and asked, "What became of the defeated Kitni?"

"We took their surrender and their troops were allowed to go home. We found out from the Kitni negotiators that a large number of Kitni hated Risard for what they had done to their country and their families. Now that he is gone they are mostly going home and some are committed to getting a new Kitni state up and running with the old code of ethics and democracy."

The terrain now began to take on a mountainous atmosphere, the same one that they had ridden down. Suddenly they saw the beginning of the cavern which started off about a thousand feet above the entrance of the corridor which had been constructed by the Kitni before Risards poison took affect. They dropped down and landed on the ledge beside the guards crudely constructed guard house which had stood erect for thousands of years. There were two guards on duty on their arrival, they queried who we were, the approach of newly elected General Ottilin put their minds at ease and they asked eagerly about news of the war. The general replied, "We have victory men, we have victory, but only for these people we would not be here and the war would have been lost." He looked at the mercury wall of metal and enquired, "Has there been any contact?"

"No general," replied one of the guards. He turned to Jack and said, "It might have been a false alarm?"

Jack replied, "That is possible but we can not afford to be wrong." Thinking for a while Ottilin turned and said, "We will open the gate and accompany you in. We now have effective body shields and would be useful in a close quarters fight, after Jack of course." The tall Castorian soldier walked over to the entrance and removed a chain from around his neck which had a small key for the console on the side of the entrance. He inserted it into the hole and the crystal technology fired up and started a searing noise, Ottilin turned and said, "The other thing that opens it is a special frequency that only the Empress has and also now you," he opened his pouch attached to his weapons belt and handed it to Heir Straus, "You are always welcome back, all of you." The strange metal opened up into a corridor from where they heard the commotion. Straus looked at Jack and realised that his worst fears had been realized. His other team in the tomb was under attack and by the sound of it were in a bad way. Ottilin said, "Stand clear," looking at his men he roared, "shields on, five at a time, now," then he activated his shield and started to run up the corridor the five closely behind, then it was Jacks turn he and the remainder of his security team ran after the Castorian guard. The corridor seemed to be longer than he remembered it was then he caught the dull light of the tomb and eventually they came through to the gate room and its ancient but beautiful splendor. There was a small but terrified research team who were in a corner of the room huddled together. Ottilin said in a booming voice, "Worry not, for you are safe now," the research assistant replied that Joe and what were left of the security team were holding out at the mouth of the tomb and were being slaughtered by the minute by a force who seemed hell bent in getting into the tomb. Ottilin looked at Jack and then said, "We will help you then we will get out of here,"

"Agreed," Jack went first through the tomb guiding the guards to where the fighting was happening. The roar of machine gun fire was deafening but reassured Jack that there were survivors fighting off a bigger foe. They then walked through the last hall that was covered in mosaics and statues and then finally past the large statues of the young Greek man and woman looking at each other with love and devotion, until they came to the rope ladder at, the bottom there was one of the security detail severely injured. Jack looked at him and the injured man nodded and said, "Knew you would come," then the man shouted up to the top "they're here," and then fell into unconsciousness. Jack shouted to Michelle to help him, he went up first and there was Joe firing off his hand gun and dropping an attacker. Jack cradled up to him and he turned around, "oh thank fuck!" said Joe. He looked Joe in the eyes and said in a calm manor, "I brought help," suddenly he noticed that he still had his sword that King Riceos had given to him and held it close. Out of the shaft climbed general Ottilin, sword in hand he ordered ten up with him and proceeded to engage the enemy. The shock many got from seeing this massive warrior charge into the mist of battle, the gunfire directed at him was relentless and the bullets just bounced right off him. Driving his sword deep into the first combatant he met, he squealed in horror as the blade disemboweled him. General Ottilin retrieved his sword and then switched to his side arm which was a lot more powerful than the weapons which were in use by the enemy. Jack then decided to engage the combatants with his own men firing off shots at close range. There were about fifty left and the Castorian's were going through them at an alarming rate, there was no place to hide, it was a slaughter. At the end of the battle two of the strange force were found cowering behind a large rock formation further on down the side of the cliff, Ottilin walked over with the two of them by the scruff of the neck and then said, "All yours." Jacks men then pulled the two in for questing and it was then that Jack and Ottilin said their goodbye, asking Jack to visit when or if he ever got the chance. They shook hands and the warriors climbed down into the tomb and into the complex to complete their journey home, they went through the corridor and closed it from the other side. Jack went over to what was left of the mobile command centre and took a good look at his two prisoners. One who was shivering was wearing dress trousers and a shirt, "one of their officers perhaps," said Richard walking over to them. Nicolas bent down and said, "Oh I know who this is. It's the son of the chairman and I have a feeling he has just betrayed his own father," to Jacks surprise the other man was covered in burns and bandages and had a slight resemblance to the rat Aseare, the bandit who the Egyptian government was after. Jack said, "Hold this one Nicolas; I would think his father would like to have a word with him." Looking at him with disgust Nicolas replied, "Oh you've got that right

Jack." After that all the bodies were bulldozed into a hole made by anti tank mines and quickly covered over before the Egyptian troops arrived. As promised by Joe when they got there, one of Heir Strauss' political attaché's smoothed things over with the Egyptian minister. Jack and Straus climbed into the 4x4s and made their way to the first available air transport helicopter. The rest of the initial team followed behind, sitting back in the seat he said, "Well Jack my boy that was an adventure and a half."

"Are you ever going to use the key again?"

"I do not know right now but who knows what tomorrow will bring," smiling at Jack and putting his hand on his shoulder he said, "you're the closest thing I have to a friend, do you know that?"

CHAPTER 19.

"Yes Heir Straus this I know. What about the contents of the tomb?" looking sincere he said, "It will be removed and donated to museums all over the world." After three hours driving Heir Straus told the driver to pull over and asked Jack to come with him. They walked into a German war graveyard and followed the last row of tomb stones until the old man stopped and looking down he told Jack that this was the only other friend he ever had. It was the grave of captain Hans Muller, the old man had a tear in his eye and explained to Jack that Muller had been the first to find the tomb but was killed, "With his death I took it upon my self to seek out this great place and make good of it and I think we both have done the bravery of this man honor," he then quickly turned and walked away. Jack looked at Strauss and he stopped and said, "He saved my life in an air raid." Heir Straus walked off into the awaiting jeep with Jack and sped off until they reached the makeshift helipad. Getting out of the jeep and getting into the helicopter with Michelle in his arms as they said good bye to this deadly, mysterious and beautiful land. The Professor then said, "I had the time of my life." Looking at Heir Straus he said, "If you ever go back, you know where to find me!" The entire crew burst out into laughter as he replied, "yea, yea, no problem Professor."

Back in the leafy suburbs of the Berlin restaurant, a young woman walked into and sat down at a table, across from her was Jack who was tapping his hat, and said, "you're late,"

"As were you the first time we met," replied Michelle, smiling at each other Jack was holding a tumbler of brandy and touching her hand. She said, "I miss the Empress, does that sound odd?"

"Not at all," replied Jack, "She will be fine, as will we."

THE END.

Lightning Source UK Ltd.
Milton Keynes UK
15 January 2010

148674UK00001B/62/P